MW01028043

WHAT THE CRITICS SAY ABOUT KATHERINE DUNN
AUTHOR OF <u>GEEK LOVE</u>, <u>TRUCK</u>, AND <u>ATTIC</u>

ALSO BY KATHERINE DUNN

Attic

Geek Love

TRUCK

KATHERINE DUNN

WARNER BOOKS

A Time Warner Company

Warner Books Edition

This Warner Books edition is published by arrangement with
Harper and Row Publishers, Inc., 10 East 53rd Street,
New York, NY 10022

Warner Books, Inc., 1271 Avenue of the Americas, New York, NY 10020

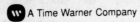 A Time Warner Company

Printed in the United States of America

First Warner Books Printing: March 1990

10 9 8 7 6 5 4 3

Library of Congress Cataloging-in-Publication Data
Dunn, Katherine.
    Truck / by Katherine Dunn. — Warner Books ed.
        p.   cm.
    Reprint. Originally published: New York : Harper & Row, 1971.
    ISBN 0-446-39153-0
    I. Title.
PS3554.U47T78   1990   89-48862
813′.54—dc20   CIP

Cover design and illustration by David Tamura

To Dante P. Dapolonia, for Eli

*Being a bird ain't all sunshine
and shitting from high places.*

—DANTE

TRUCK

*G*oing to go up on the mountain and be king. If I'm the only one up there, I'm the king. Be the goat king. Lose goats. Nobody will own me anymore. Crouch on the rocks where the water comes down and send out fleets and haul in fish and rubbish and rock on my heels in the sun singing no words as loud as I want. Never speak again. Push little things into the dirt and sprinkle from a can and come out early in a clean soft dress and have the wind blow all the way up my crotch. Dry it out in the crack where it's always fusty. Set down here any old way and adore my knees with no help from anybody. I'm so lovely when nobody sees me. Such perfect knees. They bend. Anybody comes up the road I go crashing back into the trees, creeping after, spying out of rocks and following secretly until they go. Sing my little song, good old hopsy-dopsy sunshine shining shine shine all in my bones, good old sun sunshine. Do my little dance and fall down red. Let bugs crawl wherever they want. I don't care. Stand around naked in the rain, or even with clothes on. Mondays I can go around all kind and soft not stepping on bugs and Wednesday swing rabbit heads against the rocks and rip off the skin with my fingernails. Sing I liku du water; da water like meeeeee. This water absolutely worships magnificent me. Leave all the lights on when I go to sleep. Go shit in the woods crooning oh pew I stink sooo bad and if I don't like the goat *one day I'll just kill it and hang up the skin and feel all gushy and melancholy later chewing on the leg. Do all that when I'm the king.*

Mario's in the Roosevelt Hotel. Gray and wet and inside warm, the reds heavy around the chrome. Doesn't get busy until night. Now, in the afternoon the back counter and lounge dark with men moving. Instruments gleaming vaguely on the dark little stage. A flash of blue-veined thigh in fishnet as the waitress bends to set a table. Her uniform is black. She is black and invisible except for the thigh. The counter seats are thick, red leather stools and the waitress bored. The Levi seams press into my crotch and I can feel Heydorf's sweater smelling heavy on my shoulders, the wool chafing over my nipples where they're cold and tight. His long hands are moving slowly in the pizza crumbs. Weird square pizzas cut in thick rectangles instead of wedges. That's how you can tell it's a high-class joint. Doesn't taste the same really, not as good but don't say that. It's high-class. The hands move without wrists or arms. It doesn't mean anything. The nails are flat, pale like the rest. He can't do anything with them, curl around glasses, edging the slipstick back and forth slowly with just the tips. It's all numbers. The hands are numbers. She's leaning against the other arm of the counter, head down, almost asleep. The pizza is gone. The Coke gone. My elbows in the crumbs on the shine. He barely bends his head toward me. He barely speaks, "Say look a bird." My hands slap down on the counter flat, the fingers spread and the crumbs brittle in my palms. I half stand up, eyes wide, and her head rocks up, the eyes clicking open, lunging forward and pointing back over her shoulder into the darker, into the far part of the lounge where the men are arranging furniture. Almost a whisper, just the right tremolo of surprise. "Look! A bird!" She swings around, her arms up, hands flopping, and I'm running with the stool spinning behind me, into the lobby, my sneakers sucking at marble, the pizza heavy in my gut and the hurry all through me like hide-and-seek when you're desperate. The revolving door almost carries me back in. It's wet suddenly and gray and I shut off the excitement. Straighten out my face and catch up with Heydorf casually. We both just walking slowly, hands in pockets, heads down. I want to laugh and run up and down and talk about it. Crow and let myself feel good but he doesn't say anything. Looks for cars and crosses the street to the park.

He isn't paying any attention to the wet so I don't. We sit on the bench. My ass is wet and my face. He doesn't look at me. We talk very slowly thinking a long time between. We are very impressed with the words. We do not trust each other. He is nearsighted and does not wear the glasses. The eyes are never open. They are heavy. He is heavy to himself, all the thin pale stooping his shoulders and he caves into the bench. His head too huge and drooping. He always looks exhausted. "Should sit in a tree there by the parking lot. When people pass say, 'Chirp, I'm a bird.'" Slight twitch at the elbows. That's exciting. I swallow it and sit still looking at the asphalt shining until it doesn't show in my face, then look at him. My eyes are always wide. The white shows under the color when I'm just looking straight ahead. I can't help it. When he looks up he tilts his whole head back till the eyes go onto me without opening futher. The long fingers touch his ear, his lips, his chin where the pimples were. I

wore the sweater and he didn't say anything. It was in the
suitcase with the underwear and shirts, everything smelling heavy when I opened it. He left it and didn't come
back for a while so I opened it and washed everything
and put it all back but the sweater. It hangs below my ass
a little and drops straight from my shoulders except
where my nipples get hard and poke up a little over the
ribs. He lets me talk and listen and be here because there
are no tits and my Levi's hang from my pelvis and my
hands are scruffy. I don't have as much hair as he does.
My sneakers are black with high tops and thick white
soles and rubber toes. They think I'm his kid brother.

They are frog hands and want to fold on themselves,
the long way thin instead of in half the short way. They
have no muscles. The tips are soft and splayed. Frog
fingers feeling themselves. He never notices them. He
only touches with the tips blind, never grips anything. If
he plays with it, if he has one, it must be thin and soft and
pale. It must be just a little thicker than his finger and the
hair pale around it and thin like on his head. Straight
hair, not curling, and his balls pale and small, look
unused, unusable. If he has it and plays with it. Probably
hardly noticing, just picking at it delicately with two
fingers at a time, only the tips touching it, never gripping
it, only sliding absently on it. It couldn't get hard, only
thicken and hang a little further out. Could never get
darker. Never shoot out, only drip, thin and pale, absently,
him not noticing.

He went away right after graduation and we wandered
around not knowing it was him that was missing. The
next fall the letter came: "Dear Dutch, I'm coming to eat
your food. Heydorf." On yellow paper in the clear black
rapidograph printing. All the letters capitalized, all the
same size. We had all learned it. Spent hours copying it.
Learning the curve of the letters and not to let them
touch each other. We each claimed it, not knowing where

it had come from. After a week or so I heard him in the kitchen after everyone was asleep and went down. His suitcase was by the door. He stood at the table spreading jelly on white bread, holding the bread flat on the table with two fingers and spreading the jelly thick on top. I went behind him to the refrigerator for milk, the moving cold on my skin and warm inside and only the Levi's hanging below my navel and the five buttons shining. Two glasses and the peanut butter and I sat down and he sat down in the long raincoat dripping and his hair spiky from the rain and he lifted the bread flat on the tips of his fingers and his eyes flickered blue in my direction and away where I was brown and flat and naked above the Levi's. I very excited, want to ask. Move very slowly, reach so far across the table leaning on an elbow that I can smell my own pit and take bread and the knife and open the jar and slowly, deliberately, as though I were interested in it, spread peanut butter and then jelly. I remember when she made it. I picked the blackberries by the road. The whole bush and the trees behind were white halfway up with the dust. Then milk and I put my foot on the chair right in front of my ass and the knee in my armpit, the other leg curled under and sat hugging the leg with one arm and the other elbow propped on the table and licked the knife slowly, carefully, looking at him, trying not to show in my eyes how I was waiting, knowing he could see it and would make me wait. "I've been in Missoula studying philosophy." He takes a bite and chews stroking the fingers on his hand with his thumb. He lifts the glass, only the tips of his fingers touching it, and drinks. I can't see his Adam's apple under the white shirt collar. I bite into the bread very clearly and chew looking hard at the bread. He finishes the milk and turns sideways in the chair, elbows on his knees, hands hanging, head down looking at the floor. He looks like he's about to get up and I put the sandwich down afraid he's leaving. "Where do I sleep?" I run barefoot, silent on the wood, the air cold on my arms and chest and belly, creak open the cupboard afraid to wake my mother. Bring blankets and a pillow back to the living room. He is standing in the dark with the kitchen door bright behind him. He is picking his nose slowly and wiping just the tips of his fingers in the folds of his pants. I put the pillow at one end of the couch and spread the blankets thinking how the pants show the crack in my ass when I bend and how my back looks pale and the bones make shadows in the light from the door. I stand back with my toes digging into the rug, hands inside my pants on my belly, shoulders hunched. He takes the coat off and drops it on a chair not looking at it. He sits and takes his shoes off, the socks falling at the ankles. I turn and go back upstairs, sliding out of the Levi's and into the cold bed. Lie a long time thinking of him being down there. He doesn't know I have a cunt. He wouldn't be here if he did.

"I'm gonna go to Los Angeles and study hypnotism." He is looking at his feet mostly. The shoes are wet black. His eyes slide toward me and then away. "You hit a bank president over the head and drag him off to your room. Tie him up." His voice doesn't change. It is low and runs on slowly no matter what he says. "When he wakes up you hypnotize him into opening the vault and filling up a suitcase. You can't make him take it or hand it to you but you have him put it on the table. You take it and truck off. Give him a post-hypnotic suggestion that it was a pink bunny rabbit. Also give him a suggestion that he can't be hypnotized again. He tells the police the pink bunny rabbit did it. They come and haul him off. No matter what they do he keeps hollering about the pink bunny rabbit. They haul him to the nuthouse and you're driving up the street in a Cadillac with a big seegar." I'm nodding trying not to show how cool all that is. I don't believe it but it's so cool and they all think I'm down here working.

Dialing numbers, spieling magazines over the phone for thirty dollars a week and green stamps. He smiled when I told him that. They give you bonus green stamps when you make a sale, and only half a day's school if you have to work. Standing in the rain waiting for a ride into town, and they all running to class and the company folded after two weeks but I never told. Just keep coming into town. Nobody checks when I walk out of the library so easy with the books. I black out the numbers with a felt pen, cut out the flyleaves with the card envelopes glued in. Seventy-five cents for an illustrated *Don Quixote* in good condition. A dollar and a half for *The Great Books: Freud.* The little man in the bookstore doesn't look too carefully. The dust and the *Illustrated Mechanics* in piles leaning over him. Thirty cents into town. Thirty cents back. Nothing if I hitch. Tell them I'm putting the money in the bank. She doesn't know if I never ask her for money. I went into the office and the gray lady was so sorry but she was packing the cardboard boxes. The telephone man was taking out the six phones and the mimeographed speeches taped on the walls in front of each phone and the window to the wall with only rain getting in, the lists. Sixty dollars goes a long way. It made my throat sore and they hated me. They were busy and thought it was somebody they knew or the old ladies who talked and talked because I was somebody to talk to. He just got off from the navy and his folks didn't know he was home. They were out so he answered the phone. He would buy some magazines if I would go out with him. Sure, and I so scared, but sure and gave him my real address in case he queered the deal and he came, that night. I forgot and came home and he had a big nose and buck teeth and glasses but I in the Levi's. He was sitting on the stoop waiting for me and his pick-up was out front. I saw him and knew it was him and my mother doesn't let me go out with boys and he was ugly. I was barefoot with my sneakers on their strings around my neck. I had been wading for crawdads in Fanno Creek, putting out leaf boats sailing to Byzantium and standing on the bank groaning and heaving rocks at the boats with my eyes closed and then peeking to see how close I'd come. So there was mud and wet. It's on the way home from the bus stop. I didn't know what to do. He stood up as I came near the house. I put on a blank face. Froze my eyes. Walked up the steps without seeing him. Into the door. He followed me grinning nervous. His Adam's apple sliding up and down his long neck. My mother wiping her hands on her apron. "Why, dear, where have you been? This young man has been waiting for you for nearly an hour. Jean?" I stood not looking at her, my eyes frozen on nothing, knowing my hair had mud all in the brush of it and my Levi's were wet above the knee and muddy-butted and the mud making the hair on my arms look dark and all run in the same direction where the sleeves were rolled up above the elbow and I cut my cheek on the blackberries when I was turned into a swine on the island and rooting for truffles. "Jean? My God! What's wrong?" She grabs both my hands in her hands. "She's so cold!" She lays her warm hands on my cheeks. "She's in shock of some kind!" She'll always make a fuss if you need it. I would not speak. If he would only go away and not stand there gawking and gulping I could come out of it. She's worried. I know she'll think somebody did me. "Jean, Jean! Little? What happened? Tell Mama what happened!" I close my eyes slow and then click them open. Turn and smile at her, all innocent. "Hiya, Maw, can I have a sandwich before supper?" and then let my eyes roll up and fall in a heap. I'll have amnesia like before when I clonked into the wall roller-skating and woke up with twenty pounds of bandages on my head. She's crying and godding. She picks me up and carries me into the living room. I come awake when she puts me in the chair and look at her so puzzled. "Jean! What's the matter? Where have you been? What's happened?" I turn all slow and puzzled and speak slow and low like junkies and nuts in the movies, "I came straight home from school, Maw, I just got off the bus outside and came straight in, Maw." Not letting my voice change. A little breathy but monotone. Too corny for the movies but scary when they think it's for real. "My God! She doesn't go to school in the afternoons now!" And that guy is standing there looking worried and flabbergasted and wringing his hands. "Is there anything I can do? Maybe she should see a doctor. Maybe she was in an accident. My truck's right out here. I'd be glad to drive you, Ma'am." And my mother is running for a coat and he stays so I can't even make a face at the developments and she comes back and goes to pick me up and he says let me and picks me up like I'm wounded and I limp and quiet, eyes wide and bewildered, cussing to myself for having started this mess but it's too late now and got to be gone through. She sits by the door and almost holds me in her lap and I let my hands lie limp on their backs like Heydorf and don't speak and don't move but only look straight ahead and she's telling him how bright I am and only fifteen and it comes out how he met me or didn't meet me really and I'm cringing inside wondering if they'll figure it out but they're too scared to think and maybe he's relieved he doesn't have to take me out and what a hell of a thing his first night out, and all he wanted was a little action. Have to get hooked up with some crazy accidental dame like this, looks like a fuckin' nine-year-old boy. He could have asked Marge next door or one of the bleached-blond beehive babes that lean on the rail at the wharf. Fat butt with tits and an ass and they know what action's like. I feel a little guilty he's being so nice. Just run smack into a mess like this all unsuspecting, but it serves him right, blind date over the telephone.

Probably couldn't get anybody he knows, he's so ugly, his head eggy and scrawny. Dumb-ass sailor for chrissakes, get me into a jam like this. We're at the county hospital. Eight o'clock at night emergency entrance and she carries me in. The intern asking questions. He's feeling me all over asking if it hurts, pulling my legs, my arms. Poking his fingers into my head on the white table. I just sitting, not looking at anything, with my legs hanging over. He is going for the resident shrink. I always wanted one, you know? To talk to all the time about nothing but myself and he'd always be interested. But it's a woman like a house. Short brown hair and a grim efficient look. The nurse flips me on my back and takes off the Levi's and jersey with me still limp and embarrassed but I won't look or speak and they put my legs up in stirrups and she's got something shiny and a glove very pale and she puts the stool between and looks and puts something in me and it's so cold and hurts a little and she tries to put her finger in with the glove and it hurts and I yell or maybe just grunt and she says, "What happened, young lady? Your mother is scared to death you've been raped but you've never been touched as far as I can see." Not my fault. Not because I didn't try. Not because I didn't want it. She's looking at me hard. "I was on the pipe crossing the creek and slipped. I remember falling and then I was home." "Does your head hurt?" "Yes, here," and I touch the top of my head in front where the concussion was before. She feels it hard till it does hurt and I know she can feel where the soft spot is and think that's why there's no lump because the bones haven't grown all the way together like the time before. My head does hurt now and I feel very shaky in the knees and stomach like the first day of school. She's not angry anymore. She must have thought I was putting on an act. She writes on printed cards while I'm pulling on my clothes, very slow and only half acting I'm sick. They're waiting, both white, sitting close together and she looks at the doctor begging and I'm walking but slow and shaking, and the doctor says I fell and is there a history and Maw talks about the other time and he's sitting with his mouth open looking, listening, believing it all. "That was when she was nine," she says. "Last year?" The doctor is writing down what Maw says. "Oh no, she's fifteen now." The doctor looks at me funny and they go a little ways away and the doctor's asking more questions. I know it's because there is no hair under my arms or between my legs, only the one pale hair just below my belly button that has always been there and all the rest fuzz. Invisible in the winter and dust in the summer. He was leaning against the door of the English room. I walked toward him and he was looking a little ways behind me. Someone said, "Hey, Dutch! You dropped something!" I turned around. Fred and Pete behind me. Pete pointing at the floor. A man's white hanky folded into a rectangle, the red in a streak the long way. I bent and pick it up by the clean corner. "It's not mine. Somebody must have a bloody nose." Looked up at them, Pete collapsing against the wall shaking, his ears red. Fred's mouth open long and black and the long loud laugh, and behind me Heydorf saying "Haw-haw." Never laughing only saying haw-haw. And Pete gasping, "It's true! She really doesn't!" I stood up and pulled my gut in, felt the air between me and my pants, hands in my front pockets, flat, facing me, felt the shoulders hard and hot around my ears, walked off, not hurrying, my sneaker soles squeaking on the floor. They still laughing. I am laughing. He leans on his knees, hands flipping aimlessly to touch his points. "Hong Kong. Hypnotize a whole Chinese family. Tell them they're Easter bunnies. They go around breaking into paper houses with baskets of eggs. They all get arrested and you sail off in their junk. Become a pirate." He's even a little interested in what he's saying. My guts are jumping with it. But he's going. Going away and I'll be here forever, scraping excitement out of Portland, Oregon, with no one to help and no way out and I'll marry a service station attendant and never see or go or know anything or do anything or ever feel myself all over full of possibility like now because he is so possible and anything is possible now but when he goes it will be high school again and the nothing and the nothing after that in the rain because girls cannot. Even girls who are not, because secretly they are. And will always be trapped and I want to be free. Why couldn't a girl be? Only because of a hole there and there can never be anything else. But maybe not even the hole, maybe nothing, and I could. "When do you think you'll go?" He puts his hands in his pockets and his legs flat out from the bench, lying on the bench and looks in the direction of his feet, being cool, being speculative and acting, always, but a good act and I'm not ashamed to believe even though I want to believe. "I've got a few hundred dollars coming from an insurance policy I'm cashing in. It should come this week or next. I'll get some good clothes. A pearl stickpin. You have to look like you don't need a job to get one. Even in crime you need money to make money. Then go down, scope out the crime scene." I don't know how to say it. He knows it but I have to say it and say it right. The fountain is squirting up and the rain comes down into it. His sweater is heavy with wet. I can't look at him. "I wish I were eighteen. I'd go too. I want to be free, you know? I don't know what from but I'm not and it'll take a real move of some kind, something desperate to get me out." It's embarrassing. I can't look at him. He just sits. He won't help me. "And it's three years. I don't know if I can make it." I can't do it alone. He won't help me. It's so hopeless. The lovers stroll slowly, not noticing us or the rain, heads together, wet. And we wet sitting close but not touching anywhere. I am very sad and the time seems

impossible, gray, too late already for me, because he's
going. DKW rattling through Eugene looking for a pool
hall. I in front. Heydorf in back. Vince driving. The horn
wires hang out from the radio hole—red and black. One
in each hand, at each intersection Vince yells "Contact!" I
touch the copper ends together—white sparks, blue in
the dark. Beep. Hit a bump. The trunk lid slides off
clanking. Jerk stop. I hold the break while Vince jumps
out. Trunk lid rocking in the road. Lights. Horns. Rocking
on its belly in the road. He picks it up, fits it on scraping.
Heydorf's knees high in front of him, his hands white on
green corduroy, limp. "Look a dog. Think hate thoughts.
Don't blink. Don't move. Think bad hate thoughts. Dog
runs away. Won't come near you. You can always stare
down somebody dumber." Vince driving again. Shifting
noise, laughter, "Yeah! Like you did to poor Sooty that
time." "Yeah." Forget the wires. Turn around in the seat
to look at Heydorf. "One time Judy Leben was over at my
place. I was looking at her upside down. Talking to her.
Looking her right in the eye. After a little bit she got
really scared. I felt it too, like she was a fish. She wouldn't
talk anymore until I was right side up. She thought I'd
hypnotized her." "I can psych you out." He's looking at
me. I can see all the color of his eyes. Cold blue. Pale in
the lights from the street. I stare. He stares. Vince yells
"Contact!" I don't move. Have to look to touch the wires.
Can't look away. Blink slowly. Not very often. Swallowing
ice cubes, cold all the way down, hard in my stomach.
Numb. When they melt it's the warm in me, not in them.
Heydorf's eyes full and cold. I falling into them, not
moving. He doesn't care. Nothing touches where the eyes
are. I put the black all around in a thin line with the
eyebrow pencil. Just where the lashes come out, on top
and bottom. A line going out from the corner of my eye.
Egypt. So they know I'm a girl. It helps. Makes them even
bigger, don't look so bulgy. When I look they can't help

but look back. Except Heydorf. He looks past. Not looking
at me. Looking at my eyes. Vince is getting mad. We not
talking. Not playing contact. Just looking at each other. "I
thought you people wanted to play pool." No answer. No
move. The eyes. "If you want to play pool you've got to
help me look for the place." I want to. Want to play pool.
Want to stop looking and move my eyes. Want to look
away but he'd think. No expression in his face. None in
mine. Just looking. Yes, let's play pool in a little bubble of
yellow light on the old chalked green. Let's play Screw-
your-buddy. Let's move around and admire me when the
balls sink. The click. The moving all clear with numbers.
Blue chalk, and the cues always warping. Can't see each
other except the hands. Except when you're shooting
bent into the light. The rest in the dark. Let's. But it's
serious now. Can't stop now. Can't give in. On the ancient
sleazy green. Compare bridges. He taught me at the
smoke shop. The floorboards gaping. The tables on cement blocks. Sammy's Smoke Shop. Sammy dripping over
the stool. The back room always dark but the bright
green shining. After a while I'd come alone because he
liked it and I wanted to be good so he'd like me. Hours
till my back ached over the table. Not giggling. Not
holding the cue like a broom. Not like a girl. Sammy
watching. Selling greaseburgers and Bugler and purple
pop with his thumbprints in the grease. Sammy grunting
and not charging me. I'd brush the tables for him. Let
him put his hands on my ass. The long soft brushes
sweeping the chalk into the gutters, into the pockets. The
blue dust drifting in the air. "You gotta get yer English
cold, kid. Soft, kid, soft. Ya shoot power or ya shoot pool."
Miss the last bus home and sleep on the snooker table.
Phone Maw and tell her I'm at Lebens'. Go see *The Hustler*
with Heydorf. Then out to Sammy's. He lost interest. I
beat him once and he wouldn't play anymore. "Dumb
game." The car stops. I almost fall backward into the

windshield. Lose his eyes. He's looking around. Vince is lifting off the trunk. Swinging Heydorf's suitcase onto the sidewalk. I look at Heydorf. His eyebrows go up a hair. I don't know. Vince swings open the door on my side. "Get out!" I climb out, legs stiff, looking at him. He's really mad. Holds the seat up for Heydorf to climb out. Slams the door. Jumps in the other side. Buzz off in the dark. We stand on the sidewalk. Quiet, dark, lawns all around, pale wooden houses very neat. A few street lamps. The blond suitcase sitting on the sidewalk. Hands in his pockets, whistling, no tune. "I guess he's sore." He looks at me and grunts. Sits down on the suitcase. I sit on my heels pulling the pea coat up around my ears. Around midnight. I'm supposed to be back at the sorority house by twelve-thirty. My girly debate partner back there talking to the college girls. Putting her hair up in pink sponge rollers, practicing her speech. My speech is on the floor of the DKW. "Do you think he'll come back?" His hands flop exasperated. "I dunno." "You need a place to sleep." "Un-hunh." "Maybe if we go over to the Student Union there'll be somebody you can ask to put you up. I've got to go back to Sigma Coy or whatever that place is. I've got debate finals in the morning." Walking in the dark streets. I carry his suitcase to show I can. He doesn't mind. Somebody in a letterman's sweater directs us. Crowded, bright, orange pop, good old Tom Grow, red hair, white eyelashes, you remember him, he was in the class ahead of yours, oh yeah, and they go off. Tom carrying the suitcase. I go back out into the dark. All the buildings dark. Got ten minutes to get back there and I don't know where it is or what it's called. Just went in to dump my toothbrush. White, looks like a house. I could walk past it and not know it. It's cold. The rain starts. Duck into a freight entrance. Ventilator fans blowing. Dusty but warm. Dry. I want to lie down. Soft. Sleep. I'm really tired. Lean against the warm grate. Not really warm. Just warmer.

My ears are cold. My hands. The pea coat collar is wet. Got to get back there. Might as well go. Wet and the wind. The streets empty. Really empty. No cars, no people, the street lights bouncing in the wind. Yellow crosswalk signs dancing on cables. I've got no money. If I carry money with him I end up paying for everything. Just my jackknife in my rear pocket. Vince is mad. Heydorf will be sore at me for getting him in bad with Vince. Probably laughing at me for putting the black stuff around my eyes. Looks weird. Creepy with my dungarees. Scrub at it with my fingers and palms. My face is wet and my hands come away streaked with black. Bad Breath Smith in the john at school: "That's really so *effective*, Dutch, you ought to wear it at the debate tournament." My legs ache below the knee. Can't sit on the grass. Wet. Screw the tournament. Screw Marcia Smith. Screw Vince. A tree, naked. Easy to climb. The bark smooth, soft, lot of thick branches. Crawl up in the tree and straddle a branch. The Levi seams in my crotch. It's cold. It's wet. Unbutton the pea coat and button it around the branch so I won't fall out. Tiger hunting. It's uncomfortable but it's cool. Seems all the things that make good war stories are miserable at the time. Heydorf on an air mattress in Tom Grow's dormitory. Lights down the street. A car. Rip the buttons open and swing down on the branch, drop too far, hurts my ankles. The car is past, campus police pale on black on the door. They stop before turning at the corner and I'm running down the street yelling, "Hey, wait!" and they're gone and I'm standing in the middle of the street just tired. I find the place when the sun comes up. Marcia Smith in her white nightie, pink curlers. She sat up all night. The police were looking for me. "Quit dorkin' around, Dutch, it's cold out here." I come out of the cubicle and march across to the steam room door. The floor is wet, concrete, feels soft, like there's moss on it, fungus. Everything gas chamber green. Heydorf's long towel, twenty-five cents extra for a long towel, once around his waist and over his shoulders, toga, his legs stick out pale below the knee, arms hidden in the towel. Pete and Fred in short towels. Once around the waist. Knees bony. Goose bumps from the belly up. I in the short towel. Safety pin. It almost makes it around twice. My square feet digging in the wet. It's a big room, the far walls invisible in the steam, the ceiling low. We sit on the concrete steps jutting out of the wall. Cold on our asses, the air thick and wet, very warm. The drain in the middle of the floor gurgles. The water comes off the walls, off the benches, us, up out of the floor. It stinks, horsy man, my tee shirts at the end of the week. We're already wet. Can't tell if it's sweat or from the air. Running out of my hair. From under my arms. All down my back and belly and legs. I'm in a puddle. I can barely see them. Fred, moving slowly, gets up and crosses in front of me, sits down on my right. Heydorf lying down, looking dead with his eyes closed. The wet warm as a bath. Pete on his belly, his head on his arms. He has to do this for his back. We just here to see. The queers. Everything gray, sleepy, hot. The water around me is hot. A man comes out of the white and splashes through the pool in the center. He looks very pale, his skull gray and wet, gleaming dull in the thick folds behind his head. His chest hangs down in a sack, nipples wide and pink, the belly flopping out and dark gray hair streaming thin down into the towel. He doesn't look. He goes out the door. Fred sits, elbows on knees, his thin belly creasing the loose skin as he hunches. He's only a little bigger than me. His hair white, freckles pale, the towel droops around his waist. I can see darker hair curling up toward his belly button. The crack in his ass shows dark. "Fred," my voice sounds thick, soggy, "does pubic hair get gray too, when you're old?" "Yeah, just a little later." He looks very tired. He looks at me, and then looks at me. "You haven't got any under the arms." I lift

my arms, turning to show both, shrugging, what can I
do? "Does she have any in the groin?" Heydorf on his
side, his head propped on one hand, the other hand
picking at the towel. Only his feet and hands and head
uncovered, his hair dark and flat with sweat. Fred looking:
"Do you?" "No." "Make her show." I stand up. The towel
hangs lower in front, the safety pin holding it to itself. It
is wet. It drips. I'm dripping. I don't look at them. I look
at the safety pin. It takes a long time to open the safety
pin. I turn around, facing Fred and Heydorf, my back to
Pete on the step below. I open the towel, hold the ends
out to the sides, still over my ass. Fred looks, sitting still. I
look at Fred, not at myself. Heydorf sits up and leans over
his knees, picking at his lip, looking. Pete says, "Lemme
see." I start to close the towel. "Show him." Heydorf lays
back down arranging his towel around him. I turn around
with the towel open. Pete is propped up on his elbows. He
looks up, looks for a second and then flops back down,
chin on his arms. "I guess that proves she's a girl. I always
suspected she was a nothing. My five-year-old sister looks
just like that except her belly's smaller." I wrap the towel
tight around, the long streaming wet as though I were
pissing warm down my legs. Pin it carefully on the side so
it doesn't flap open between my legs. The steam is hissing. Can't tell where it comes from. The cars hiss by in
the puddles. The rain, always. My room small. Deep
clutter, clothes, papers, books, the bed never made, the
walls pale blue. I wanted them black and the windows
black and no bed, no furniture but a rug and a pillow. I
sit, tired of reading. I am sick of books. I can't tell where
I leave off and the books begin. I'm nobody. I'm a
polluted nothing. A confessed sin, an open door, the
clutterer in the clutter. We are wet. The water shines
between his fingers, running from behind his ears into
his collar. Another block to the bus station. It's crowded,
the park sitters moved in out of the rain. We sit, wooden

arms between, so you can't lay down. He goes on talking.
"These lifeboats off surplus navy ships. Scrapped at Zeidel's.
The ship never sank so the boat's never been used. A
little engine. A sail. Seaworthy. You can get one for about
a hundred and sixty. Sail it down to L.A." I see him sick in
the back of the boat, not steering anymore. I go back to
steer. The sea comes in all the time. "Yeah. Where can
you find out about it?" "There's a guy. Night watchman in
the scrap yard. Lives in a tin hut with junk piled around.
Gives me booze." It's dark out. I have to catch the next
bus home. Hate to leave. Its Friday. Can't come in again
till Monday. Empty till Monday. "Wish I was eighteen."
Just wishing. He doesn't look at me, looks at his shoes.
"Why wait?" "What?" "Why wait till you're eighteen?" He
wants me to come. I can come. The rest doesn't matter,
the why. He only steals from his friends and we are
honored and steal for him. Fall. The sun. Walking in the
streets electric because I'm with him. The farmers' market
open. Humming. The fruit shining gold, red, orange, in
numbered piles. The green is golden and not poisonous.
The smell, the smell moves with us, ripe. Small scales
hanging from the beams and the small men in the shadows in the stalls. He stands looking, head down. I waiting,
expecting. "I want a banana." I can barely hear him. He
turns and walks away, his feet pointing out, his shoulders
hunched. I'm scared. It's pounding, all the people. He is
almost at the corner, the bananas have black streaks
arcing in the yellow. They lay in bunches on their bellies,
fingers curving in bunches. The shopman is weighing
tomatoes for the fat lady. Her children are nagging. His
face is tired. The gray circles under his arms and his
hands on the scales. Maybe he puts this thumb on the
scale. I edge through the crowd. Heydorf is out of sight.
The table is pushing against my ribs. I lift my arm and
with my whole forearm brush a bunch under my shirt,
down from the table and up under the black jersey. My

arm against the bananas, holding them against me, push directly out from the table into the crowd, away from the man at the scale. I'm not tall enough for him to see me through the crowd. Push, edge, too short to be seen, into the street so I can move faster, between the cars. I did it. I made it. Running, to the corner and around, down faster. If I miss him he's gone. He's looking in the window of the bakery. I know what he wants. I'm scared again. The bananas aren't enough. It's never enough. The briefcase is on the sidewalk leaning against his leg. It's unzipped. I go to it, crouch and drop the bananas in and then move away, not speaking, not looking at him, toward the entrance of the bakery. I can see him reflected in the window. He bends uninterested, picks up the briefcase and walks away. He'll be in the park. I wait till he's at the cross walk and then go in. There's a girl alone behind the counter. No one else. I take the bill folded into a tight thick square out of my back pocket. Five dollars. Five trips from the library to the secondhand bookshop. She is lifting the cake off the rack. "May I have it in a plain bag instead of a box?" She is careful with the dark cake on its thin cardboard. She doesn't notice me. She doesn't know I should have robbed her but am too chicken shit. I carry the bag flat on my palm. Stop in the next doorway to take off the stapled register slip. Tear the brown bag artfully, jounce the cake a little till cracks show in the frosting, wrap the bag haphazardly around the cake. Into a little grocery for a quart of milk. Ditch the milk bag. Put the carton up under my arm under the shirt. It's cold. Loose shirt, not very obvious. Cross the street, another block, another crossing, the park. He is sitting on the green bench by the water fountain. He expects the cake so he sat by the fountain. He's eating a banana. It's pale in his fingers, peeled, the yellow skin hanging in a crack in the bench. I sit down beside him, put the cake between us. He looks at it, puts the rest of the banana in his mouth and lifts off the brown paper. The cake is cracked raggedly across the middle. "It's broken." I look at my shoes, the toes white thick rubber glued to black canvas. "I had to get it off a rack instead of out of the window, almost dropped it." Take out my jackknife, being careful not to jingle the change or show him the side with the milk carton. He opens it and cuts a square out of the round cake, lifting it on the tips of his fingers. The frosting is thick and soft and his fingers sink in it. He bites and chews. I wait, looking at him. "Yeah, that's pretty good chocolate." He hands the knife to me handle first. I cut a wedge in the cake and lift it out, biting carefully to get the proper balance of cake and frosting. My stomach steadies and my breath is easier. Hold the cake in one hand and pull the milk carton out with the other. Prop it on my knee and open it, offer it to him. "Ah, that's a thought." He is a little surprised and I'm very pleased with myself. He thinks I stole it all, I hope. But then, he gets cake whether I bought it or stole it. I take the risk, I pay. I'm the sucker. If I bought it I'm just a sucker. If he thinks I stole it then I'm a cool, handy, useful sucker. But I'd rather be his sucker than theirs. He gives me something, the excitement maybe. Not the other, not the touching or the other. He couldn't give that. If he knew I wanted it he wouldn't let me near him. But it's enough for now, since it's all I can get. The sun is warm. The grass is green. The gypsies are walking in the park. We are laying in the grass in front of the keep off sign. He is on his side, one hand holding his head. He picks at his lip with the other. Me on my elbows on my belly, picking clover, chewing it, spitting it out, fingering through the grass for clover. The gypsies take a long time to go past. Sing and play and talk and laugh. We look at them from the corners of our eyes. I want to ask, I know but I want to have it said. "You think I'm pretty dumb, hunh?" I look at him, at his eyes not looking at me. He wipes the tips of his fingers in the folds of his pants, picking at the corduroy. "Yes." The eyes flicker toward me, see how I'm taking it. I still looking. "You don't use the brains you've got." I try to decide whether he wants me to think that's a lot or a little, relieved he's not lying, looking for clover. "You find a guru. He's drunk in an alley, half dead, stinks. Follow him. Feed him. Live with him. Clean his shoes. When you're thoroughly guru-ized you kill him, so you can go on living." His eyes are open, looking at me. The cold blue chills my guts. Maybe he doesn't let people see them out of kindness. He looks away. "If he ever says he's a guru, he isn't." The gypsies are crossing the street against the light. Satin skirts away over the asphalt, purple and crimson and scarlet. Only gypsies have those colors. For other people it's red, just red. "Wanta go down to the bus station, watch the old ladies faint in the heat?" Why wait? I'm scared. They'd drag me back and it would be worse after, watching me all the time, everybody mad, questions. Even without that I'm scared. "It's easier for a boy, and you're eighteen." He looks back at me, looks away, shrugs. He doesn't care one way or the other. Ain't his machine. "I'd have to wait till June. School lets out. It's a month and a half." Looking at him I can feel my eyebrows go up, asking. Put 'em down. I know he won't wait. "That'd give me time to get some money." "Yeah, you'll need money. Bus trip to L.A. is twenty-two forty. Need at least a hundred." He's interested now, knows I'm hooked. "I'll leave next week sometime. Write you when I get settled in someplace." His hands flop as he talks. "Need camping gear. Sleeping bag. Take the bus to L.A. I'll meet you. Pull a couple of jobs. Disappear into the hills. Walk into the Baja. Down to the tip. Get a fisherman to take us across to the mainland. Live like a king in Mexico on a hundred bucks a year." My bus pulls up. Jump up. He's picking up the briefcase, going now that I'm leaving. I put my hand out, square, grubby.

"Deal?" He takes it, loose, his pale hand covering mine.
He nods. Not interested anymore. "Deal." Bus moving in
the dark. The rain. Inside the light is blue, fluorescent,
dark around the driver. The people old, tired, lavender
in the light, and gray. They scare me. Three of them. Two
women in white uniform shoes, man with a lunchbox.
Going home. Every night. The same. The work. It makes
me sick scared. I think of leaving and it's not scary
compared to this. I'm the last one off. It's late. The town
dark. Another mile in the rain home. The cars pass. The
creek sounds big under the bridge. I'm a little scared of
the dark. Nothing in it, just the dark. They're all watching
TV. Yell "Hi" and up to shower. Not for the clean, for the
warm. Come out cozy in flannel. It's good, the comfort,
especially now after the rain. Peanut butter thick, soup,
milk. She worries about me. I sit tasting everything, climb
into bed with a brainy mystery. The comfort doesn't scare
me now I'm leaving.

"It's fifty cents a night. Can's down at the end." I can
smell it. The door doesn't close all the way and the piss
soaks into the wood. There's no way to get rid of it. New
floor maybe. Even then when it's warm, the smell, puke
and piss and spraying shit, black and soft and sick. The
beds line the walls, six on each side. Army cots, steel.
Steel wire strung across the frame, a mat across and the
pillow sewn onto the mattress. One blanket, khaki wool. I
sit down on it and feel the stiff spots in the blanket. Dry
and stiff in spots. Would be paler in the light, from old
scum or piss or puke. A hole, crisp around the edges,
darker. Cigarettes and the smell of burning wool. It's
early. Nobody else here yet. Heydorf on the next bunk
kicks off his shoes and lays down, ankles crossed, arms
under his head on the pillow. Closes his eyes. I wish he
didn't look so dead with his eyes closed. The fat man is
going down the room looking under the pillows, under
each bed. He stoops and his belly nearly reaches his

knees. His khakis slip down in back and hang straight to the floor. No ass. He comes back toward us with a green bottle under his arm. His tee shirt is gray, stretched around the neck. The gray hair curling dark beneath his chins. His chest looks like tits resting soft on his belly. He stops at the foot of my bed, opens the bottle and sniffs at it. There is a little clear liquid sloshing in the bottom. He looks over the bottle and winks at me. "Brothers?" He jerks his head toward Heydorf. I nod. "Where you from?" "Missoula. Hitchin' down to Corvallis. Dad works down there." It comes out easy. I look straight at him. His cheeks drag down the bottom lids. The pink shows below the whites of his eyes. He sucks his left cheek in between his teeth looking at me, speculating. The cheek doesn't cave in where he's pulling at it. The stubble moves over the fat. His mouth is very small, the lips thick and arching. No teeth after all. "Nice-looking boys, yep. Nice-looking." He waddles away capping the bottle. I lay down, my sneakers still on. Look at Heydorf. He's picking his nose with his eyes closed. Wiping his fingers on the blanket. I can hear the rain. The window is too dirty to see it. The neon red blur goes on and off in the window. Alaska Card Room downstairs. Somewhere the click of pool. It's almost dark. The forty-watt bulb over the brown-spotted toilet shows yellow through the half open door. We lay not talking on the beds, watching them come in. They're all tired. Had to get the money for a bed tonight. Too cold. Too wet. They don't speak much. Quiet for those already sleeping. They take the bottles out from under the old coats and share a little. All pale from the rain. He comes to the bed on my left and sits for a long time. Too tired to lay down, head down, hands hanging loose, the lean old body already dead, only forgetting to lay down. He stretches across the blanket. The hat falls off. His trouser leg hikes loose up the shin, the thin pale leg bone-shaped into his shoes. No socks. Shoes cheap, old, the laces broken and retied, the knots tight against the holes. His mouth falls open, hangs to the side, gray inside, the bare spotted gums shining wet in the dim. I turn over to face Heydorf. Curl up to ease my stomach. His eyes are closed. His long white hands laced across his chest. The john smell is still there but it doesn't burn in my nose anymore, and the smell seeping dead from the old man's stomach, sliding out at his mouth in shallow breaths, almost gone when I turn away. She had orange hair, the powder white on her face, black lipstick. Naked she was so thin. The brown hair curled thinner at her belly button in a cone to the deep thick mat between her legs. She propped her leg up on the bench to dry from the shower. I sitting, watching, couldn't see the slit through the hair. No paleness showing through. Her long breasts hanging on either side of her knee as she toweled her foot. "You don't have to worry. Lotsa girls don't get boobs till they're lots older'n you. Or hair or anything and they come out real pretty." She talks low so the others won't hear. "And if you'd wear girl's clothes and some makeup you'd be real cute even with your hair that short." She drops the towel and reaches for the grimy bra on the bench. The cotton is sweat colored and the wrinkles in the elastic are stiff with sweat. She puts it on over her shoulders and reaches around shoving her chest out and fumbling to fasten it. Standing up her belly sags a little and the heavier hair hangs away from the thin on her belly. I can see the neat blue letters tattooed just above the crotch, "REPENT." "Didn't it hurt to be tattooed there?" "Sure, a little. But it's sure a good joke on some of these *men!*" She laughs tipping her head back, her crooked teeth pushing each other and dark in places. She puts on the too tight sweater. Cheap nylon panties with the lace hanging loose at the legs, the elastic broken. The tight plaid skirt. Goes barefoot to fix her hair and make up for the next class. The hand rubs low on my spine. Warm.

Soft. Lower. Slow. The fingers kneed in the soft at the crack. I am almost awake. If I wake up anymore it might go away. It stops rubbing and slaps me sharp on the ass. I turn over quick remembering. The fat man is leaning over me. I can smell the liquor. Someone sits at the foot of the bed. A man. Drunk. Dirty. His shoes beside his feet. I can smell his socks and the fat man's booze together. "Shhh. All the beds is full up an' I need a place for this fella. If you'd double up with your brother I'd appreciate it." His low voice grates. I fumble for my shoes, remember not to put them on, swing my legs off the other side of the cot and put the sneakers next to Heydorf's shoes. The fat man is laying the drunk out on the bed, spreading the khaki blanket over him. Heydorf is on his back, his clothes on under the blanket. There is only a few inches on either side of him. I can smell puke clearly from somewhere. I lift the blanket a little and lay down balancing carefully against him, my head on my right arm, belly to his side. My feet have plenty of room but my ass hangs over a little. He is still asleep. I put my left hand on his arm to steady myself and push against him with all that touches, trying to move him a little or get him to move. The fat man is moving down the aisle toward the john. Somebody is snoring. The bed squeaks when I move. There's more room now. He's warm against me, against my chest and belly. My crotch bone is hard against his hip. It feels good like rubbing there. I want to rub against him but if he woke up. I put my hand between his chest and arm. Warm. Close my eyes to feel it all. I can hear him talking to her even when he whispers. The tire iron is against my back. It hurts but I can't move. My knees are up to my chin and my stomach hurts. It's plywood between the trunk and the back seat. Loose in sections. Rough against my cheek looking over and between. Moving carefully, only tiny inches at a time. Heydorf has more room. Almost stretched out. Only his legs curled up. I can't see him. I can't see myself. Sometimes I can't tell where my hands are in the dark even when I move them. They aren't paying attention to the movie. The window is rolled all the way up holding the speaker. I can see their heads. Two making one darkness over the seat. They are holding each other and touching. The light from the screen makes his pale hair shine. Her hair is dark, loose. I cannot see them touching. "You are so beautiful. I've wanted you so long. So long." His voice is low, interrupted, just breathing. "Oh Fred, Fred." She sounds like she's crying. In class she sits very straight, her hair tied back with ribbon. Black hair. She is nearly as short as me but with curves. The blouse always tucked in. Skirt fitting tight at the hips. Her legs curving gold in the stockings. Her shoes always look new. They always match what she's wearing and the ribbon matches and her long pale hands, small face, serious, turning pages carefully. She always looks so clean. In the locker room her bra and slip and panties all white and new, the lace narrow and the straps untwisted. Amanda. Her eyes are purple and she walks quickly, books in front of her, arms across her chest, looking down, her face almost too small to be pretty. He is my friend. Fred. I don't care about her. She sounds like she's crying. They are almost lying down. I can't see her. Only Fred's head and his shoulder above the seat and he saying "Please, please." He is almost crying. He borrowed the car from Vince. It's Vince's car. We got in before Vince took it over to him. We climbed into the trunk and pried the board further away from the seat. Widened the cracks with the tire iron. Vince wanted to come too but there wasn't room and how could he deliver the car? He shut the trunk on us laughing. We laughing and watching. Fred getting in. I smelled his hair tonic. The pale hair stiff. The smell oily and thick drifting in to me and he singing "Da da da" and whistling. Looking in the rear-view mirror at himself as he drives, not knowing we are here. He sings "Amanda" to the tune of "Granada" and stops the car, parking carefully. Sits quiet a minute, leaning his head on his hands on the wheel, whispers, "Please, dear God," and then snaps his head up, runs the comb through his slick hair and checks it out in the mirror. Jumps out and slams the door. I can hear the cleats on his dress shoes sharp on the sidewalk. He's gone a long time. We getting bored. Not talking. I'm embarrassed a little already. The passenger door opens and she slides in very smooth and proper and the door shuts. Her head turns watching him walk around the front and get in. He slides in front of the wheel. She is not touching the far door. Sitting somewhere between close to him and away from him. He bends to put the key in, his face turned to her, grinning, freckles pale. He looks very tight. The tops of his ears are red. "You look very nice, Amanda. But then you always do." She smiles and I put my hands over my mouth and roll my eyes even though there's no one to see. They talk about school. Teachers. He borrowed the car from Vince. "You all seem such good friends," her voice hesitant. "You and Heydorf and Vince and Pete." I tense, waiting. I'm offended at being left out. "Yeah. They're kind of wild but they're all really pretty bright. I think you'd like them if you got to know them." He drives intensely, his knuckles white on the wheel, shifting raggedly. "Flanagan's all right with you?" "Sure, that's great." They talk a little too quickly. Too politely. She's easier now. Looking at him as he drives. "What about Dutch? I always thought she was just a dumb juvenile delinquent." I hate her. If Fred lets that get by, I'll never speak to him again. "Well, she's weird all right." I wish Heydorf wasn't here. It wouldn't be so bad if I were alone. "I didn't mean she wasn't nice." Trying not to seem catty, cat, puss puss. "I don't really know her. I don't think any of the girls do. It's just that she's always skipping class and she dresses like a boy. Look like a boy really, you know?" She looks at him, hoping she hasn't offended him. She's offended me. He's offended me. All the times he'd walk with me and sit in my basement eating peanut butter and listening to records and telling me, telling me things he couldn't tell anybody else. And I listening and liking him and he's ashamed to like me in front of her. Sniveling little superclean bitch. "She's not dumb." Thanks a hell of a lot, Fredsy Poo! "She's easy to talk to." She's looking down. "Not nearly as nice as you though, and nowhere as pretty." She's smiling again. I may puke. The carhop brings hamburgers and milk shakes and french fries. Fred not looking at her bare legs. Looking at Amanda. Talking about debate. His summer job. Her folks. I'm hungry. The hot sweet relish, french fries. Should have brought provisions. The light comes in through the crack. Heydorf looks asleep leaning against the board. He picks his nose with his eyes closed. Not looking anymore. Just listening. I lean back and close my eyes. My stomach's grumbling. Feel a little faint. Getting colder. It's very dark except where the light from the screen touches, the back of the seat, the dashboard, Fred's shoulder. His head's out of sight now. They aren't talking anymore. Only the breathing, quick and sharp. He sits up, pushes his hair out of his eyes and starts the car. "We gotta get out of here." It doesn't sound like Fred. So hoarse it scares me. He puts his right arm on the back of the seat, peering back into the dark. I freeze forgetting he can't see us. I can see the sweat beading on his face in the light from the screen. His face looks dark and mean. She sits up, pushing at her hair. I can see her head bouncing as she pulls at clothes. She doesn't speak. She is sitting close to him now, not looking at him, looking down. "Jesus, Mandy, don't touch me." He's driving fast, looking left and right and in the mirror. I'm scared. If he gets in a wreck. Nobody will know we're here. If it catches on fire. I can see us burning and screaming, burning and nobody knows where the screaming is coming from. The traffic thins. No street lights. The moon pale and the stars rushing in the window. I can barely see anything but the shadow of their heads against the headlights. His hands on the wheel. We turn sharply and my back hits the tire iron hard. A gravel road, dark, the headlights touch the tombstones sliding white. He slows and turns off the lights, the car rolling silent, stop. He seems calm now, tired. He turns and touches her, "I'm sorry about this baby, it's the only place I could think of." His hands on her cheeks. He's kissing her like a movie. Not hurried now. Smoother. I can't see their faces clearly, only pale in the dark and hands pale. He reaches in back of her seat and pulls the lever that makes it lie flat, then his. Now there is nothing between us and them but the plywood. My legs ache, numb and aching. I have to piss. I'm hungry. I want to go away and leave them alone and be alone. I don't know him anymore but we can't get out of the trunk till somebody outside opens it. Maybe we could push the plywood down and crawl out through the back seat but there is no back seat anymore, only the seats flat and bare all the way under the wheel, under the dashboard and Fred kneeling and her kneeling, facing each other, shadows against the windshield and he is fumbling with the buttons of her blouse and she half helping half preventing and he is kissing her to keep her from stopping him and they do not speak but touch and her shirt comes off slowly. He pulls her sleeves inside out. The cuffs are too tight, and her bra is paler than she is and it's all vague and dark. She looks very small. She doesn't help him with the bra. He tries to reach around her kissing her to do it but he can't and she turns around and he takes it off and they don't seem very big at all, just pale and small with darker dots and he turns her around and her skirt wrinkles up at her waist, at her thighs and I can see the paler in between her stocking tops and her girdle.

She shouldn't have worn a girdle, and he is looking at her and his hands are moving slow around her breasts. His hands cover them and she puts her hands on his shoulders looking at his face looking at her breasts. "Amanda, Amanda, you are so beautiful. Amanda." He sounds like he's crying again and he is reaching around to her skirt, her hands stopping him. "I'd better." She sounds scared, and he stops and starts unbuttoning his shirt looking down at the buttons fumbling and she unzips the skirt and puts her thumbs under pulling down, falling back on her elbows until I can smell her hair, and lifting her hips and pulling the skirt and the girdle down together and the stockings without unfastening them, all off with her shoes and her panties pale across her pale body and he is out of his shirt and kicks off his shoes and socks and sitting down to pull off shorts and pants together, not looking at her and she is sitting with her legs curled leaning on one arm watching all pale down from her hair. They must be cold. I'm cold and I can feel Heydorf shaking. It's not too late. We could giggle. I could giggle. But Fred's kneeling and he's different. He's thin and pale and small but something not as pale stands up from him and she's looking at his face and he is reaching to kiss her not looking at it but I can see it moving with him, stiff, swaying, and he lays down and she lays down beside him and their heads are inches from us but I can't see their heads or hear their breathing. I can see that. He is touching her shoulders softly, slowly petting her, kissing her. He lifts up and looks at her and his hand runs down her shoulder. I can see her breasts flattened on her chest and the darkness between her legs in a triangle. She lies still, her arms at her sides and her legs together and his hand runs over her breasts and down her stomach and along her legs outside not touching the triangle and her hand touches his knee, just touching and then petting and I can see the thing pale and stiff against the dark.

She must be able to see it, and her hand lifts from his leg to his arm petting and he bends and kisses her long. "Fred, I've never..." "Me neither." Whispering. Me neither, and Heydorf shaking though I can't see him. I can feel him shaking, or I'm shaking and I wish he weren't here, to know I saw this. To know I didn't giggle. I'm sick. Fred is climbing onto her, her legs between his legs, and she looks very small though he is small and his ass looks flat and square, two pale squares. If we breathe they'll hear us. I can see the crack but I can't see the thing in front anymore, not just his old pisser but the new thing, hidden, he is over her, resting on his elbows. I can see his hair and his long familiar back and his legs on either side of her, not his face which I don't know anymore, not her face, and he is moving against her, his ass going up and down slowly, gently, and I can hear him breathing. I can see her little hands just barely the same pale as his back but the shadow in the fingers. "No," she says, clear, "no," and he says, "Please, please," almost crying and she is pushing him up and pulling her legs apart under him and he comes back down between her legs and he puts his hand under him between her legs and it stays there. He is pushing up on one elbow and the hand is fumbling between them and then she breathes in very sharp. I can see her fingers digging into his back. He is groaning like he hurts. "Please, please, it hurts, Fred, please." She is crying and he is pushing down very slowly one low groan all the way and she yells, harsh, once, short, no word, and stops and he stops and lays on her, in her, his head beside her head and I can see a little bit of maybe her chin and her fingers tight in his back. "Oh baby, Amanda, Amanda, are you O.K.?" Whispering and she whispering "Yes Fred" and he starts moving again, his face tight against her neck. I can't breathe and his ass moves up, his toes flat on the vinyl and then down hard, fast, all the way down, and groans and she groans, not his voice, not her voice, and he comes up again and down and then very fast once, twice, and he is crying again lying on her and she is holding him, her arms around his back, petting his head and "Fred, Fred, I can feel it in me, Fred." Her voice is like a child's, and his shoulders shaking. He's really crying. I can hear the ugly sound in his throat and I'm shaking hard now and the sick comes up rough in my throat and my face is wet and I can't see and I close my eyes and lean my head against the plywood and shake and somewhere next to me in the dark, carefully not touching me, maybe Heydorf is shaking too. It's a long time to get dressed and make sure everything is straight and their hair combed. They touch easy now but the talk is harder. They put up the seats but I'm not looking anymore. Not really listening, just laying all crumpled up, tight and tired, with a full bladder and an empty stomach. Want to go home and piss and eat and sleep. Not talk to anyone or see anyone. It's cold. Maybe raining. I don't know whether I can hear it or not. The car starts to move, the vibration hard all through me and something is knocking somewhere. We're stopped. I look through, the headlights are on. Fred getting out. He walks forward and looks at the left front tire. He sticks his head in. "It's flat, baby." She moves over and pulls his head down to kiss him, long, soft, I can taste it. "I've got to change it, baby. It'll just take a minute." No. Oh no. Oh no. Too late. The trunk opens and the cold and the bright flood in and there's no place to hide and I can see Heydorf suddenly and Fred leaning over, his mouth open. Too dark to see his eyes. My eyes are burning in the air and I can hardly move, everything stabbing me, everything asleep, and Fred staggers back a step and sits down in the road and puts his head on his knees and his arms around his legs and sits rocking, making no noise. I start to laugh and then stop. We climb out slowly, looking at Fred, not looking at each other and she calls, "Fred, Fred," very

softly and I can hear her shoes on the gravel coming
around and we are too stiff to move fast enough and we
are still there and she sees us and stops and sees Fred and
runs to him bending over him and his face turns up and
it looks dead and pale, no expression and the moon is up
there somewhere and it is all still and pale and his voice is
strange and hard not changing. "They were in the trunk
all the time." And we are running in the grass and the
stones come up at me so fast I can barely dodge them,
running, and somewhere I can hear running in gravel
and Fred's new voice yelling, "Mandy, please! Amanda,
wait!" and the feet keep on running and I can hear the
blood in my ears and we come to the road and Heydorf
turns left to Vince's house and I turn right to my house
and we run away from each other as fast as we can. My
pants seams hurt me. Where I was laying on the rivets in
the hips, they bunch and hurt me. I pull at the fly front.
The buttons pop all the way down and the pants are loose
and a little air comes in and I can feel the wet there at my
crotch, the wet that takes so long to dry and so slippery, it
doesn't really have a smell or like medicine, some medicine I don't remember. It's dark and I can feel him all
bones with softness. I have to remember to call Leben.
Make sure if my mother called her our stories are straight.
Lying is so easy, like just sitting very still. I'm not here and
if they don't ask I don't say anything at all. Just climb out
the window in the dark over the roof to the porch posts
and down and they never know or else I just don't come
back until I'm ready and if the story is good, if I'm cheery
and polite, not guilty, they only talk and I apologize and
in the night when there is no one to see or explain I on
the roof against the moon soft-footed over the shingles
and running through the fields wild with the moon,
crouching till my breath comes back on the wheat knoll
with the long blades waving all around and no lights, no
houses, and I wild with my breath, excited by the blood in

my ears and how quiet my running and my voice, my own voice rising till it screeches, breaking at the moon and coming down low until I can't hear it but only feel it rumbling through me and then silent walking the special way so I don't get tired but can go on across the fields and orchards never stopping, seeing everything in the dark, seeing better in the dark. Never on the road but over lawns and fences and feeling how I move and how I breathe and how the frogs stop and the crickets and the dogs turn in their sleep but don't wake when I go by but the horses turn at the fence and run white-eyed from my scent. At the road I have to cross and sit waiting, watching to make sure no cars, no people, then run with the cold tar foreign. Once a truck came around the curve. Its sudden lights, I jumped from the yellow line to the ditch, rolling into the high reeds and the water and lying still with my eyes pulling at each other and the water banging in my ears. It stopped and backed up, the headlights above me. He must have seen something, my feet in the air in his lights, but I don't move, though the truck stays seconds, seconds, and then goes on. A dog, or a rabbit he thinks, but he knows something is out here moving in the night and I know he's out, know someone else is awake in my nighttime. It makes me mad. If he'd got out to look, I would have jumped and taken his throat in my teeth with my own voice snarling to be alone again and the night silent again but the gray light and the voice and a bell somewhere . . . "Everybody up. Out by seven-thirty or another half a buck!" The fat man by the john door. The stink from behind him, Heydorf looking at me. My arm is on his chest. Last night's old man sitting slowly and reaching for his shoes, the hat for his pale-skinned head and then shoes. "That's nice, boys. That's real cozy." His eyes glitter wet and red with no other color and the mouth falls lipless back into his cheeks. Heydorf jerks away from me and up and the others are reaching for pants and shoes, their bareness feeble, gray-spotted asses cracking over maggot-white legs, and Heydorf moving to sit up. The drunk in my bed rolls over and looks at us. Just a flash of eyes and broken skin knitting around itself and he rolls back and picks at the blanket weakly, covering his head and hunching into the piss smell of the mattress. My tongue is thick and my face feels very big, the flesh too heavy on my eyes and the sneakers a long way off. Heydorf moving quickly, tucking his shirt in. My feet hit the floor too hard and sting in the cold. No socks. My socks are gone. The sneakers are heavy and hard to tie, everything thick and my mouth cruddy. I stand up shaking my shirt down, Heydorf not looking, standing at the foot of the bed, pale. "Button your fly." And I look down and the paleness, the smooth under my shirt with the Levi's flapping, go down toward the john pulling in my big gut, walking bowlegged, fumbling with the buttons and feeling sticky in the thighs where the wet was.

Saturday's breakfast. French toast and fried eggs. The eggs on the bread. Cover with syrup. Lots of syrup and cutting into the egg running gold over the brown and the syrup thick and sweet slipping on the eggs and soaking into the hot bread and milk and the sweet heavy going down slow and she's there from the head down putting more on my plate and the morning sun through the window hot on my back but it will rain later and I won't grow anymore anyway, Maw, it's no use. He's sitting across, telling war stories about school. I can't see his face. They all laughing. He's only ten and four inches taller and fourteen pounds heavier and she's tall and full and getting old, worrying and getting old and I don't like looking at her face. Too soft. Too innocent. I'm her child, her only daughter, and a wolf bitch at night. Maybe if I got pregnant I'd get tits. But you can't get pregnant without tits. Walking into the Baja. I'll be so miserable, hungry, hot and cold and dirty. Make the bed and pick up all this crap so I can think. Neat piles of papers folded in between books. Clothes stashed out of sight. See the floor again. Dark wood shining and it's raining again. Always raining or remembering the rain or waiting for it. Make a list, neat, the square printing filing down the page. Ways to get money. Sell books, make up a list of all the books I have here, hardbacks fifty cents, paperbacks a quarter. Dime for trash. Show it around at school. Sell what I can't peddle at the bookshops. Sell my skates, Chicago shoes and precision wheels, humming blue. The clothes, nothing there. Tee shirts and beat-up Levi's. Dad's booze, water it, sell it at school. Should be able to get away with a couple of quarts. Sell it high for an ounce at a time. Mow lawns, return pop bottles. Don't eat lunch. Find old tires. Two dollars apiece to the recapper. Hubcaps. Write English compositions for people. Monica Gunberg will give me five dollars for a Charles Lamb paper. Copper wire to the junkman. Think of more later, I'm tired. Fold the page carefully, a small square, insert in the crack under the desk. I feel like I've started already. Sit reading about men living under the sea. They didn't want to come up. School again Monday. I can't. But there's twenty-six forty in the sock already, left over from the phoning job. That's the bus fare right there, so all the rest is gravy. Just go. Up the steps and look, up more steps and look again. He's not here probably. A wasted trip and days more before I find him. The steps go down behind me, wide with the double banister in the middle and the curves gentle all the way and nothing to stop me at the bottom. Just a little rise at the end so I can sit facing down, not hanging on the slick of the banister and the slick of my pants and my feet dangling wild and faster and faster till at the bottom the faces of the people coming up blur and I fly off at the end maybe eight feet and land on all fours soft and run out before they can say anything with the books flat against my belly under my shirt. Up more steps. The sign is right. This is the room. I stand in the doorway and look carefully, starting at the left, turning my head slowly looking at every figure crouched over books at the long tables and hunching at the stacks with their hands on books. The room is green, pale and the wood dark and all the people are awkward and quiet. His head is enormous. I didn't know it was so big. Pale like a lion's on his skinny body. His back to me. Papers and books spread on the table. The rest of the table empty. I jaunt over. Feeling good. He's really here. Don't speak. Sit down across from him, don't look at him. Look at the librarian. They're all the same, suspicious. Catch my breath. His papers are typed, neat, and a few notes in the square hand. Paperback Hobbes. All fits into the brief-case. I reach into my back pockets for the sandwiches, waxed paper soggy. Open them slow in my lap. "Would you like a peanut butter and jelly sandwich?" He looks down and taps the desk. "I don't like peanut butter." "Would you like the jelly half of a peanut butter and jelly sandwich?" "Gimme." The bread is dark, stiff. Peanut butter and jelly soaked in, wet, bent, crystalline. Slide the slices away from each other, not lifting so it won't tear or leave all the gop on one side. There's still jelly thin on the peanut butter, thick and lumpy on the other half. Slip the jelly carefully so the librarian doesn't see. We sit eating slowly. Chewing carefully. It's better this way, soggy and stiff. All the flavor soaked into the bread. She is looking in our direction, looks alarmed. Starts moseying over, straightening books, pushing chairs up to tables. He's still eating, his back to her. "Hide it." I put mine on my knee under the table, open the Hobbes. He slips his into the briefcase. Flat on the desk. Catch the glaze at the corner of my mouth with my tongue. She's looking and we're not looking. She can't figure out where the food went. Strolls away patting at books, her lumps wagging around her, looking puzzled. I want to giggle. Yawn instead. And yawn and lean back and stretch and scratch. She doesn't let you sleep here. Old Irene Meyer with her purple birthmark and her knobby nose. Absolute cow. Greasy long black hair, all the way down her back but it's never clean and she curls it in corkscrews at the ends and froths up greasy bangs to hide the acne on her forehead. Big purple birthmark on her right cheek and she's so holy going to Youth for Christ and Future Teachers of America and shushing and pursing her mouth whenever anybody says anything. Her father's some kind of minister and she always talks trying to be smart to make up for being ugly. Love thine enemy shit. Give aid to Red China. "That's stupid, Irene. We can't give aid to Red China!" P. J. Bushbaum's going to be president. "I think you'll find our present posture with regard to the question of U.N. membership, the increased possibility of a nonproliferation agreement with the U.S.S.R. and our already expressed blah blah blah would preclude the possibility of any sustained economic contribution to any Asiatic Communist blah blahs." "You're all nuts! We can't give aid to Red China!" Heydorf gives me a nudge with his foot across the aisle. I sit up, look serious and say, "With all due respect for the scholarship of Mr. Bushbaum, it should be obvious with only a tentative grasp of the available data that the problem in question is one of such delicacy and portent that the impact of a hasty decision might negatively far surpass any possible positive effect which would in any case be arbitrarily obtained in an obverse geometrical progression in probability." Heydorf says, "We can't give aid to Red China!" Vince howling and beating on his desk: "We can't give aid to Red China!" P. J. Bushbaum: "Come on, you guys, you know we can't give aid to Red China!" Pete jigging on his football helmet: "We can't wa wa wa give aid wa wa to Red wa China wa wa!" Stamping our feet and slapping the desks chanting, "We can't give aid to Red China!" Singing, "We can't give aid to Red

China!" Another chorus, Heydorf conducting: "We can't give aid to Red China!" Mr. Hittner puts his head down on his desk. Irene Meyer swings her head back, all the hair swishing back like seaweed, wet and black, and we are standing up singing, "We can't give aid to Red China!" She grabs her books and runs to the door with her knees together and her birthmark flashing lavender to maroon and disappears. I jump into her seat and stand leading the rondo, "We can't we can't, give aid give aid, to Red to Red, China China, we can't give aid to Red China!" So they put us all on detention for a week but we didn't go and nobody said anything. It's quiet and the rain has stopped. Everything dripping, everything gray. I'm hungry. Pad down to the kitchen, sniffing and looking. She's there copying recipes onto file cards and popping them into the tin box with the flowers and Mom in pink. I painted it in second grade and the big cup she still drinks her coffee from. She looks up bright and smiling, "Hungry, child?" and I can smell her soft of soap and lotion and cinnamon and feel like crying. Want to go sit in her lap and get all folded up in the soft and cry and be fed, sit watching a scary movie with her to hold my hand. Grinning, "I sure am, Maw," trying not to cry. Go into the refrigerator for milk, checking out the possibilities and she starts bustling. "None of that peanut butter now. It clogs your innards and doesn't do a bit of good that I can see." Opening doors and slinging pots, "It'll just take me a minute here." So I sit down at the table with a glass of milk, my feet on the heat register. Feel the grate hot through my socks and the air hot up my pants legs to my knees and watch her square-dancing around the kitchen. Do-si-do from stove to sink and allemande right to the refrigerator door, humming crazy and she comes up red to put a big yellow bowl of Scotch broth down in front of me, thick with barley and mutton. She makes it at night in five gallon lots and my brother drinks it from a mug all day. Open-faced grilled-cheese sandwiches, mild cheddar bubbling brown crust and yellow cream inside. Mayonnaise spread thick beneath the cheese and cocoa. She sits down to eat with me. Tells me how she stole her mother's red silk pantaloons for a flag on the pirate raft. Railroad ties strapped together in the slough in the North Dakota plains. The red undies flying in the wind and her mother came riding by with the minister's wife. She laughing, gently imitating the minister's wife and I laughing, swallowing the hot sweet cheese and wondering how long before it's all funny. Wish I could stay and be comfortable here with her forever but I can feel the minute going and the new minute and all the new minutes that will have to come and I wish I were old, very old, sitting on the porch in the sun. Too old to move but just sit warming and remembering and have it all over and done, all the pain and the growing and even the good things over and just sit far away inside remembering. But she thinks maybe I've grown. I seem taller. So I stand against the door jamb and she sights at the mark on the wall and sighs and brings the scale out from under the sink and I stand balancing careful not to touch anything but it reads an even seventy-two. "And you just ate." Her eyebrows peak in the middle and her gray eyes swim behind her glasses. I am always eating, trying to stretch. I feel so tight on myself. I need more room. To hate in. I hate. I hate everything. Everybody. Why are people so afraid of being alone? I'd like that, to be all alone. To know they were all dead forever. Never look at anybody again and see so clearly what I'm not. Have them all gone away into a hole. A big cave or a deep mine shaft. But I'll have to go into the hole. Too many of them. Like in the fireplace. When I sit in the fireplace. Nothing has ever been burned there. Just pink bricks all around me and cold and hard with the opening smaller than the inside. It bothers her when I sit in there. Somebody told her it's Freudian or some-

thing. The truth is it's just a good place to sit because
there's only room for one. All the other small places,
under tables when the tablecloth almost touches the ground
and the packing crate in my room and tree houses or just
trees, or sticking my leg up straight in bed so it's like a
huge tent with Bedouins dark and hot and goats in the
corner. Anyway not her belly, I know. Maybe my own if I
have one. I just fall down inside myself, close red and hot
all around me. I'm a secret and I wait for friends to come
and visit me but they never do. Sit peering out the door
and would really rather not come out but in the end I
always do. I don't understand what men have instead.
Theirs is all outside and mine is all inside so there must
be space left over in them. Maybe that's where their soul
is and I have a hole instead. That's why I'm a beast. She
said, "There comes a time when everybody has to choose
whether to be a human being or a beast." I chose but I
didn't find out it wasn't nice until later. That's why I
didn't learn arithmetic. I kept sliding lower and lower in
my seat until I was sitting on the floor under the table.
Crawled around for a long time looking at legs and socks
and shoes and finally I couldn't resist and bit this goldy-
pink calf just below the knee in back. There was a lot of
yelling and trouble. After that I had to sit up straight and
look at the board but I wanted to be crawling around
under the table and couldn't pay attention. There are a
lot of people in the world and they are almost all silly and
disgusting. If I see too much of them I begin to think I'm
like them. Want to die and not see myself again. And they
all give me trouble. Just by being there if nothing else.
About the most disgusting thing they do is die. Only way
to stop that is kill them all off. Turn them all into mud.
Stop this awful constant dying. Just blast them all away at
once so I can forget about them. But they don't go away
and I don't have a button. So I have to go away. I always
wanted to go away but I knew too much about conse-

quences. Consequences is why the little man runs down
the track in front of the train instead of jumping out of
the way. He doesn't know what the consequences would
be. He doesn't know what's to either side of the track and
he's running too fast to look. But he's got to come to the
point where he jumps anyway, regardless of the consequences. Or maybe he doesn't. But I do.

There are two kitchen chairs in the field. They are
thirty or forty feet apart facing northeast. The timothy
and vetch twist green around the legs and the feet are
deep in the dirt. The field runs off into sky on all sides
and there is nothing to see but green and sky and the two
chairs. He sits in the chair, one ankle propped on a knee,
notebook open, book in the grass beside him. He picks
his nose and stares out at the horizon. When I first came
here it was late summer and the field was pale sharp
stubble, thin rows distinct and shallow. I crept around
from the road looking for his house. Walked up the hill
with the straw stabbing at my legs, over the rise and the
field goes on and on and the chairs in the middle. Far off
I almost don't believe them, but he is sitting there. Gray
clothes and his pale head fading into stubble and straw.
Vince in the other chair dark and jerky against the yellow.
I dropped to my belly and, stung and stickered, crawled
on my elbows closer. They mustn't see me. Mustn't know
I'm here. The sun is hot on my back. It heats my shirt
and lays on me heavy as water and the little armadillos
come and spiders and flies and I lay watching out of
earshot, flat in the field and not quite behind them, off to
the side. They each have a book and a pad of paper. Both
slumped in chairs ignoring each other. I don't think they
speak, only read and write and stare off into the edge,
and I watching every stretching of legs and nose picking.
They are small out there. When it isn't raining I come
here after school. Sometimes Heydorf is here alone.
Sometimes nobody. I watch the empty chairs and wait.

When he is alone I come closer, edge around to face him.
He's nearsighted and only wears his glasses to drive. It's
always dusty. Sneezing is the greatest danger, and having
to piss. I squat in the trees before I crawl out into the
field but sometimes I forget and drink too much before I
come up. Twice I've had to squirm backward down over
the brow of the hill and leave before they did just to piss.
Afterward I was too tired to crawl back. Usually I stay
until they go. Heydorf doesn't like the cold so it's always
before night. His head turns toward Vince but he still
looks at the ground. Vince jerks up in the chair and nods.
They both bend and pick up their books. Vince jerks
along on his bowed legs, twitching and waving his arms.
Heydorf slouching after, head down, hands in pockets. I
can never hear anything. The wind is wrong. The field is
green now and deep. I could come very close now without being seen. But he's in Montana. Nobody comes here
anymore but me. I lay for hours watching the chairs.

The map is huge but I can see it all, from one ocean to
the other, without moving my eyes. The light is very
hard. It is all white with thin black lines and redheaded
pins clustered and spotted all over. There are thousands
of pins. Each one is a murder happening. They pull and
glow and push into me until I can see all the gray rooms
and black alleys. The hard light naked in the rooms,
seeping in the streets. See flesh hazed rosy and flat, the
arms rising and falling, fingers clutching steel, teeth
meshing, eyes shrinking and popping and closing. All the
hasty jerking of murder being done. It's all one room
with the light cruel and weak from a wire in the ceiling.
All these million rooms with blood springing into the air
and the man alone with blood screaming to come out.
The murderer, forgetting the murderee who is, after all,
dead. He's so incredibly alive, this murderer, with every
cell conscious and roaring, for this one second utterly
loves himself, in all the little rooms after all the gray years

for one second he finds the beast who loves himself above all and then stops, too late, and reaches for somebody else, the one he always thought he loved best, who is probably already dead. They make checks on the clipboard, watch the pins flash and then fade to red plastic. When they're cool they are removed and analyzed. The spectrograph records the residue. The slag from the burning is caught up in heaps and watched for smoldering.

It hurts when I bite my sweatshirt. The hard gritty cotton grinds up through my skull and hurts. It says "PAX" on the back. All the Latin I know. My feet are in Fanno Creek. He leans against the abutment and looks down at the water. His hands push air when they move at all. He calls everybody by their last name. It eliminates intimacy. "Hittner's just like everybody else. He thinks he'll be out of town when he dies and somebody will send him a telegram to let him know." Me too but I nod and push my feet into the water further. The cars hiss above us and the boards in the bridge clunk as they go by. Maybe the bridge will collapse on us. Push us into the mud here. I take my feet out of the water and peer at them in the dark. The rain mists in a little, spraying off the wind. It feels like sweat. His voice is low. It slides under the wind and the cars and the brush scraping on the banks. It pours warm into my ears with creek sounds, soft and thick like breathing through phlegm. I don't have to listen, as though I were thinking the words to myself. "You're all screwed to begin with. They'll all get their diplomas and go to college a little bit. Then they'll join the army and get their asses blown off. If they survive it's nine to five and home to the fence and the kiddies for the rest of their lives. You're even worse. You'll marry the service station attendant at the first Flying A you come to. Never do anything. Never see anything." My eyes are sliding out at the corners. I can feel my face tight in the wind. I know he's right. I hate it. I can't. I can't do that.

"What about you?" Keep the voice cool. No irony. No anger. "I'm gonna study law. Become a pirate. It's all a lie that you have to do anything. They just tell you that to keep you quiet. You don't even have to die. You can kill yourself." I can't see his face in the dark. His hands show a little. Pale blobs hanging at his knees. No use looking for his face.

I'm luscious. I can feel myself all over beautiful. My hair is white and falls to my crack. I'm purple and long and walk calmly on the tiles. Feel the cool smooth beneath my feet. Even my toes are lovely, Jesus feet, a neat pale scar on each purple arch. They want me. They are afraid of me and their trunks poke out in front like my toes under the sheets. They are all staring though I don't look at them. My eyes are black and my eyebrows white arching on my purple face. Every bone is perfect. I have tits. My mouth is huge and the lips are thick as plums, so heavy they part and my teeth show. The air moves on my belly and under my arms and between my legs. The hair is white and curls heavy. They forget to talk as I go by. They forget to be cool in front of their friends. I can feel them hunching over their pricks and rubbing against anything in the heat. They are wearing boxer trunks, elastic broad at the waist and loose down to the thigh so there is room for their erection. I allow no jock straps in my gym. The moss is warm and wet and they are still following me. They are ridiculous poking out and swaying through polka dots and pale flowered cotton. Everybody I know, their brains ripped out, all the talk and gestures and cool blown away and only pricks left, follow me out the gate down the path to the swamp, single file. They don't notice each other, only me. They stumble and their breathing is hot all around me and the sun hot in sprinkles through the leaves. I feel it dapple me violet and glowing down to my toes but my cunt is red. Though I can't see it, they know and I know, and the warm all

around and my hair tickles my ass and I can feel my tits
bouncing and all those silly with their muscles and pricks
and hair everywhere dark and curling and all my hair is
white. They are only in their pricks and the pricks see
only me. The moss is soft here, the shade. I'll lie down I
think, and stretch a little and let them look if they like,
but they aren't stopping, they're all around me, grabbing
and pulling and biting. The pricks are coming at me hard
and red and hot, pushing into me everywhere filling my
mouth and cunt and ass, rubbing between my tits and
under my arms. They rip and shove until there are three
in my cunt and two each in my ass and mouth and the
rubbing and burning and I'm choking and gagging when
the tips touch the back of my throat and the white scum
drowning me and my hands held to pricks on either side
are burned by the friction and they come and are replaced
by new pricks fresh and anxious and I am full in all my
holes, the sticky scum spilling out with every stroke lap-
ping down my cheeks into my hair, splashing out onto my
legs and soaking me hot and wet and thinning white over
my purple skin. They slap me when I fight and beat me,
ripping at my hair if I bite the cocks in my mouth. When
they have all come in me or on me I lay still on the moss
and rest awhile. The flies wade happy in the scum and
they all lie around me with their balls loose and pricks
tiny and soft. We doze and wave at the flies and smile at
each other gently. It's nice. We do it every day.

We're looking for my little brother. He didn't come
home from school and my mother came in and worried
in front of us and went to the telephone next to me to call
all his friends. Heydorf sat in the big armchair and
fingered his lips listening and I let my eyebrows go up
just a little and puckered the right corner of my mouth.
He wasn't anywhere she called and her voice got meeker
and softer, Heydorf crossed and uncrossed his legs. I
said, "Don't worry, Maw. He's as late as this four times a

week and you always get at least this worried." So she told me all about his one kidney and how he has convulsions if he gets a high fever which she tells me every time and which I know having been the one to throw all the pillows into the tub and hold his arms while she held his head and we all got drenched while he kicked and rolled in the cold water. We tried to hold him but he was slippery in the water and shook all over and broke three toes once kicking the side of the tub in spite of the pillows. He was smaller than me in those days but he kept growing and I stopped. I wonder who she calls and what she remembers when I don't come home. Her eyebrows go up next to her nose. Mine raise on the outside. She has a little anxious tent of wrinkles in her forehead and her square red hands rest in her lap, helpless for once. "Well, look, Maw, I'll go find him. He's probably just found somebody interesting to talk to and forgotten the time. Don't worry." She looks relieved right away. She knows he hates it when she goes looking for him. "Would you like to come, Heydorf?" Always very polite to Heydorf. "Hmmmm." He unfolds slowly and follows me out. It's raining. I'm not wearing shoes this week. I like the cold and feeling the wet and gravel on my feet. Feeling everything. So we trucked down to the creek and crawled in under the bridge to talk. I was wet anyway so I let my feet go into the creek. They say it's polluted. "I'm hungry," he says. "Vince's house has a freezer full of steak." Uh-hunh. Yep. We are walking on the railroad tracks. I stub my feet on the ties. It's too cold to walk smooth and the cold makes the bumps hurt more. Say nothing. It's darker here, away from the road. No lights. Dark barns on either side of the track. Wet smells, sacks of nitrate and piles of moldy horseshit. Climb down off the tracks and cut through the woods. Come out in the cemetery. The grass soft. A few old blue street lights wash the grass pale, the trees and stones dark, a negative swimming in the tank. He's angry.

I can feel it. It was all right and now he's mad. He walks a
little faster. Everything else is the same, but I can feel his
anger. It rolls at me. I stop splashing in the water and
slide my feet. Walk bowlegged so he can't hear my pants
seams rubbing. Open my mouth to breathe quieter. Did I
do something? Is it me? Please don't let it be me. But he's
got some goddamn gall being mad at me. I didn't do
anything. I haven't said a fucking word since we left the
bridge an hour ago. The road is smooth tar and feels
good to my feet. Warm in the wet. I stop trying to be
quiet. Splash, stomp as I walk, let him know I'm mad too.
He isn't the only motherfucker who can get mad. If he
says anything I'll call him a flabby-assed queer. Kick him
in his two little pea balls. One word, that's all it'll take. But
there is no word. He walks along in his usual way, head
down, hands in pockets, a fast lope, and then stops. He
turns, half facing me. The rain falls on us and between us
and runs out of our short hair. His face is white and
there is a muscle twitching at the jaw. I never saw that
before. I can see now, he isn't mad at me. He's just mad.
His eyes swivel half toward me. I always expect them to
be pale but they're bright. Don't seem to change at all.
"You know who lives there?" His voice is indifferent,
nonchalant. It's a little yellow house with a lot of flowers.
"Sure, Vince's grandmother." "We're gonna raid it." He
lopes into the hedge and I follow. The lights are all out.
She's very old, Vince's grandmother. Kind of cheery and
crickety. Vince mows her lawn and his sisters sweep and
scrub. She can't walk very well, a lot of flesh-colored
elastic bandages wrapped around her legs. They look
thick with the bandages but she's tiny everywhere else.
Vince took me there once and she gave us something to
eat. I don't remember what it was but she made it herself
and it was good I guess. I don't remember. He's crouched
behind the hedge. I hunker next to him and peer through
at the back door. "Is that the kitchen?" "Yeah." "Go scope

the place." I hunch over and move quietly around the house. Stop below each window to listen. Just a little house. Three rooms and the screened porch. No sound. All dark inside. Old ladies go to bed early. Get up early. Don't sleep good. I come back around the corner and he's standing on the kitchen step fiddling with the screen door. "Here, do this." He's no good with locks and things. I grope around in the flower bed, come up with a thin tough stick. Screen doors are nothing. Slip it in and lift the latch. Let it down slow and ease the screen open. Lift it against the hinges so it doesn't screak. "Second, I've got something." He pulls out a plastic pocket calendar and I take it and slip it in against the silly old lock and it slides right in. The knob turns all the way and the door pushes in. Dark. Smell of old lady. Moth balls and Vaseline. Lavender and liniment. Curtains. Think they were pink. Probably pink. "Where's the refrigerator?" He's standing near me in the dark. I can feel a heat and a little movement. Think it's straight across, a table in the middle, reach and feel, wood table with oilcloth, a chair. "Watch the chair." I slide past and reach the flat cool metal smooths against my hands. There's a scrape and a crash. He hit the chair. He mutters and it scrapes again. I stand with the metal cold against my hands waiting and he moves up beside me. "Open it." "Wait a minute. She might come out. She can walk still, I think." She walked then, when I was here before. Just slow and it looked like it hurt. "Open it." Hold the door, pull out the handle, a crack of white when the bulb goes on. Let the handle in and swing it open. The motor is just a whisper but I can hear it change, going faster, working harder with the door open. Cottage cheese. Prune juice. Cucumbers. "Bah, old ladies. She keep cookies?" His face is white and sharp leaning into the refrigerator. "I don't know." I stand back. He's holding the door, swings. His arm swings and the door flashes past and the black sweeps across him and it slams. Refrigerator door slam, cushioned, springs, magnets, but loud now, here. Very loud. "Why'd you do that? Dumb thing." "Shut up. I want cookies." He's fumbling and a scratch and the match is yellow and he's yellow in it and yellow shadows move in the dark kitchen. "Who's there?" Scraggy voice. Cracking old voice. Must be her. Not near. Calling from somewhere else. "Who's there?" The match goes out while I'm looking at him. A door cracks somewhere. She's opening her bedroom door. Going to come out and see what's going on. Doesn't really think anybody's out here. A cat got in or the wind blew the door open. Not really gutsy. Heydorf's turning to go out and I reach and grab his arm. "Wait." Then I do my Inner Sanctum laugh. Deep and cracking and it sounds great in the dark and I really get into it, roll into it thinking about the old lady in there shitting her pants. I'm still doing the creepy laugh when the door slams and there are clicks and bumps and scrapings. She's locked the door and she's pushing stuff up against it. I let the laugh die out slow and eerie. Crazy laugh. Practice it in the tree house along with the Tarzan yell. I'm still hanging on to Heydorf's arm. "She won't come out now. Light another match." He fumbles and the yellow light comes up and I'm grinning at him when he looks at me. Mush over to the cupboards. Bang 'em around. Make all the noise I want now. A coffee can full of store-bought cookies, for the grandkids and their friends. We're friends. Chocolate cream filled. Cheap. Not great but O.K. Toss Heydorf the can and he drops the match and I bump against something. Cloth covering something. Bird cage. The canary. Forgot about the canary. Ricky. Vince says she gets a new one whenever they die and always names it Ricky. There's a rustle under the cloth. He's awake but it's too dark. Won't say anything. "Let's go. We got cookies." Heydorf's feeling for the door. It's open and the dark outside is gray and the dark inside is black. "Wait. There's probably something more." "Naw, come on. We'll go get a steak out of Vince's freezer." "Yeah...wait though. I'm going to do in this canary." Mealy-looking canary anyway. Make the old lady think it was a maniac. "Shit. Too much trouble. Come on." He's going out the door but I'm going to get this friggety canary. Ricky. Jesus. "Leave me the matches." He stops and digs them out and I edge around in the dark and get them. "I'll be out on the road." He goes and I edge back into the kitchen. No more noise now. But I hit the chair and it scrapes on the floor. No sound from the bedroom. The phone's out here. Safe. Light a match and go through more cupboards. Nothing. An old dried-up jar of peanut butter. No good. Flour and sugar and shit. Nothing good to eat. Bird seed. Gonna get that fucking bird. Another match. Lift up the cover and he's over in the corner. Feathers in the shit on the bottom of the cage. Bright eyes. Black eyes. Pale yellow. He never sang anyway. Chirpa tweet. I can see him breathing, or maybe it's heartbeat, very fast. Another match. Gas cook stove. Perfect. Fool around with the buttons. Oven. On. Teach him to sing. Another match. Put it to the hole and there's a push of air and the flame goes on blue, curling up. All the flames shooting down and then curling up. Take the cover off the cage. He doesn't say anything. Too dark. Can't talk in the dark. Put the whole cage in. Ain't gonna put my hand in and chase him around in the bird shit. Just fits. The heat comes up from below. "Watch out for wooden soap." Close the door and look around. Nothing good to take. Hokey old lady stuff. She wanted to show us postcards. Had a lot of postcards. Pictures of Vince when he was little. Old lady crap. Creep into the living room. Dark. Potted plants. Put my hand out and stick it into dirt. Wet dirt. Chairs and tables and knickknacks. Fancy painted cups and saucers.

Pottery animals and ladies in long dresses. The bedroom door is shut tight. Muttering in there. Prayers. Not a woman's voice. Not a man's. Just old. Turn the knob and push. Nothing. Locked. Give her a thrill. The muttering stops. I turn it again. Rattle it. "Oh dear God! Let me die now!" The scraggy old voice screaming. Pitch my voice low and hollow, far away and strong. "Sure thing, baby!" Rattle the door again hard. Something falls down inside and I run out giggling, my hand over my mouth. The oven's roaring and there's a thick burning smell. Slam the door behind me and let the screen swing back. Run off up the road laughing to where Heydorf's waiting, eating all the chocolate cookies.

He's gone. Left today. Took the bus to L.A. Two and a half months till school lets out. Got to get money. Got to get out of here. Two and a half months. Get out the lists and unfold them.

Ways to make money

Sell things I have
Steal things and sell them
Put jars in the halls with "Save Dutch Fund" on 'em
Lunch money
Pop bottles
Old tires to recapper
Copper wire
Write papers for people
Mow lawns
Baby-sit

Things to steal and sell

Books (from school and downtown library to
  kids and secondhand bookshops)
Cakes (from cake sales to wrestling team after
  they weigh in)
Hubcaps (from parking lot during games etc.
  to??)
Nylons (from dept. stores to girls at school)
Cigarettes (to boys at school)
Typewriter? (from old Birdsing—pawnshop?)
Also: nick change while tending popcorn stand
  at home games

Things to take along

   hatchet
   matches (waterproof and regular)
   rope
x string
   back pack
x extra socks (two pair)
x sweatshirt
x extra dungarees
x Band-aids
x antiseptic (iodine, alcohol, something for burns,
      vaseline)
   knife
   canteen
x underpants (two pair)
   sleeping bag
   compass
   fishhooks
   poncho
x needle and strong thread
   boots (good hiking boots)

   x flashlight (batteries)
      jacket
      notebook (pencils)

   x —things I have or can get from home

   Wait till it's almost time to start accumulating things. Some of it too noticeable around the house. Could keep it in my locker at school. Do that. Keep it there till the very end. Leave right after school lets out. No use hanging around after. Maw'd just start making plans for me.

   Sold the skates to the rink today. Fifteen dollars. Minus bus fare, $14.70.

   Jake doesn't notice anything. Carry books out by the armload and he just sits there playing with his tie. A good *Crime and Punishment, Don Quixote, The Great Books: Marx.* School library books are easier to cover up than the downtown library's. Downtown they put a stamp on damn near every page. Six dollars from the secondhand bookstore on Third Avenue. $5.85 in the pot.

Fourteen pairs of nylons. Size 8, 10 and 11, medium. $7.00 in the pot.

The jars in the hall are amazing. A steady fifty cents a day. Maybe they don't read the card and think it's for a worthy cause. Maybe they think it's a good joke. Just pennies. Once in a while a nickel or a dime. All adds up.

* * *

Gave Monica her take-off on Charles Lamb today. All about how Joe Nestle, the cowherd, got drunk and let the cows eat cocoa beans. Milk came out brown. Villagers punished him by making him drink the spoiled milk. Eureka! Disgusting. Monica loved it. Get her a B if she fixes up the spelling and punctuation. $5.00.

Tried to get a typewriter out of the Business classes tonight. Birdsing always leaves the window open a little. Walked all the way out there. Got in O.K. But the typing room was locked. Tried an adding machine instead. Ninety pounds. Got it out the window and into the trees. Took me about an hour. Dragged it part way. Dirt and shit in the works. Probably no good now. Left it in some bushes. Even if it doesn't do me any good it'll hassle old "J.K.L. Semi" Birdsing. Nothing in the pot though.

Sixty-four dollars. Had it in an old shoe in my closet. Dumb. Maw found it today cleaning and came into the living room waving it and looking hysterical. "Where did you get this much money?" She thought I stole it from Dad or robbed a bank or something. I was sitting in the fireplace picking my nose. "Well, Maw, I've been saving it for a long time. From the telephone job and lunch money sometimes. Stuff like that. It's for my education." Very clever I think. True too. My education. She got all happy I'm being so wise. Sits down on the floor in front of the fireplace with her bandanna wrapped around her head like Aunt Jemima. Am I going to college or what? Yeah, maybe, or art school. Haven't really decided. We sat jawing about things like that till she hadda get up get dinner. Gave me back the sixty-four dollars. Find a better place to put it.

I told Leben I'm running away. Made her swear not to tell of course. If anybody asks her she'll blab her brains. Told her I was going to the Mission Mountains in Montana. Near a little town called St. Ignatius. Saw the mountains on the map when I was looking to see Missoula, where Heydorf was. St. Ignatius is just about a ghost town. Looked him up. Patron saint of thieves and travelers. That's me. Told her all about how I'd live in the mountains. Build a log cabin. Fish and hunt and trap. Be a hermit. Got kind of excited about it. Do all that, only down south.

Cecilia, Vince's little sister, bought four paperbacks and my transistor radio when I told her about running away to the Mission Mountains. She swore not to tell. Holy hair. Probably won't. She goes hiking a lot. Says she's got boots I can borrow. She's a lot taller. Five six maybe. But her feet are the same size as mine. Look at the boots tomorrow. Get her money.

Great boots. Infantry boots, high ankles, thick hard rubber soles, hooks for the laces and two leather straps around the top. Great. Told her I'd get 'em from her just before school lets out. They just fit. A dollar for the paperbacks and three-fifty for the radio. She got a letter from Vince in the navy. He likes it. Shoulda known.

Pietila called me in again about wearing dungarees to school. Told him I was poor and he said he'd be glad to arrange for clothes from some charity or other. Said thanks but I don't take charity. Got a roll of air mail stamps out of his petty cash drawer while he was making a call. Six dollars from Mrs. Martin at the grocery store. Told her it was for a charity. People are dumb.

Lot of trips to the secondhand bookstore. The guy in the Green Dolphin got suspicious. Won't take anymore. Have to go all the way across town to the Academy.

* * *

There's going to be an end of the year party. Mostly seniors but underclassmen can go too. Two days at Mt. Hood. Whole ski lodge. Swimming pool. Lots of food. Tobogganing. Figure I'll tell Maw I'm going to that. Have two days' head start before they start looking for me. Twenty-five dollars a head.

Told Maw about the party. She didn't like it at first but I explained how it's sponsored by the school and loaded with chaperones and all that. Told her it was ten dollars and I'd pay it myself out of my savings. She wanted to pay it but I said I wanted to and now she wants to buy me a dress for it. Aarg. Get out of that somehow. Tell her everybody's wearing pants. Something.

Time running short. Letter from Heydorf. He's staying at the Pasadena Y.M.C.A. Told me to call him when I get into the bus station. "And watch out for Mexicans who want to sell you a diamond ring for sixty bucks. They might rob you and whatever else they do to girls." So he'll meet me. It's easier that way. Feel all mushy toward Maw lately. Try to be good to her since I'm leaving.

* * *

Everybody's gone but me. Vince in the navy. Fred and Pete off in college. Heydorf in L.A. All these turds in school really get on my nerves. Never go back to school again. Sit off in my cozy cabin with a kerosene lamp and a fire and read whatever I want. Never have to count the iambic this-and-thats. Never diagram another sentence. Never try to figure out what some asshole teacher thinks is the meaning of a story. "The river is life and the river is death." My ass. My royal Irish asshole. Stupid sons of bitches. I'm passing everything but P.E. and Algebra. Two Cs, three Ds, and two Fs. That's the way it looks now. Might run into trouble.

Teddie Mote decided he's my friend. He hunts and fishes and goes camping a lot so I told him how I'm running off to the Mission Mountains. He thinks it's fantastic. Swore not to tell. He will when they ask but he's loaning me all sorts of camping gear. Told me how more than anything else he wants a son. I didn't laugh because he's loaning me all this stuff.

Maw wouldn't listen to reason about the party dress. Took me downtown after school today and bought it. I wouldn't

look at 'em. She picked it out and made me try it on and
she bought it. Pink. Cotton at least but pink. No sleeves.
My freckledy old arms stick out like a turd in a pan of
milk. At least it hasn't got any gewgaws on it and there's a
pretty good pocket. I suppose I'll have to wear the damn
thing to leave in. White god-awful shoes. Gold heels and
pointy toes. Fall off when I walk fast. Hurt my toes. And
this underskirt with lace on it and darts for tits. An insult.
But she couldn't find any with lace that didn't have the
tits in. I kept telling her everybody was wearing pants but
she called Leben's mother and they conspired. She gave
up trying to make me wear skirts to school a long time
ago. I kept skipping. Hid down under the bridge all day
so nobody'd see me in a skirt. But she figures this once
I'll wear a pretty pink dress. That'll learn her.

Dad's brandy about half water now. Have to lay off it. The
football team isn't even used to beer. Watered-down apri-
cot brandy knocks them on their asses. $20.00

All my books gone. Maw asked what I did with them.
Told her I'd loaned some out and given the rest to the
Fireman's Christmas Fund. She gave me some of hers to
donate. Down to the secondhand bookstore again.

* * *

Letter from Heydorf. He's getting a .22 pistol. Wants me to get a pile of ammo from his basement to bring to him. Have to raid the place. His mother doesn't like me. Thinks I'm a bad influence. Get Teddie Mote to drive me out. Very handy since he's decided he's my friend.

"You gotta stay right here. Keep the motor running. Getaway car. See?" He's chicken shit. Two blocks away and his face is white and his eyes are bugging. Dark and I run soft on the sidewalk. A little white house. A little grass and a lot of other little white houses. Down the driveway. Concrete steps down to the basement. Dark. Window isn't latched. Slip the screwdriver under and there's no car in the drive. Gone to the movies. Window's up and I slide in. Sink. My feet in a big zinc sink. Step out and down a long ways. Turn on the flashlight. Shelves of canned fruit. Peaches and pears and cherries all golden and pink and cobwebs. Cement floor. Over against the wall, rake hanging up and hose and beneath, on the floor, two piles. A tarp over each one. A little card pinned to each one. The one to the left reads "Leave me." Heydorf's square printing. The one on the right says "Take me." He planned it before he left. Spread out the tarp. Boxes and boxes of shells. ".22" with an eagle's head on each box. Heavy. A big fishing reel. Fold-up fishing pole. Pile it all on the tarp. Wrap it up. Dark and the air is dusty. "What are you doing?" The voice is hard and the light clicks on. Bare bulb and dust everywhere. Dust on my pant legs. The flashlight gives no light in the whiteness. She's standing on the steps. I can see all of her. All the inner tube rolls in a pink knit. Little gold circle pin on her shoulder. "I asked what you were doing." Very cold.

Not even angry. Just disgusted. I stand up and get the letter out of my pocket. "He asked me to get this stuff and send it to him." Holding out the letter but she doesn't take it. She walks down the steps slowly. The steps bend and groan. She's very fat. The makeup pale on her face and dark on her mouth and little eyes lost in the hot fat. "I couldn't get here any other time and I thought you weren't home when I came so I thought I'd just take it and leave a note." It's bad. Strained. I'm sweating and shaking. She's not angry. She's cold. "Well, I think you had best go and leave these things where they are. If my son wants them he can write to me and I'll send them." She goes to the door and opens it. I turn off the flashlight and walk past her out the door. It takes two steps to pass her. She smells warm and sweet. Some sweet thing and she's cold. She closes the door and I look through the window as I go and she is wider than the door and she's pink and soft and very cold. Ugh. Get Teddie to buy me a hamburger. Warm me up.

Had to take all the jars out of the hall. Pietila finally noticed and called me in. Told him it was a joke. He said it was probably illegal or something. Doesn't matter. Too late. Already cleaned up. Nearly time now. Four days.

Report cards. F in social studies too. Maw worried I won't be able to go to college like I want to. Told her I'd do better next year.

* * *

Derry Ragel's O.K. Has a car. Told him about the Mission Mountains. He's wild to help but has a date to go to the party. Teddie's going too. Derry'll get his friend Bryce to drive me into town to the bus station. Bryce is high society. Good grades. Escort to the May Fete princess, letterman, René Van Den Bosch's boy friend. Hotsy-totsy, I'm a Nazi.

Cecilia brought the boots today. Put 'em in my locker. Teddie will bring the pack with the stuff I asked for tomorrow. Put it all in my locker and get it out the night of the party. Maw will drive me to school, see the buses loading for the party, drive off. I'll run in and pick up the stuff and meet Bryce out behind the cafeteria.

There's a bus at nine. Express to L.A. Perfect. Leave the school around seven-thirty. Plenty of time to get into town, buy the ticket and get on the bus. Then I'm gone. Out of it. I went away.

Dear Maw,

    I am in Montana in the mountains. I'm fine and am a hermit now. Don't try to find me. I am really all right. I'll write again soon.

Love to Dad and Nick
your daughter
Jean

I lick it all up and put it in an envelope. Already stamped. Already addressed. Put it into the larger envelope with the note.

Postmaster,
St. Ignatius, Montana

Dear Sir,

    I am an avid collector of postmarks and am interested in obtaining the St. Ignatius postmark. I would appreciate your forwarding this letter with the appropriate stamp to my home.

yours truly,
my father's name

*   *   *

I know the letter is hokey as hell but a person writes hokey things to their mother. She'll know it's me. Does the job.

I've never really given her any trouble before. Tried not to shit on her. Nothing ever gets back to her of what I do. Never ran away before. That was because I was chicken shit. Not because of her. That time when we were in Nevada and I was going to ride my bike to Oregon and live in a hollow tree. Had it all planned out. What I needed to take. How much money I'd have to have. How long it would take me. Didn't have the money. Never even started. Kept thinking how obvious I'd be on the road on my bike. Too scared to hitchhike. Kept seeing my scraggy body laid out on a rock in the desert with snakes crawling all around it and flies buzzing over it. Too easy to get caught and dragged back. Never even started. Never even tried. Too many consequences. All planned out now. Has to work. If I've got the guts. If I start thinking about consequences now it'll make me sick. I'll end up being a good girl and staying here. Stop going out at night. Stop walking on the tracks. Stop laying under the trestle when the freights come through. Stay here with Mama and let my hair grow. Get a job at the supermarket and never nick anything. Never pocket any change. Spend all my money on clothes and sit at night with Maw in front of the TV sewing on my hope chest and waiting for the right Flying A man to come along. Too much. Too much to stand. I really would end up killing somebody. Feeling the knife one day and red and anger and all the lost minutes and wasted hours come pouring out. It'd be whoever was there. It wouldn't matter who. Just whoever was in the room and I'd put my monster face on and not laugh and not take it off when they laughed. They'd take too long to know it wasn't a joke and by then it'd be too late. Too late for them. Too late for me a long time before. Maybe I'd learn to embroider. Dish towels and pillowcases and monogrammed handkerchiefs. Once I found out what the monogram would be. But it'd be too late and the knife would come into my hand and somebody's true blood would fall all over my embroidery. I have to go. I have to. Doesn't need guts anymore. I've got the machine moving and so many people know a version. Can't back out now. I've got some pride. I've set it up so I don't have to worry about having the guts. I'll go because going is easier than staying. It's good. I did good. Still, I wonder if I'll do it.

Thursday. Last day of school. No use going to class. Speeches and bullshit. Cutesy farewells. Drag all the stuff out of my locker and into the nearest can. Boots and Teddie's pack and all the stuff from home. Brought out in little bags and pockets and folded between books. Relayed for weeks. All here. No good jacket. No sleeping bag. Get 'em in L.A. Less to carry for a while anyway. Sit touching it and packing and repacking. Good Japanese army knife. Teddie's old man's souvenir. Heavy and black-bladed for night fighting. No shine to shoot at. A heavy webbed belt with holes for the canteen and the knife. No vaseline at home. Out lately. Got Vicks VapoRub. Probably no good for burns. Burn more than the burn. Throw it in. Never know. All smooth and tight. Shove it in hard and pound it all smooth. A back pack and a side pack to hang on one shoulder. Across the shoulder maybe. All there. All finished. Nothing more to do. Put it all into the locker. Efficient looking. Smooth. Go wandering around the halls. A few other people wandering around. Laughter and speeches coming from behind the doors... Though I've overworked and failed you, though I've bitched at you and jailed you... Very cute. Everybody jolly and sweetly melancholy at parting. Lovely. Big reunion in the fall... My, what a fantastic tan! You've changed your hair! It's beautiful! Don't you think she's gained a lot of weight? Of course I'm taking all enriched courses this year... already accepted at Oregon State and the U. of O. but I'd really like to go to... But I won't see it or hear it. I'll never have to hear it again. Never have to be in it and cold and outside in it. Never again. Go down to the gym. All the mats empty. Trampoline's down. Get up on it with my sneakers on. Not allowed but there's nobody around. Walk around. Springing, flying, jump and jump and the floor goes away and my head is wild and my arms move the right way without thinking about it. Fly and the harder I fall the higher I fly. Fly clear away and my foot goes between the springs and I fall flat and still bouncing and it's nice and easy and feels good. I was ready to stop anyway. Get down and go rustle around in the equipment cupboards. Bats and helmets and spikes and pads and gloves and wrist guards and bows and arrows. I was always pretty good with the bow. If we'd had archery all the time I might have passed Phys Ed. They're green fiberglass twenty-pound bows and fiberglass arrows with a plastic fletch and slightly pointed target tips. Take one along. Anybody tries to take me back I'll get 'em in the balls with my trusty bow 'n' arrow. Take a bow with a good string and a handful of arrows. A strap to hold the arrows. Amble down the hall and stow it in the locker. Long day. Nothing doing. Everything already done. Go sleep in the back of the library. Rest up for the trip.

* * *

Wanted to eat a lot of supper. Couldn't. Belly acting up.
"That's O.K., Maw. They'll give us a lot of food at the
party." Nick wants to know what the ski lodge is like. How
many people will be there. I can't talk. I can't even listen.
I just look at them. Maw thinks I'm feverish. No, just
excited. "My, I never saw you so excited about a party
before." They don't know. It's funny. They have no idea.
Like Ma and Pa Kent now knowing the kid is a weirdo.
"It's nothing, Maw. I just like to go around in these weird
pajamas." She zips me into the dress and puts some smell
water behind my ears and tucks my pajams under my
arm. "I've got something I hope you'll like." A new
raincoat. Trench coat. Black cotton. Pretty cool with the
belt and the collar goes up high. I kiss her and don't cry.
Don't cry. You'll fuck it totally. The shoes hurt. Helps
make me tough. She drives in her apron and she's telling
me about some party where she wore a sky-blue dress and
I can't hear her, I just see her silly face against the lights.
The school grounds are lighted and the buses surrounded
and the parking lot crowded. She doesn't try to drive in.
"Have a lovely party, Little, and call when you get in and
I'll pick you up." One more kiss on her cinnamon-soft old
cheek in the dark. I'm out and running. Wave once and
she's gone and I'm gone. The shoes keep slipping off and
I have to stop for them. People all yelling with luggage.
Whole suitcases for two nights. Maybe they're all running
away too. Crowd and lights and I'm running. The locker
is easy and the stuff comes out and swings around me
and I throw the pajamas into a barrel and I'm running
and it's dark and lights blink and there's hot-shit Brycie
Baby's fancy Ford. He opens the door from the inside

and I throw the stuff in back and slide in. "Hi. I understand you're running away and want to get to the bus
station?" "Right." I gather he doesn't approve. Tough titty.
But then he might squeal too soon. Better talk to him
about it. We're out of the parking lot and it's dark all
around and he handles the car well. Smooth and not too
fast. Not proving anything. "Can I ask you something?"
"Sure." Oh-oh. He's going to save me. Turn me back. All I
wanted was a fucking ride. Could have hitched or got a
bus. Less trouble. "Why are you doing this?" Think. It's
got to be good or he'll tell tonight. Ruin everything. I
start slow, talking in my old dreamer voice. A little stream
in a mountain valley. A little cabin, simple but adequate.
Quiet. Peace. I've been there before. The fish are good.
Only a two-mile walk to a little half ghost town. A little
solitude. A little time to learn to know myself. To read
and think and be alone. I'll tell my parents when I get
there but they wouldn't understand. Things are happening too fast. The world won't slow down for me so I have
to step out of it for a while and allow myself to adjust. It's
so sweet I could puke. He loves it. I can see the picture
growing in his eyes. He wishes he were going. He likes me
and admires me for my depth and perception and sensi-
tivity. He eats shit. But at least he won't tell until somebody asks him. Naturally he wouldn't lie. He stops for gas
and won't let me pay. Goes into the station and comes out
with two bottles of pop. I thank him and we go on and he
talks about how he'd like that too and it's funny he'd seen
me around school and heard about me but never thought
I had, you know, any depth. He regrets now that he didn't
get to know me better. Maybe when I get back we can get
together sometimes and talk. Lovely. I'd love it. Town.
Lights. Bus station. I've got the door open and I'm
pulling at stuff and he wants to carry it for me but I
thank him and tell him it'd be conspicuous. "Wait, here's
something." He reaches into the glove compartment and

holds out two books. *Edible Plants of the Northern Temperate Zones* and a pocket Bible. "They might help. You're welcome to them. And...and I wish you luck." "Gee, thanks and thanks for the ride." Bye-bye Brycie Baby, shoulda knowed you'd be a fucking Holy Hair. Toodle-oo, so long. And I'm trucking along with my junk hanging on me and it's too late and I'm glad. I didn't have to worry about going through with it. It's done and I'm free. Now just be careful and it's all open. The world. I'll be king. If they don't catch me first, I'll be king.

It's this same huddled old gray bus station full of sailors and Indians and bums, and the benches have arms or at least knobs every foot and a half so you can't sleep here but they do. In the summer when it's hot we'd come here eating ice cream and sit around waiting for an old lady to faint in the heat. Once one did.

Now it's dark and the bulbs are dim and make it darker and I don't even feel ridiculous in my pink party dress with the packs slung on my shoulders. I feel electric and the money is folded in tight neat bundles, one for the ticket, one for secret. To keep and live on for a while. A year maybe. Who knows how far a hundred dollars goes? This twenty-four dollars is a thousand miles and it's wet in my pocket where my hand sweats on it. I walk across to the ticket window stepping very carefully and standing straight as though the packs aren't heavy. Can't look worried. Be sure and clear or they'll start wondering where I'm going alone. He's glasses, I don't know what else, and I say, "One one-way to Los Angeles." No please. He might look up if I say please. The ticket slides out and the money slides in and the bus leaves in twenty minutes.

I sit down behind the Coke machine and lean back into the shadow feeling in my pockets the package of fish-hooks and the toy compass and the pill bottle of water-proof matches. The cop cars go by too often in the street and my sweat tickles running down my ribs. If they come in and grab me or question me I'll go softly and be quiet. No screaming and groveling. Make it a little easier next time. Somebody could've told and they're looking for me already. All the whys and the tears and they'd lock me in my room for a while and then forget but whenever I wanted to do something she'd remember and say something and all the hurt looks, aargh! It's just too much. In a couple of weeks, maybe a week, I'll send the letter to St. Ignatius and in another week they'll have it and I don't ever need to go back. I can get by. With the bow and Brycie's plant book and hooks and string and nick things. Creep down around an old farmhouse in the night. Make friends with the dog first. Sit up on the hill watching for day or a few days and then stroll down so nobody sees to make friends with the dog. Maybe wait till they go into town to the movies and then go down wild and starting at everything and look into all their rooms and drawers and sit on the bed and not brush away the creases and eat a genuine peanut butter sandwich again, it will have been months and months, with jelly and take a steak and canned peaches away and leave a little note: "I have eaten your food. Thank you. The Green Phantom," and then sit up on the hill to watch when they come back. Old man in suspenders and a chubby lady with a white collar and apron and kids and they'll slam doors and run in and out and the voices will carry up faint in the air and they'll wonder. Pin the note on the screen door so they see it right off. But if they come back at night I couldn't see. Maybe they'd just be in the house talking about it and I couldn't tell. Maybe anyway it'd be cooler not to leave a note. Leave everything just the way it was and then I could go back again, when the fruit's ripe in the orchard or lots of times and they'd never know at all. Be careful to take things they couldn't be sure were missing. One can each of things they had a lot of, a piece of meat from the bottom of the freezer. My stomach hurts. It always hurts when I'm really scared. The intercom says Omaha and Phoenix and Dallas and the voice is clear how they are flat gray towns and I don't want to go there. The people move in lines with luggage out the doors. She'll be sick with it, worrying, and maybe take it out on him. If they catch me, as bad as I've made it for them they'll make it worse for me. The intercom says "and Los Angelees!" I count quick, the pack and the bow and the shoulder pack and my ticket. Standing up is confusing and my legs are asleep a little and ache. The line is long in front of me. I might have to sit with somebody. I want to sit alone and think. Moon out the window and not have to be polite. Thirty hours. Maybe the driver looks at me funny. With the bow I'm asking for it. Even unstrung it's obvious. I'll tell them I'm on my way to Mexico City for an archery exhibition. I'm the Oregon Female Champion and there's a tournament. Most people wouldn't know this is too piddling a bow for that kind of stuff. Thin green fiberglass with "Tigard H.S." in black felt pen on the belly. But the driver punches the ticket and I go out. The bus is dark in the dark and the aluminum siding cheesy in the neon. He said they had stewardesses. Maybe they serve you meals like on a plane. Thirty hours. That ought to be long enough for four or five meals at least. But I ain't hungry. They all in the bus going to Mt. Hood for the party. They say there's a swimming pool and sledding and skiing and lots of free food and pop and they all dancing and necking but chaperones, I don't know who they got and then they all come back home. They all go in their houses and wash their brassieres and rinse out their stockings and hang up in the bathroom. Wash their hair and put it up in curlers so they can drag Broadway the next night in souped-up cars.

It's crowded but I get a seat alone and put my new raincoat in the rack. Fold it up so the goodies don't fall out of the pockets. Lay the bow on it in back and put the packs on top. I'll change clothes in L.A. before I meet Heydorf. He wouldn't want to be with me in a pink dress.

The motor goes on and people fiddle with the reading lights and play with the blowers and their hands show white above the seats and the tops of their heads and nothing else. The thumps and bangs stop and the door closes and my stomach flips a little and then eases back into ache. This is it. We're moving. There's no going back now. Out of the garage and the familiar street dark and empty, I stare hard out the window but it doesn't feel like a big farewell or anything. It's just scary. I know I don't know what I'm doing but I'm doing it anyway. But the bus doesn't cross the river or turn onto the highway. It goes down under the bridge and the dark comes thick and the puke burns hot almost coming up. They know. They just going right to the police station and they'll take me off in front of all these people and then go on to L.A. without me and I won't even be able to get my twenty-four dollars back. I'll stand there ridiculous in my pink dress with the bow and packs and the stuff in my pockets and they'll laugh and my mother will be grim and maybe cry. But the bus stops at a big service station and the pumps hum and the bright lights burn my eyes through the green glass and I lean back and close my eyes and pray oh dear god oh dear god, like when I was little, don't let them get me, don't let them catch me, until the bus moves again, up onto the bridge this time and straight out onto the white wide road with black all around when the houses are gone. My arches ache where I've been pressing them on the footrest and my fingers are stiff on

the arms of the seat. Nobody can see me and it's warm
and the engine roars. My stomach goes back to a soft
ache, dies out, hardly there anymore. It's all done now. I
went away. They'll call up the school when I don't get
back Sunday from the party. Or won't wait to call the
school but will call one of the kids' houses, Leben's
probably, to see if the bus got back O.K. and on schedule.
And maybe whoever they call will tell them I wasn't at the
party and they'll start scurrying and worrying and calling
everybody. Maybe they'll think I'm lost up on the mountain. She's sure to think somebody raped me and killed
me in the bushes someplace. She's sure to think that every
hour or so. Then somebody will get feeling guilty about
not telling and the whole Montana story will come out. I
talked a little about Montana at home, I think. Maybe
she'll remember that and believe it. She'll believe it anyway. They'll all believe it. So figure I've got two weeks
before they could accidentally stumble on the right direction to look for me. But then they'll go to the police and
Brycie Baby would spill it that I took a bus and somebody
at the bus station might remember that I bought a ticket
to L.A. Any smart cop would ask at the bus station. But
say I've got two weeks. Anyway I've got two days before
they expect me home if they haven't found out already.
But at least two days and maybe, probably, two weeks.
And when the letter gets there postmarked St. Ignatius
that should keep them in that direction a while longer. At
least another week till they get the postmaster to say he
just forwarded a letter that came originally from L.A. So
maybe even three weeks and by that time I can be totally
gone. Take a bus to San Diego and another bus as close to
the border as possible and then get out and walk. Just
walk out of town into the hills and across the border.
Even if they patrol the border on horses they couldn't be
that hard to get by. Even if there's barbed wire. Just
skinny under it and walk on into the Baja. Walk across to

the Gulf of Baja and down the coast to one of those little fishing villages in the south and get a fisherman to give me a ride across to the mainland. Maybe work for the fisherman awhile. Cut bait and haul nets. He wouldn't know I ain't a boy. Must be hundreds of miles down the Baja. I'll be so miserable, hot and dry and no food or water. Rattlesnakes. Maybe I better get a snake bite kit. Razor blade and a suction cup. You have to cut an X over the holes and use the suction cup to draw out the poison. Tourniquet. If you swallow it or have a cut in your mouth you die anyway. My gums always bleed. They will by then anyway. No oranges. A little scurvy. Zits and your gums bleed. And bug bites and sunburn. I can get a cowboy hat same time I get the sleeping bag. White straw cowboy hat. My nose will burn off. Eat rabbits. Shoot rabbit with my bow and arrow. Got to be careful with the arrows. Only five but if I can find 'em they work again. Roast rabbit. Rather have peanut butter but can't carry jars or bread or anything like that. Too heavy. Too bulky. Wouldn't last long enough anyway. Can't even take candy bars. Melt. Life Savers maybe. Quick energy. Butterscotch and wild cherry. They put my tongue to sleep after a while. Stiff. Can't taste anything. Maybe he will come with me. He was talking like that. We. And he does know I'm a girl. The letter said, "...whatever else they do to girls." I'd be scared to rob something big like he wants to. It's so easy just to get by but something big and they always catch you. Wreck everything. And the hypnotism. But maybe he will come with me. I know I'll be scared of the dark if I'm alone.

It's dark and the sway is smooth and it feels warm in the seats with heads and seats dark against darkness and black against white when a car passes going the other way. It's not the coast route. Too straight and smooth for that. A big highway. Down through Salem. Straight through the middle of the state. I don't know the towns on the way. Don't know. He knows, the driver, up there alone. Dark and soft, the noise soft and steady so it isn't there anymore. Thumps from behind me, one seat behind and across the aisle. I lean over a little to peek. A little lady. Chubby but little. She looks gray. She sits very straight with round hands on her purse in her lap. Her skirt hides her legs and it's too dark to see her face. The thumps come from the window seat. I can't see. A man in the window seat across from me lifts himself up and looks down into the seat next to the gray lady. "If he doesn't stop kicking me in the back I'm gonna stop the bus and kick his ass off!" His voice is a little louder than it needs to be. Just a little. He falls back down in the seat and disappears behind the woman in the aisle seat. The little gray lady opens and shuts her purse, just nervous, click-click a couple of times. Another thump and the man in front lurches up again and leans over. She drops her purse and leans into the seat and I can see her pulling and tugging at something. The man in front falls back down and she pulls for a little while longer and then sits back and picks up her purse again. Black leather. I lean back in my seat and look out the window. Scrape something, knees cracking maybe. I look again and a long man is crawling out over the little lady. He puts his hands on the arm of her seat and his knee comes out but not far enough and then goes down and there is a sound of tearing, and he shakes his foot and throws it out into the aisle. The bus lurches just a little and his elbows fold and he is laying over the little gray lady with one foot in the aisle and one foot on the other side of her. Her gray round head shows over a black shoulder. He lifts up and her head disappears into her armpit. I can see her chubby little hands, one on his arm and the other pushing up on his chest. He lifts away and the round hands give a little pat as he goes. He stands in the aisle with his head a little bent. He's tall. He wobbles and puts his hands on seat backs and walks slowly back and opens the door of the toilet. The light flashes a second and then he's inside and shuts the door. I am sitting on my knees on the seat and can just put my eyes over the back of the seat without lifting up. It's too dark for anyone to notice unless they look right at me. The gray lady is folding at her skirt. The fold parts in her hand and I can see that it's torn jaggedly up from the hem. She folds slowly and holds the fold closed and holding the skirt and her purse she slides out of sight into the window seat. I can just see the edge of her, faintly gray, and maybe half of her head. The john door cracks white and black comes out. I scootch down in the seat because he's walking toward me. It takes him a long time. When the foam rubber sigh comes from his seat I look again and he is all dark and very long. He lays back in the seat and his legs bend into the aisle and past me. His feet must reach the back of the seat in front of me. I can hear him breathing. It's short but deep. Maybe I can smell vomit. I'm not sure. Maybe it's my own. I'm not sure. My legs are almost asleep. I stretch them into the next seat and lie propped in the corner with the window cold against my cheek and the seat warm against the rest of me. I like a cold pillow. All the rest warm and the pillow cold. When I vomit I like to stop and rest and lay my face against something cold. The toilet tank or the wall if it's tile or the floor if it really feels bad. My eyes closed and my head hot against the cold and my whole body shaking and sweating, fingers jerking and the hard outline of the sick inside me. I can hear my blood then and my heart and feel all the organs working. I can feel where my lungs end and how they flap, and the floating dark things inside that don't turn red till they hit the air. Usually they're not there at all. I can't feel them. I don't believe in them. But when I'm sick or scared I can feel them all. It's nice.

He's lying on the floor kicking. He was groaning a little

and he started to twitch and shake. I could hear his heel
rubbing fast against the floor and I looked and he was
sitting straight with his head tilted back looking at the
ceiling. Not much noise. A little rubbing, and I could see
his hands, pale blobs that changed shape very quickly.
Then he slid down off the seat onto the floor. He did it
on purpose. He didn't fall. He put his hands on the seat,
and on the arm of the seat and slid down onto the floor.
His legs jerk and kick. Sometimes the knees or the shins
hit hard against one of the seat legs. I don't think he
knows he's doing it anymore. The man by the window
pushes up in his seat again and looks over into the aisle.
He turns around and leans on the back of the seat and
down. His head begins to shake and keeps going from
left to right, not very far and each swing is a little shorter
and a little bit faster. His head stops moving and his voice
a little too loud. "Jesus. Why in hell do they let drunks
onto a public bus?" Then he turns back around and
settles down into the seat. I can see the edge of the little
gray lady, her arm, and she's leaning over looking at the
man on the floor. After a while he stops kicking and lies
very still. I can still hear him breathing over the engine.
He breathes slow now, and I listen and can't see his face
but only a section of his legs where they pass my seat.
Later when I wake up he's asleep in the seat with his head
on the gray lady's shoulder.

Heydorf doesn't go with girls. Maybe he's queer. The
time he stayed over at Vince's house and Vince went to sit
with him on the bunk he yelled, "Help, I'm being attacked!"
Probably a joke. But maybe half a joke. Maybe he hates
'em like my old man hating niggers and him so dark-
skinned. But I saw him watching the girl in the hall at
school, kind of crazy, hungry and plotting blank all over
his face. And he followed the lady in the green dress for a
long time. But he never does anything so he wouldn't do

anything. I'd have to do it all. He'd just lay back with his
eyes half closed and his fingers twitching and he wouldn't
get hard, just a little bigger and still soft. Just sticking out
a little further and still hanging down. I couldn't do it.
He'd be watching, not really there, just off at the other
end watching. If I put it in my mouth I'd always know he
was up in his head and not there in my mouth. Couldn't
do it. The bus stops at a restaurant and the motor hums
rough and people get off and go inside. It feels bad
stopped. Ain't getting anywhere. I want to grunt forward
in the seat, pushing to make it go again. There's no
reason to stop. There's no gas here and there's a toilet in
back. They don't need to eat so soon. Fifteen or twenty
minutes and the wait lays dead and pulls down on my
stomach and I sit straight up waiting. I'm stiff but I can't
lean back till the bus moves on. The lights make a pool
and the bus lays in it and I'm tight and straight in the bus
and a grease smell of cooking comes in. The driver has to
piss. That's why. He drinks coffee and pisses and the next
while he'll have to piss again and then he'll drink more
coffee. Maybe having to piss keeps him awake. It's warm
out and I can see the bugs beating around the lights on
the porch. The sign says "Roamers Rest" in white light
bulbs and the black spots on the light bulbs are burnt
bugs. The ashtray is full. The lid is up a little with paper
sticking out. I put my finger in and feel wet tissue and
cigarette filters and ash grime. I take my finger out and
wipe it on the back of the seat. No bugs in there yet. The
air conditioning makes it almost too cold. Except me, the
scorpion. My mother was born on Halloween. What does
that make me? Nothing, Scorpio, The insect in the ether,
The bug in the sky. Bugs don't know their mothers. Eat
'em when they meet. I just don't care anymore. They'll be
hurt and crazy worried and do dumb things and hate
themselves and me but that isn't as important as this. This
has got to be done. If they catch me they'll take the

money. After all the work it wouldn't be mine. They'd
take it so I couldn't run away again and it'd get spent on
oil bills and hamburger and detergent. It'd just go away.
I'll split it up. Five dollars for spending money and the
rest, where? I could pin it inside my underpants but if the
cops took me they'd search me and find it and give it to
Maw. The door of the restaurant slams and the bus
bounces a little as somebody jumps on the step. He comes
all the way back. Tall with a red plaid flannel shirt under
his black suit jacket. He stops at the seat just behind and
across the aisle. The little lady smiles at him. She isn't
gray like I thought but powder blue with pale yellow curls
and old pink cheeks. He stands straight and his left arm
jerks out with sandwiches wrapped in triangular waxed
paper. "Eat one of these!" The voice is urgent but low.
Pushing the sandwiches like she's denying herself. She
smiles and shakes no, and he throws the sandwiches into
the overhead rack and flops down into the seat. He pulls
at his collar but it's already open and he falls back with
his eyes closed. The other people come back and the bus
moves on. I like it. When it's good in a car I want never to
stop. Just keep going forever. The stopping makes me
feel sick and tight like it's time to die. Just drive on,
whoever was driving, not me. And I'd sit in the seat and
we'd stop to piss and for gas and at drive-ins for hamburgers and get candy bars at gas stations and just go on
fast down the road, not turning, just curving and I'd
sleep sitting up or crawl in back and cover up and the
driver would never sleep but just drive and the car would
never break down or run out of gas. In the morning we'd
get a whole package of coffee cake with nuts and jelly and
a lot of frosting and paper cups of coffee with a lot of
milk and sugar and I'd sit cross-legged on the front seat
and eat gooey cake and sip sweet coffee and go on fast
with all the windows closed on a purple road with everything pink and purple before the sun touches it. Behind

me the soft voice says, "Gimme a cigarette," and there's a rustle and a scratch and a deep breath going out. They aren't getting along so well. He gets off the bus and she doesn't. She doesn't eat and they don't talk. She's mad at him for getting drunk and ripping her dress. Probably say "I was never so humiliated" later. Maybe he lost his job and they got to go to a new town so he got drunk. The girl across from me has her hair up in wire rollers with a pink shiny kerchief tied over. Comb it out just before she gets there. Look nice for the folks. Whoever. Pedal pushers. Maybe she'll change clothes too. She isn't with the man by the window. How can she sleep in curlers? She's even got curves in her arms. I got muscles in my arms. My hair feels like a paint brush. A camel's-hair number three, short and tickly but soft. I got a curve too. My belly curves out and in again as smooth as can be but the ribs stick out on top. The rat in the ribs is just walking around now. He strolls down under my stomach and rubs his back against it. The stomach gives and quivers and he walks across the liver with it sucking and mucking like a mud hole. When I'm scared I breathe too fast and the lungs beating push him down out of the cage. He gets angry and chews on things. Just biting at anything. His eyes are light brown and his skin is very pale from the dark. It must be icky inside me. Wet and hot and full of bad smells. Everything slimy and elastic with little jerks and pumps and rolls and when I move only ribs to hang onto. Maybe he gets seasick when I walk or run or turn somersaults.

Heydorf might not even be there when I get there. I'll call him from the station. Pasadena Y.M.C.A. Bright lights and palm trees. If he's not there I'll have to keep calling and waiting and calling. More bright lights and the bus is stopping again and the man gets off and brings back more sandwiches and the woman smiles and he throws them in the rack with the others. Nick's old underpants ride up my crack and I scootch around to get them out and the bus goes again and the pink dress gets tangled and itches. Must be every two hours the bus stops and the man gets off and throws more sandwiches in the rack. I can't sleep when the bus is stopped and wake up with everything tight and tired. I wonder what kind of sandwiches he has in the rack but I can't get off the bus when it stops. I might not get back in time and somebody might speak to me. I have to piss but the can is past too many people and the man with the sandwiches. The arm between the seats pushes up so I curl up and sleep. The sun comes and we're in the mountains. My ass hurts and I can't wait to piss any longer and the bus stops for an hour in Redding. It's California already and I leave everything on the bus but the money and climb out. It's hot and my eyelids are thick with pillows underneath and the town is small and flat. I walk slow once around the block with low buildings and there's a sporting goods store. I go in quick and ask to see snake bite kits. The man leans over a tall glass case and takes them out carelessly. Throws them on the counter and I look close. Red rubber bulbs like a douche or an enema. A one-sided razor blade and a leather strap. Three dollars. My ass. My royal Irish ass. Three dollars. No thank you. He throws them back into the case not even disappointed. As though he didn't expect me to buy. I have to piss. I'm so stiff I forgot. Back quick to the station. Hard lights and hard benches. Posters of New York and Miami. The john is full of women and it takes a dime. I haven't got any change. Back out to the magazine stand for an Almond Joy and change. Back into the can. Standing in line in front of a mirror. My dress is wrinkled and my arms look pale jutting out and my face is round and spotted with fuzz standing up all around it. Thick lower lip and no upper lip and the boxer's nose. All puffy and too big for my body and the women are big and smell hot and thick of eau de cologne and sweat and hair spray. I am close to their armpits and the heat is wet there and their elbows shine and they put on dark lipstick and draw on eyebrows and lean into the mirror combing and brushing and the long hair comes out in the brushes and falls slowly through the air. I stand back so the hair won't fall on me and put my hands up to rub my hair and my hands are square with broad palms and thin gray grime past the wrist and dark lines of grime at the knuckles and under the nails. It's my turn and I go in, close the door and sit down too quick and get my dress wet. Got to hike them up in back or they hang down into the toilet. The pissing hurts. I've held it too long and it burns and my insides are stretched from holding it. But it is good and I can think again and sit for a minute afterward with my head in my hands just feeling better.

Most of the women have gone but the girl who sat across from me in the bus is putting hair spray on her curlers. The pink kerchief is laying on one of the sinks and her legs slope smooth from pedal pushers to penny loafers. I go to wash my hands but there is hair in the sink and I feel sick to the stomach from the hair and the hair spray. Out in the lobby I sit looking at my legs under the skirt and eating the Almond Joy very slowly. My legs are very white because I wore dungarees all winter. The hair is pale and short and just fuzzes in the light. Straight down from my knees with big bony ankles and big square feet. The silly party shoes gap at the sides when I walk. My foot is as long as my lower leg from the ankle bone to the inside of the knee. The toes point in and the heels are far apart and my knees hit each other when I try to walk softly. After a while I remember and put my knees together because I'm wearing a skirt. Take another small bite of candy and chew very slowly and carefully tasting and feeling the coconut and almonds and chocolate all separate in my mouth. The bus is called and I go out.

Almost fall down climbing in. Put my foot on the skirt. The ashtray is empty and the aisle is swept and the sun comes in warm through the window. People got off in Redding and other people get on and a lady in slacks and short boots with her shirt sleeves rolled past her elbows sits with the girl in curlers. The man with the sandwiches and the little lady must have got back on before me. He is already asleep and she looks out the window. The window is green and the town looks gold and bright through it, and the hills and the rocks are lush and the sky very blue. The sun comes in on me and my hair is hot and I sleep. The man says, "Jesus H. Christ! Haven't you got anything but these Canadian cigarettes?" and the little lady laughs embarrassed and says no and the bus is stopped again and he gets off and I look up and the sandwiches are still in the rack and I wonder what kind they are and I can't get off because I don't know how long the bus will be and I might miss it. The man climbs back on with two big chocolate ice cream cones. He holds one out to the woman and says, "You got to eat this or it'll melt all over both of us!" She shrugs and smiles and takes it. She's a licker. He's a biter. He takes big bites of hard ice cream and chews and swallows and bites into the cone and eats it all in just a few bites. She licks carefully and slowly. She doesn't let any drip off. It makes it last a long time. I'm a licker myself but I've always admired biters. My jaws are running looking at the ice cream and I can see the stubble working on his jaws and he picks the pieces of cone out of his teeth. His nose has been broken too and his hair falls back and loose over his forehead. He looks younger than her. I meant to get some more candy to bring on the bus, but I forgot. Sometimes when I wake up I'm sick to the stomach and can't think or talk or pretend anything until I eat something. It doesn't matter what, anything, and a few minutes after the first bite I'm O.K. again and can just eat to fill myself up. But before

that if I can't find food soon enough I fall down on the
floor and my stomach heaves and cramps and I puke
clear foul liquid that burns and hangs from my teeth and
sometimes Maw finds me like that and she runs to start
breakfast while I lay there puking white on the floor and
I can't get up and I can't tell her to just give me a piece of
bread and I'll be all right but she's gotta fry eggs and
bacon or make oatmeal and I haven't got time for that
and I'm still awake and I still hurt but I can't move and in
a while she comes and picks me up and takes me back to
my bed and I just lay there while she washes my face soft
and calls me her only little one and I can't even really see
her but can see moving and then she brings me breakfast
and gives me a drink of tomato juice first with her hand
shaking so the glass clicks against my teeth and after a
minute I'm O.K. again and sit up and eat and tell her she
saved my life I was so famished and she gives me a lecture
about how I don't eat right anyway and it's all right and
it's nice afterward but when I think about how bad it was
it really scares me so I put cookies or something in the
drawer for a long time after that. It's been that bad four
times in the last couple years but she never learns that
hungry isn't for something good. Hungry is for anything
at all. If that happened where I couldn't get food right
away I guess I'd die. I'd just lay wherever it was even if
there were rabbits dancing on my head. It was dumb not
to bring something on the bus. If I slept a long time and
woke up really hungry I'd make a scene and they'd haul
me off and question me and send me back. I'll get
something next time we stop. They're talking about booze
and bars. The new lady brags and slaps her knee and
hooks her boot heel on her knee. "I've slung drinks in
every bar west of the *Mississip!*" The man with the
sandwiches grins. "Me too, but I sling 'em down my
gullet." The lady hikes up in the seat and looks back at
him through the crack between her seat and the girl in

the curlers. "Yeah, you look like you have." She looks down at the curlers. "You a big drinker, honey?" "Just a little bit, at parties." She blushes and her voice is rinky and high and surprising. I lean against the seat and the window and watch and listen and feel warm and far away and only a little bit sick to the stomach. An arm reaches back from the aisle seat in front of me and offers cigarettes to the girl and the barmaid and the sandwich man. "God, American cigarettes." He lights eagerly and leans back sucking and his pant leg hikes up and his socks are frayed at the ankle and his shoes have hooks instead of holes. "Give *her* one of these too!" He reaches and the arm reaches again with the cigarettes and he takes one and gives it to the little lady. She starts to shake her head but then takes it in chubby hands and lights and smokes and smiles and says, "Yes, it's very nice," and the man nods and gestures at the barmaid. "All she's got is Canadian manure and rice paper and I had to smoke 'em all the way since Seattle!" "Men!!! My Lord, whyn't ya buy your own smokes? Any man'd bum cigarettes from his wife when he smokes another brand and then complain..." "She ain't my wife! I never seen the lady before." The barmaid looks and I look at the sandwich wrappers in the rack. Grease makes them dark and the ends hang limp down between the bars. "Hell, no. My wife left years ago. She's rich now back east someplace in perfume. Sells perfume. I send her an anniversary card every day on the day the divorce came through." He's looking at the sandwich wrappings. Maybe they'll start dripping soon. "My, but she was a woman. Year after we's married I come home from logging and she gave me the clap." His teeth are straight and his face splits over them. The eyes wrinkle and the cheeks fall in sharp and dark beneath. "Said she'd turn over a new leaf and by god she did. She got worse." His voice is low and clear and they laugh and I laugh low and then look out the window quick so they won't know I was watching and listening. "But they call me Happy Jack now and I wouldn't get married again unless I found me a beautiful dumb oversexed blonde who's rich and owns a liquor store." It makes me sad. Too bad. But his voice is nice and he tore her dress but he gave her sandwiches. And ice cream. "Don't think I'm snoopy, honey, I was just curious." The barmaid has her hand on the girl's knee and she looks at her warm and serious and the girl blushes again. "I don't mind. I'm going to see my boyfriend in the navy. He just got back on leave, but he couldn't come up home so I'm going down to see him. My mama didn't like it but I'm going anyway." Her voice sounds like wire curlers rubbing against a window. The barmaid leans back against the window and drops her arm down on the girl's shoulder. "You engaged to him, honey?" The girl nods. "We haven't been able to get a ring yet." She's older'n I am. Boyfriend. Dumb word. She's running away too, maybe. Her mama doesn't know she's gone off to take her curlers out just before she gets there and put on her lavender toreador pants and the pink fuzzy sweater and kiss and hug and no Herbie we mustn't, oh Herbie, in the navy, take her to a motel in Pasadena, it's O.K. if we're engaged, because we truly love each other, isn't it Herbie? and oh Herbie do you still want to marry me? "Ed 'n' Edie's." Tacky. Beanery with both gasoline and diesel pumps. I get out this time even faster than the sandwich man. First to the can for a long warm easy piss and then into the diner. Knotty pine. Wagon wheels and big yellow lanterns and a cute souvenir knotty pine plaque, carved in red. Eat your beans with pineapple and get Hawaiian music. Postcards of Mt. Shasta. The sandwich man is eating huge bites of peach pie with hard white ice cream. The bus driver is drinking coffee. Must be Edie in the apron. Her upper arms spread and hang and flop as she moves, her hair gray and brown and yellow, munged into a net. Thick glasses with rhinestones at the temples. My feet don't touch the footrest when I sit on the stool so I lean on it. "I'd like a peanut butter and jelly sandwich to go, please." "No peanut butter, got tuna, chicken salad, salami, ham, ham and cheese, hamburgers and cheeseburgers." She doesn't look up. She slops a gray rag in a plastic tub of cups. No time for a hamburger. I slide off the stool and remember not to spin it. Trail over to the candy counter. A big glass bowl of chocolate-covered mints in green tin foil. I put some in my pocket because she didn't look up. When she walks over I can hear bedroom slippers or maybe thongs slapping and hushing on the floor.

Burnt peanuts. Two Butterfingers, and three Hersheys with almonds. I should have got something to drink. Orange pop. Or a chocolate milkshake to go. There's warm green sun on my hands and face and I lean back staring out the window and watching the chocolate make gushy pads on my fingertips. Mt. Shasta, far off, white even in summer. The mountains of the moon. Maybe they're in Africa someplace. In a Tarzan book. I bite carefully and lush my tongue around in the chocolate till it's thin and watery and runs down almost without swallowing. Lots of people don't eat chocolate 'cause it gives 'em zits. Gives Heydorf zits but he eats it anyway. I don't get zits. Or only one or two once in a while if I don't wash for a couple of weeks. I get freckles. Once I had a zit on the end of my nose and poked at it till it got really big and red and sore but wouldn't bust and put Maw's powder on it but it showed white on me, and told people it was a bee sting from getting honey out of a bee log. Br'er Bear. They probably figured it was a zit all the time. Freckles aren't so bad. Mine aren't. Some people got red ones like P. J. Bushbaum and they look like zits anyway. Some people got fly shit black ones. I got nice spready goldy brown ones. Better'n zits. If I got zits from choco-late I'd eat it anyway. Live in a tree and get somebody to

fill up a bucket with chocolate and peanut butter and
haul it up and sit there with the sun warm and my
big-nosed sneakers on, eating peanut butter and grape
jelly sandwiches and milk and fudge with walnuts and
Hershey bars all day long and not even bother when the
zits come popping out. Not even pick 'em. Just sit there
and let 'em swell up and pop and run down my face and
if anybody ever tried to talk to me or climb up into my
tree I'd scream and throw my red-pussy-zitted face at 'em
and they'd fall down and have convulsions and their hair
would turn white before my eyes and when people came
along and found them lying there at the foot of the tree
they'd carry 'em off and nurse them but they'd be gibbering
idiots for the rest of their days.

I don't think Heydorf cares he has zits. He never puts
anything on 'em and he don't wash. He just picks at 'em
'cause they hurt good. The chocolate's all gone and I
spend a long time sucking my tongue until it's clean and
then very carefully lick the chocolate off my fingers. For a
couple of hours afterward, every once in a while, my
tongue bumbles onto a piece of nut or a little well of
chocolate in a tooth. It's nice and I feel good and the
sick's gone out of my belly and my ass don't hurt for a
while and it's warm.

It's dark coming into L.A. Been dark for a long time.
Sign said Los Angeles city limits and it was still dark all
around. No lights. No town. After a while service stations
and a few houses and then more, thick and white but flat,
and the sky is pale and fuzzy from the lights. I'll tell
Heydorf war stories about the bus. The lady who had a
nervous breakdown and was coming back home from the

sanitarium. She showed me pictures of her great Dane but she didn't have any pictures of her husband and kids. Talked all about her great Dane. And the big red cow all gentle and slow and quiet. She got on in a tiny town in the desert and a skinny little man, very dark and quick, holding a blond baby. He walked her to the bus and kissed her and stood to wave goodbye. She's going to her sister's eighth-grade graduation that wanted to be a nurse. The cow had wanted to be a nurse but she couldn't get the education so she was going to help pay for her sister's education. She was warm and flowed over into my seat too and kept me warm and she got off at another little town in the desert and got into an old pick-up and went away dusty and rattling. Maybe I'll even tell Heydorf about the man who laid down and got sandwiches.

The town's still flat. No big buildings. Just like Portland except more spread out and white and gray instead of green and gray. I thought it'd be a big town. Call Heydorf as soon as I get off the bus. Then either I'll go out to Pasadena or he'll come in to meet me. I'll have time to get out of the dress before he comes or before I go out. Change in the bus station. Got to buy a sleeping bag.

I got the wrong raincoat. It's black and it felt the same but it's too long and the pockets are empty. No compass, no hooks, no waterproof matches. Some lady gonna find herself pinched in the shoulders and flashing her ass. She gonna think the pockets is weird. No big deal. I'll throw it away with the dress and shoes.

I'm almost the last off. The pack cuts a little in the fold of the raincoat. The bow is awkward, bangs the seats and catches in the door as I fall down the steps. Got everything but the raincoat. It's very dark and the open doors are bright. A painted yellow stripe runs in one door and I follow it. It's brown, dingy cream-colored paint and old wood seats, brown. In Portland it's gas chamber green. A short hall with an open side. They're unloading the bus.

The little sandwich lady from the bus stands at the window with a powder blue coat tight around her. A pale blue hatbox and a small suitcase slide toward her. Her purse is blue, not black. She picks everything up daintily and goes out. No sign of the sandwich man. More luggage comes slamming out and the hands are big and black, the arms black. It's warm and his shirt is off. Black and shining. There aren't many Negroes in Portland. The muscles all cut and smooth and his throat running deep into his chest. Old Levi's. They hang low and loose and the elastic of his shorts shows above, white against hard black. They all want a white girl. So they say. Maybe he'll look. His face is clear and sharp. I thought they all had thick lips and flat noses. He ain't much older'n me. He might look. I've seen a few in Portland with shiny clothes and a fat blond white girl. Ugly. Rolling and pasty with crooked teeth and a high voice. She couldn't get anybody else and they don't care as long as it's white. All that clean hard black cutting into gushy white fat. Sow belly. They have to eat that too. And pig's ears. Put a black wood spoon into a can of lard. Have to boil it to get the grease off. Icky. Black fat's nice. She worked in the laundry and it looked solid and healthy. Big boobs and her ass started ten inches below her neck. Warm and clean.

   He doesn't look. I have to phone Heydorf. There's a clackety-clack from somewhere steady. Out into the waiting room. Same two-bit picture machine. A separate café and magazine store. Dark wood benches and a row of telephones in the corner. I walk over to them. No telephone books in the booths. I have to look up the Pasadena Y.M.C.A. There are ten thick books hanging upside down in a rack on the wall. Different names stamped on the binding. Pasadena. I put the side pack down between my legs in case anybody tries to snatch it. Roll the shoulder pack down and prop it in front of me. Lay the bow and quiver against the wall. The pencil's in the pack. Have to tear the number out of the book. Flip up the book. It's heavy and the stand is too high to see over. Hold it down at an angle and thumb through. The Y.M.C.A. page is gone. Ask information. A lot of people around. Take the junk into the booth with me. The bow falls out on the floor and somebody picks it up and hands it to me. "Can I help, miss?" A spick. A Mexican or something. Thin and not much taller than me. His pants are orange and tight at the cuff. Balloon around his legs. A checked jacket and a polo shirt. Yellow and greasy. They carry knives. Try to steal. Put his hands on me. "No, no." I stand up on the pack and pull the door closed. He stands in front with his hands in his pockets. Gonna sell me a genuine diamond ring for sixty dollars. He smiles easily and nods. I look away quick and fumble in my pockets. Just bills. I spent all my change on candy. And I didn't separate the money. Bastard'll get my money. Pull a knife and walk me out quiet into an alley and take my money. Heydorf would laugh and laugh. He leans against the wall looking out into the waiting room. I'd have to go back and they know by now, or almost by now. They know I'm gone. I'd have to phone and get bailed out like a kid on a prank. He strolls away. I throw the door open and pick up the stuff. I remember I've got a skirt on about halfway through and bend my knees. All I need is flash my knobby ass at a roomful of spicks. I've got it all slung around crazy hanging and banging and the skirt gets tangled up in my knees and the bow drops and I trip over it. The café section is crowded and there's nobody at the counter. I don't feel like taking anything. If I got caught it'd be a bad end. My belly hurts again and the pack straps are heavy on the folds of the raincoat. Dig and cut. Finally a little lady in a hurry. Yellow uniform. A doily in her hair. Can't decide what to get. Have to get something. Nobody just gives change. She's tapping and looking toward the counter. Two Hershey bars with almonds and

a pack of butter rum Life Savers. She grabs and throws
and I end up with a quarter and a half a dollar. My own
fault. I should have counted. One Hershey or one and a
Life Saver or even two Hersheys. Greedy and dumb,
that's my problem. A quarter. I don't give a fuck. I'll put
the goddamn quarter in the phone. I drop the change
into a pocket and cram the candy in on top. Only reach
one pocket carrying all this crap. Out to the phones
again, not looking anywhere. Pack all the junk in and
stand on it. No seat in the booths. Somebody might rest
there. Or sleep there. Put in the quarter. A deep bong
instead of a ting. Information and I get the number
turning it quick on my tongue and saying it out loud. The
quarter makes it back and I plug it in again and dial fast
hoping I haven't fucked the number already. It rings a
long time. "Hellooo?" A little too long and high. A queer.
Even I can tell. "Pasadena Y.M.C.A." "I would like to
speak to Mr. Heydorf, please." He thinks I'm a man.
They all do on the phone. The operator always says sir.
"One moment, I'll see if he's in." I never heard it for real
before. Just jokes and comedians. I didn't think they
really talked that way. The queer again. "I beg your
pardon. Can you give me the name of the party who's
calling?" "Just say Dutch." "All right, Dutch." A little
giggle at the end. Aarg. Heydorf thinks it might be his
folks. Caught up with him. I'll be cool. "Hiya, Heydorf.
I'm in the L.A. bus depot with fuzz on my ass." Too
much. How about "I'm here, what do you want me to
do?" Too slavy. His voice comes on the phone. It isn't him.
It sounds different. Maybe I never talked to him on the
phone before. "Hello, Dutch?" "Yeah." "You in the L.A.
depot?" "Yeah." "I'll come over, but there isn't a bus until
6 A.M. Wait there." "O.K." It clicks and he's gone and my
stomach is gone and there's just a sickness. I'm tired.
Tired all over. Tired inside. Must be getting old. Wanta
lay down in my nice soft bed and pull the covers up.

Stretch out, never get up again. The other booths are full
and people stand around outside looking restless. Got to
move. He'll catch a bus at six. I don't know what time it is
now. Time enough to change in anyway. I come out of the
booth and slide all my junk out. Somebody edges in and
shuts the door while I'm still picking stuff up. Where is
the can? Up there. Must be up there. Concrete steps.
Rubber grip pads and steel ribbon edges. A cracking
color photo of a beautiful American couple smiling at the
Rockies through a Scenicruiser window. Probably needs a
dime. Have to spend either a dime or fifteen cents or
thirty cents or like that. Back to the candy counter. I can
smell hamburgers and onions. Hot and greasy with a lot
of ketchup and french fries and a big old chocolate
milkshake. Lot of salt on the french fries. Lick it all off
my fingers afterward. But there's just stools and they all
full and I've got all this junk. The lady with the doily
comes back and looks at me funny like I'm a glutton or
something. Get a jumbo pack of chocolate-covered peanuts. Thirty-five cents but I get the dime and a lot of
chocolate-covered peanuts. Out and up the stairs. The
intercom's blaring and bus engines going and people
buzzing and that clackety-clack. It's hot in the can. A lot
of women and a fan spitting in the window. A long row of
pay toilets and one free and they all lined up in front of
the free one. Even the rich-looking ones. I go right up
and put the dime in and go inside with all my stuff. Very
superior. My own private can. Open the pack and pull
out my Levi's and the old washed-out red sweatshirt with
the spade drawn on the back in red felt pen. Pull out the
heavy socks and Cecilia's hiking boots. The dress zips
down the back and I have to stretch and twist to get at it.
Flop it up on the hook. Off with the underskirt. Lace on
it. Baggy in the chest. Kick off the dumb white party
shoes. Little gold heels and pointy toes. Stand on the tile
stretching in my tee shirt and undershorts. Letting my

sweaty feet dry. Sit on the edge of the toilet. Lot of old
scars and scabs on my legs. Just from scrapes and scratches but they show white and crescent-shaped and the fuzz
don't grow out of 'em again for a long time. My toenails
are dirty. Black and there's wet mung between my toes.
Rub it out with my fingers and sniff the musty smell. My
elbows are dirty too. A little gray crust that rubs off if I
pick at it. Shake out the Levi's and put them on. Fresh-
washed and snug. Soft they're so old. The five buttons go
up easy. Little easier than usual. Got to eat my candy. Pull
on the sweatshirt and the socks. The boots come over my
ankles. Thick tough soles and heels and they lace for a
while and then hook and then the leather straps on top.
Rough hide laces. Very nice. Wrap the laces once around
the top and tie in front. The Levi's just cover the arches
and won't drag in the dirt like they usually do. My feet
feel heavy and invulnerable. Sit back on the toilet seat
and dig into the raincoat pockets for the Hershey bars.
Throw the wrappers into the bloody rag bin and sit with
one heel hooked on a knee. Very comfortable and warm.
Out of sight. Alone. Eating my Hershey bars. Toward the
end I get an inspiration. Roll all the girly clothes up in
the raincoat, put the candy and money into my pants
pocket and close up the pack. Load up all my junk and
step out. I'm taller, maybe an inch and a half, in the
boots. Feel loose and good but a little awkward. A few
women look at me as I walk by. Catch sight of myself in
the mirror. Ain't any way you could tell I was a girl now.
Clump, but carefully so I don't trip down the stairs and
into the hall where the luggage comes in. Lockers. A
quarter for twenty-four hours. I go over to the old man
checking bags and get more quarters and put it in and
put in all the junk except the bow, which is too long. Lock
it up and put the key in my pocket. Free and light and
easy now. Back into the waiting room. All the benches
face the front door. Church pews. Sit down in a dark

corner at the back and pull out my chocolate-covered peanuts. Lay the bow beside me and lean back. The clock over the door says four o'clock. Two hours for Heydorf. He sounded sleepy maybe. But he's always slow and heavy. The clacking is a rhythm. A beat. It comes from the shoeshine boys. I hadn't noticed them before. The high chairs line the front wall next to the door. They're naked. They're wearing pants and tee shirts and they're naked. Black and shining wet in the yellow light. He has a red beanie with buttons all around just like Jughead. He stands on the footrest and throws his arms up with two wooden brushes in his hands. Jumps off. The man with the briefcase stops and jerks back as the boy lands in front of him. He crouches and hops on his haunches waving the brushes. He holds them over his head and clicks the wooden backs together. The man looks around and then crawls up into the high chair. Cook sitting on the throne while the king's out. The black boy leans over his feet and sways to the clacking of other brushes. He bobs his head and wags his ass and bends and slides his knees. Then he grabs the brushes and starts a rhythm of his own. High and loud and fast. Each pass over the shoe the brushes hit each other and his back is toward me with the arms and shoulders working in the rhythm. They're all young and black and lean. They sit by the empty chairs bobbing their heads and working their brushes together. The rhythm comes up high and thin and floats across the ceiling and then down through the floor. A little tickle in the benches but so steady you forget. When someone walks by they do their little dance for him and usually he goes on embarrassed but sometimes they stop and get into the chairs and the music gets higher and tighter and faster. It's silly and I really like it and want to be a shoeshine boy. Fewer people now. Scattered around on the benches in clumps. Little piles of luggage beneath the benches. Cardboard boxes tied with string. Good Will

suitcases. Duffel bags. Always duffel bags. The people sit
or lean or stand and lean. Some of them lie down. There
are ridges on the benches. The wood rises up two inches
every foot and a half, but no arms. They lie down across
the ridges on their sides and curl their legs up. The spick
with the orange pants is talking to a porter, black and old
and falling forward over the dolly. The spick leans against
a post and talks low and the old man nods and listens and
smiles. The ticket windows are open and shapes move
behind them officially, gray and official. A man with a
gun stands looking out the door. His clothes are gray and
there are little emblems sewn onto his clothes. The gun is
in dark leather and hangs square and heavy. After a while
he moves away from the door and walks slowly, pacing,
not going anywhere. When he passes someone lying
down he stops. Sometimes they get up right away. Sometimes he speaks and reaches down to shake them. They
are old men mostly. They sit up and their heads fall on
their chests and their legs sprawl wide and they are asleep
again. They aren't going anywhere. They aren't waiting
for anybody. They sleep here. They are all alike, gray and
ragged and maybe dirty. Maybe my mother would say
they were dirty. But they all sit apart. They don't speak to
each other. They don't look at anybody.

The lady goes up and down the benches talking to
people. She is round and her bandanna is gray with pink
daisies. Finally she comes to me. She sits down and looks
at me. She is as short as I am. She's very old. There's
something wrong with her skin. It's black or was black but
now it's gray. A thin coat of ashes all over her. Maybe
she's a hundred years old. Sixty anyway. She puts her
hand out and it sits on my knee. "Do you love Jesus,
child?" "Un-hunh." Her voice is weak and quakes from
her breathing. Her eyebrows go up in the middle like a
little tent and all the wrinkles in her forehead go up over
the tent. "Then think of other children like yourself as

got nothing tonight and give a little to the orphans." She believes it. She's sad because children have nothing. She pulls a folder out of somewhere and shows me. It has slots. Round slots, different sizes for nickels, dimes and quarters. It's printed in black on gray, "Our Lady of the Snows," and there's a cartoon child with his hand out. I smile my warmest crooked embarrassed grin. "You're doing a good thing." I speak low and look into her sad old eyes. "You see, I'm an orphan myself and I'm on my way to Mexico City for a benefit archery tournament for an orphanage there." I lift up the bow and grin proudly. She lights up. She glows. Her lips fall farther away from her gums and her gums are ash-colored. "You sweet child! Doing all you can for the children." She puts both her hands on my hands and looks into my face. "You must take something!" She starts pulling the coins out of the slots. Four nickels and three dimes. There's only a quarter left in the card. "You must take this." She presses it into my hands and closes my fingers over it. She holds my hand closed with both her hands and looks into my eyes. "It's for you. It's meant for you. I know there was some reason I had to come here tonight. Let me kiss you, child." And she kisses my cheek and her breath is thick and slimy, fallen apples old in the orchard and I can't breathe. She presses my hands and I smile again, "Thank you very much," and she goes off. Her stockings are rolled down below her knees and her slippers scuff. She looks back once and goes out the door. When I know she's gone I look. Fifty cents. Greasy shiny fifty cents. Makes me feel good. I'll have a hamburger and some french fries and blow my own dime on a Coke.

"You the little girl in the pink dress, ain't you?" It's the orange balloon spick in among the magazines. "Nope," I say and go on but he says, "Sure you are. Whyn't you let me buy you a cup of coffee?" and I go again and I can hear him say, "What are ya? Queer?" and I get hot and go wedge myself between a bus driver and somebody else and put the bow between my knees and let my feet dangle and eat my hamburger and french fries and an orange pop.

It's good. Good. Makes me feel so tight and full of good things so I get a package of M & M's and go look at comics for a while. The spick's gone and they don't bother you looking at comics here. They got a Dell paperback of *Crime and Punishment* which we all had to read and it was all right except I couldn't understand the punishment part. How come he felt bad? How come he turned himself in? Dumb. The crime part was O.K. though.

The shoeshine boys are still at it. Spurts of people come in and wait a while and go. They're all poor or sleazy. Rich people don't ride buses. Rich people don't have anything to do with buses. It's gray outside the door. Dark gray getting lighter. It's already started. I kept wanting it to start and then I was so busy starting it that I forgot to notice. I missed the moment. The actual moment. Maybe I'll remember later if I think about it. Almost six. A few minutes to six. Heydorf soon. I don't know what he'll look like. He won't smile. He never does. I won't either. Two months. Three months really. I won't say anything. Maybe I'll pretend to be asleep. Sitting up asleep like the bums. He'll kick my foot to wake me and I'll wake up very slow and calm and cool. Stretch and yawn, the whole bit. Shiny clothes. Metal threads running through. Lizard skin. The pant legs get tight below the knee, no cuff. Pointy patent leather shoes. Spicks and spades and po' white trash. All duded up, go hang around the bus station. Criminal lawyers with their hair greased back. Dirty fingernails. Run my fingernails along my teeth, clean 'em. A faint chocolate flavor in the mung. Not as bad as toenail dirt. That's always wet and full of old sweat.

He's halfway across the room when I see him. Heading straight for me. A black raincoat, tan pants, the sweater with a gray-white collar showing underneath. Gray-white cuffs. He walks like an old man, falling and catching, throwing himself and just barely not falling, head down and forward, hands in pockets. Same old green suede cloth loafers with the spongy soles. Same old long crew cut bushing up. Must grease it and comb it to make it stand up like that. I forget to be asleep. Just sit watching him come. Walking medium fast, lunging rough, his toes at outrageous angles. He isn't looking at me, he's just coming at me. He falls onto the bench next to me. His raincoat flops open with his hands still in the pockets. He doesn't puff but he acts like he's come a long way. Looking down and sliding his eyes around the room. It's all there again, the pulse. I want to bounce on the bench and talk fast about all the things I've seen and done but I know they're all little and silly if I tell him and not telling him makes me feel hot and secret.

"Those are good boots." I look at them. Lift one to look at it as though I hadn't before. "Yeah." Nod slowly. "Where'd you get 'em?" I put the foot back down and stretch it out to show it off. "Vince's sister." "Mmmh." I won't say anything more and he'll think I stole them. "Where's the rest of your stuff?" "Locker." "Mmmh." He lifts his head and looks around. "Let's go." He gets up and starts lunging toward the door and I follow moving slow but long in the heavy boots with the bow in my left hand. He stops in the door and looks. "What's that?" It's plastic. Green fiberglass with "Tigard H.S." in felt pen and an old brown twine twisted for the string. Silly. I hadn't thought of it. Silly. "Bow." I look at him but he's looking up the street and not at me. "You got arrows for it?" "Yeah." "You any good with it?" "Fair." "Better put it someplace for now." He always talks down to me. Leave your dolly home dear so she can sleep. Don't you think Dolly needs a nap? It won't fit in the lockers. The man at the information desk. Kind of young. Soft in his white shirt and gray tie. I walk up to the desk and look over at him, eyes wide. "Hi." He looks up and smiles. I was right. "Can I leave this someplace for a little while?" Hold the bow up in my grubby paw. He thinks it's cute. I'm a cute little fella. "Sure." He takes it and puts it under the desk and points and, "Just ask whoever's here for it when you come back." I grin wide and crooked. "Thanks, thanks a lot." Look back once as I go out. Heydorf's standing on the corner with his hands in his pockets. We go swinging off down the street all gray and warm even in the early morning. I'm almost five feet tall I bet, and I can do anything. Go anywhere, fool anybody. It's all like Burnside in Portland. All sleazy bars and beaneries and pawnshops with weird junk in the windows. We stop at all the pawnshops and Heydorf looks at guns and knives and I pretend to. Paper soggy in the gutters and gray men slow on the street. There's sun creeping in and the shops are starting to open. It's warm and the bums don't ask us for anything. A white building. Square, and the door wide open. We walk into the dim cool and it's shiny gray marble with a button. Heydorf pushes the button and the elevator opens and we get in. Empty elevator. You can do whatever you want in an elevator until it stops. He pushes the top button and it goes up fast and my belly drops and it stops and my belly flies up. "This is the county court- house." We get out on the top floor and walk around in an empty bright hall looking out the window. The sun's coming in clear and the sky's getting a dusty-red look above it. We get back in the elevator and ride all the way to the bottom and all the way to the top. It doesn't stop anywhere else. It's only about ten floors but it's fast and we fly for a long time. Practice jumping up in the air just as it stops so we wouldn't get crushed if it fell. After a while people get on at the bottom and get off in the

middle. We fly it down one more time and there are
more people waiting so we get out and walk out onto the
street again. People going to work. Lot of shops open
now. Fruit stand with the flap up and the guy's still
arranging things. I brush past and slip two peaches under
my sweatshirt and we go sit in the sun on a low brick wall
around a parking lot. Kick our heels. Eat ripe gushy
peaches. My hands get all brown and streaky in the juice
and I lick 'em and the dirt comes off with the juice and
makes salty as well as sweet. Sit sucking the pit and
watching as they all go by, hurrying somewhere, hats and
suits and briefcases. Hard hats and lunchboxes. A news-
paper in each armpit. I'm outside all that. Don't have to
go anywhere. Don't have to do anything for anybody ever
again. Just sit here and watch all day if I want to. No
explanations to anybody. I feel light and good and powerful. Invisible. That's it. They can't see me. I'm outside.
They can't see me or touch me and I don't care what
happens to them. Don't care what they think of me. Only
one can see me is Heydorf but that's O.K. 'cause he's
invisible too.

We don't talk but I think so much it feels like we talked
for hours, like I'd been talking for hours. We walk around
again and it's warmer and a little muggy and the sky's dirt
red. My eyes sting a little and water.

We're crossing a street and a little man is carrying a
stool and walking with his hand on a big spade's arm.
Heydorf nudges me and we follow them up the sidewalk
to the front of Woolworth's. The street's crowded and hot
now. The little man puts the stool down and the spade sits
on it and says, "Thanks, Lou, see you at noon." And the
little man goes off. The spade's big and rich brown with a
lot of red in it. His hair's very tight and going a little gray.
He takes off his jacket and pulls out a squeeze box. I
forget what they're called. Like a little round accordion
with no keys. He has a soft flat hat on and an old tweed

vest open over a tan work shirt. Clean wrinkled tan pants. He's blind. He looks and doesn't blink very often. He just looks straight ahead. Pulls a tin cup out of his pocket and hooks it into the shoulder of his vest without looking. Leans back in the sun and pulls the box open. He starts to play and sing, not loud, low and fine, and his voice rolls out of his chest a little rough like honey with the lumps left in, just enough to rough up your tongue. Silly old songs all sweet and warm in the sun and people put coins in his cup and we stand and watch ten feet away and count the coins and he can't see us. Mostly women. Shopping. Good clothes and their hair done and the fat beginning to settle on their bellies and hips. "He's out here every day." Heydorf speaks soft. Blind people can really hear. "He makes a minimum of two fifty an hour." I look and nod and wonder. We go into Woolworth's and I take a cheap harmonica thinking I'll learn to play it and sit in the sun and let people give me money all day long. We wander around fingering and fumbling with all the ridiculous things. Heydorf stops in front of the candy counter and looks at the chocolates, the expensive cream-filled ones. They're all in the glass case. No opening on this side and the top counter is wide. Fairly busy but it's a small cubicle and the lady tough and sharp looking. He slides his eyes at me from the chocolates. They look good but it's impossible. He knows it is. What's he trying to do? I ignore him and get a big bag of M & M's from the rack behind me. M & M's are tough because they make a lot of noise. They rattle and the paper bag is always sliding around. Heydorf strolls around the other side of the candy counter and goes out the door. The M & M's are under my sweatshirt tucked into the front of my pants. I walk carefully but easy and go on out. He's standing across the street waiting and the big spade is playing away and singing a happy old song. All about sunshine and lollipops. I'm pissed. I'm mad. Maybe Heydorf's just trying to get me screwed. Maybe he wants me out of his way. Well, I won't bug him. I didn't ask him to come down here and hold my hand. I can get by on my own. I swing across the street very easy looking. Not a care in the world. This block's a park. Grass and brick sidewalks. Palm trees all around and a fountain in the middle. The sign at the entrance says there's a mammoth parking lot under it. Thirty-five cents for the first half hour. We go into the park and sit down on a bench. I slip the candy out the side and rip the bag open. Put 'em between us. A lot of candy in the big bags. Eat 'em by the handfuls. The sugar coating comes off in pretty colors on my hands. Lick it off. Cruncha crunch. A hokey little fountain in the middle. At one end there's a little crowd. Twenty or thirty and somebody giving a speech. I look at Heydorf, a question. He looks and still looking at the crowd, "It's a nut. Like Hyde Park. You can give a speech here about anything, anytime to anybody. Nuts come down and rave all day." I can see the man speaking. He's standing on something, not very high. A red undershirt with long sleeves and three buttons open at the neck. Maybe bald. A belly. He shouts and his red arms wave and the people just stand and watch. I can't hear the words. Noise. People walk by and stop for a minute and then go on. They don't nod or laugh or applaud. They just look for a while and then go on. I'm a little sick of candy. Heydorf finishes the sack and I crumple it up and toss it into the wire basket. "I didn't get the ammo and stuff." I look sideways at him and he's wiping his fingers on his pants. Doesn't lick 'em. Picks zits with 'em so he doesn't lick 'em. "Your mother came back in the middle and chased me away. Made me give all the junk back. Says if you want it you can write and ask her to send it." He's not looking. Eyes off somewhere. The fountain maybe. "She used to be cool when she was young." His voice isn't angry, just speculating, low, to the fountain. "She and my old man

rode around the country on motorcycles and went barefoot in fountains in Washington, D.C." He stops. The
sample is enough. I try to picture the well-groomed pig
being wild enough and thin enough to ride a motorcycle.
Did they have motorcycles back then? What could have
happened? "It's hard to picture." He looks at me. Looks
straight at me, eyes open almost all the way. Glint of ice
and the flat dark green of sea ice. It hurts my stomach.
It's better when he doesn't look. I look down and feel him
looking away. He never mentioned his parents before.
"Most people seem to turn off at some point in their lives.
Maybe it's thirty or forty. For most people it's lots younger.
They stop there. Stop growing or changing or learning or
something. From that point on they're dead." He speaks
slowly, explaining. I can tell he's choosing simple words so
I'll understand. I want to yell, "I'm not stupid!" but he'd
stop then and I'm mad but I don't want him to stop.
"Sometimes people allow themselves to fall into situations
that turn them off. Sometimes they're just too dumb to do
anything but turn off." "Is that what you mean when you're
always saying we're all screwed?" "Yeah, but Fred and
them, they'll do it deliberately. They'll choose a situation
and slide into it thinking it's the best they can do. Be
insurance salesmen or run a hardware store. You, you'll
fight it but you'll get sucked in because you're too dumb
to keep yourself out." My face burns and I look down at
my feet. I can feel my hands twisting at each other and
plucking at the skin. He's right. I can feel it. Like fate or
something, already printed in block letters in my skull.
Go back home after my little fling and work at some
hokey job. Marry a service station attendant and sit in a
cozy fucking little house with a toaster bringing up sleazy
brats and reading fancy books to forget I'm dead. I'll hate
him. He'll come home all tired and greasy and simple-
minded from his simple-minded job and he'll want a
warm word and I'll throw a pan of boiling water at him.

Then I'll feel bad and be nice for weeks until I can't stand it anymore and try to kill him again. Or myself. Could kill myself. That's the only real way out of a real hole. I can just see it, painting little pictures among the pots and pans. Writing dumb poems about the moon after the kids are asleep. Little pretend ways out. And always back to the same house and the same man and the waste. I couldn't stand it. He's still there. He's still looking at the fountain in this strange town in this other state and all that is back in Portland, Oregon, and I haven't gone back yet. Maybe I won't. "So how do you get off so cozy?" He looks at his hands, thinking, his eyebrows get close together and his lids drop almost all the way. "Mainly because I'm smarter." His eyes slide and he sees me looking restless. "That doesn't mean I have a higher I.Q. It means I think better. Which means I don't have a conscience and I don't have any morals." He's looking again and I nod. "So I can do anything." Anything. He's looking at the fountain again. "I can be a poet and a pirate and a philosopher and a bum." I feel a deep breath go out and it feels like no air will come in anymore. I'm tired. It's true. I can see it. And he's still only telling me part. He's still using simple words. He's not telling me everything. He might be explaining sex to a little kid. "And for Fred and the others? There's no way out?" "No, 'cause it's what they want. What they really want." "And me? I don't want it. I know I don't. But you think this is just a fling, a prank, and I'll go back home to Mama forever and settle into the hole? No way out for me either?" It's too close, too tight, no way to ask a question. But then he won't say anything just because I want to hear it. He doesn't do that. He lies but not for other people. Just for himself. He's almost looking at me again. I forgot how impressed he gets when I'm intense about something. "Maybe, if you're crazy enough. Desperate enough. I don't know."

I have a lot of faith in my craziness. I'm crazier than anybody I know and they're all crazy. I know what desperate means. I know. He's through talking. We get up and walk slow past the crowd. A little crowd. The man in the red shirt is still yelling. Communism or socialism or capitalism or Jesus or some other claptrap.

Army-Navy Store. We go in to look at sleeping bags. "I need another pair of socks." He's unfolding long white wool. The toes tight knitted, red stripes around the top. He holds them up as though they stink already. I go over to the sleeping bags and start sniffing through. Moth balls. Ducks and spotted dogs in a brown print inside. "You don't need a sleeping bag." He goes over to the tarp rolls on the wall and tugs at one. Light green, rubber on top and cheesecloth underneath. "You get a piece of this. Waterproof. Put holes in the edges. You can wrap up in it or string it up as a tent. Cheaper. Also it folds flat, easier to carry than a sleeping bag." He looks at me trying to see if I'm intelligent enough to understand. "Besides, it never gets cold at night around here anyway." I can't figure it out. I know I'll freeze my ass off if I don't get a sleeping bag. Why doesn't he want me to? Maybe he's going to come with me and there wouldn't be room for two in a sleeping bag. Maybe he's going to come. So we get the tarp. Three yards and it's heavy and the little man cuts it and goes to wrap it and I get some khaki wool socks out of a bin and go rummaging in overcoats while I put them into my pants. Heydorf's over in the jackets. Picking at sleeves with his long white fingers. "These are good jackets. You oughta get one." He takes one and tries it on. A heavy-weather jacket. Thick and heavy. Fleece-lined. Khaki imitation fleece coming out at the neck and cuffs. Roach scarred. Patched and darned khaki canvas. Used. Maybe in battle. Vague white numbers on the back. Interesting holes. Neat holes. Bullets maybe. I get a little one and go stand in front of the mirror. The collar covers half my head. The sleeves are a little long. It comes down over my ass and the zipper is wide and strong. Good deep pockets. Somebody probably died in this jacket. Yeah, I look tough. Nobody'd mess with me in this beat-up old jacket. Heydorf's goes to the waist. Good fit. Mine's big in the shoulders but that's good for keeping warm. "We'll get 'em both! They're great!" I want to bounce again and don't. He comes over and looks in the mirror. Stuffs his hands in his pockets. He looks better with his hands hidden. Stronger maybe. Six bucks apiece for the jackets and eight for the tarp. Heydorf gets his raincoat wrapped up and we go out wearing the jackets. Rumble jackets. Take a long sharp knife to get anywhere through these jackets. It's hot and we leave the jackets open. They're heavy and I sweat and feel tough. Go into a hardware store and look around. Heydorf wants grommets for the tarp. I don't know what grommets are. A plastic bag full of metal holes. They're holes. The man has a white shirt and tie. Dark store and dust in the sun in the window. "You have to have a grommet tool to put them in." Two steel bars hinged at one end. The other ends have raised holes. "Male and female," he calls them. Shows Heydorf how to put the grommets in. Sixty-five cents for grommets and two-fifty for the tool. A waste. Could just punch plain old holes to string rope through. But it must mean he's coming too. Wherever we're going.

Go back to the park and put the grommets in. Sit on the grass with the tarp spread out pounding in grommets. Get it all set up with the tool in place on either side of the tarp and the grommet in between and then you have to pound it. We haven't got a rock or a hammer and all the bricks in the walls are attached so we stand up and stomp. I stomp. Heydorf's shoes are too soft. He gets it all in place and holds it far back and I stomp. They come out bent. Bent metal holes. One in each corner, two or three down each side. An old cop comes and asks us not to sit on the grass. Heydorf blank-faced moves over to a bench and I crouch grinning up sheepish picking up the stuff and the old cop not pushing just saying we ain't supposed to. He's O.K. I feel good. It's all silly and sharp and I feel everything, sun and clothes and the bricks through the boots and every slat in the bench in my ass. It all feels good and looks good. These are the first palm trees I ever see outside pictures and they don't look any more real than pictures. The benches fill up with people, eating lunch, hamburgers or sandwiches out of sacks. The man in the red shirt is still yelling down at the other end and there are more people standing around. There are trees and then a low brick wall, benches and brick sidewalk and another low brick wall and then grass and in the middle of the grass the fountain is low brick and squirts up in a circle. It's raining in Portland. Probably raining. The sky's red here, not clear, and my eyes water a lot but it's dry and hot and it won't rain. Maybe it never rains. He's sitting beside me, a foot of bench between, stretched out, the long hands folded white over the rumble jacket. He doesn't sweat. His eyes might be closed but they're watching. "What have you been doing?" I look away out into the grass so he won't think I'm too eager. His eyes go down further and he picks at his sleeves. "Scoping things out. The crime scene here is not good." It's embarrassing and I don't look at him. "Everything with any possibilities here is organized and controlled. All the rest is penny-ante stuff for small-time punks. You gotta have a big operation to make any progress in this town. Gonna get a good job in a bank and work into a position to embezzle a good big hunk. Disappear into the south seas. Never be heard from again." I nod. That lets me off. No big heists or anything. But what about going with me? Sounds like he's going to. Have to make the question right but before I can think of the way to ask he's hungry and we go walking to find food.

A yellow chili place. Bright goldy yellow and chrome and the flies circling silent a few feet below the ceiling. A little crowded but two stools and a big bowl of chili. Two big bowls of chili and the man in the paper hat has a long nose hanging over his mustache. Crackers and chili and Coke. Don't really want it but the place is yellow and full and Heydorf breaks the crackers up on top and the spoon is limp out of his limp fingers. Heavy chili. "I ain't got no money." A spick. Shiny green polo shirt and the silly hat with the teeny brim and the feather. Just the quiet voice. Not fighting and the chili man leans on both arms on the counter and looks at him. The eyebrows come down black and the nose comes down past the mustache. "What the hell you mean, you ain't got no money? Forty cents for chili without meat. The sign says so right in front of you. You think this is a soup line? You come in here ask for food and then you ain't got no money!" He's not really mad. He's trying but he's not. The spick's soft voice explaining, "I just sat down here and you ask me what I want I say chili. I don't ask for it. Didn't say give it to me. You put it in front of me I eat it. That's all. You di'n't ask me before if I going to pay for it." His dark eyes look up innocent and the mustache twitches and the arms flop up into the air and the mustache yells, "Ah! Get outa here!" and the spick goes. I look at Heydorf. A little shrug. You couldn't get away with that in Portland. We pay.

Back in the park. Most of the people have gone back to work. Some of the people from the bus station have moved out here now and sit sleeping on the benches in the sun or talking low to one another in little groups. We sit down near a speaker. He is standing on the brick wall and talking to another man who sits on the bench across from him. They aren't old. Thirties maybe. But their clothes are torn and thin and all the gray of the men in the bus station. The speaker shouts but no one stops as

they go by. We listen and watch and the man on the
bench watches and nobody else. He is talking about Jesus.
Maybe he stutters or there is something wrong with his
mouth. The words garble and I want to laugh. He says
Jesus is wonderful. The world is beauty and nobody looks
but Jesus can help you. The sentences are broken like a
foreign language lesson. The pen of my aunt is in the
room of Jesus who love all bird and tree and earwig. You
too. In the lovely hand of Jesus who cry from cloud to
cloud you come and you cry in the dark but these bricks
love and the sky and the grasshopper and the lion and the
hair on each hand, the each hair on the toe loves. . . . And
his arms go up against the sky trying to pull it all down
and give it to the man on the bench and his voice cracks
and the words roll into themselves and are lost until he's
crying and I don't want to laugh anymore or look anymore and the man on the bench is nodding and moaning
and the speaker's voice is harsh and low and he can't
shout anymore and he gets down off the wall and the
man on the bench jumps up to him and takes his arms
and sits him down on the bench and climbs onto the wall
himself and raises his face up and reaches up into the sky
and talks loud and begins to shout and he's giving it all
back to the man who is now on the bench and the people
walk by between them and pay no attention. Walk quickly
by and the man on the wall talks to the man on the bench
and they are invisible and we are invisible and the day is
too hot now and my head hurts and Heydorf is not
watching anymore but almost sleeping and I lay back
against the hard bench and feel all the slats against me
and my belly is heavy and tight and the rumble jacket is
too hot and my sweat doesn't cool but sticks and slimes. I
don't really feel it. It hurts and doesn't feel and I can't see
except trees and people and buildings and from way high
up I look down and see this ridiculous sick ugly in some
kind of costume and want to smash it like when you see

an ant carrying something much too big and being so stuck up. Can just see him coming into the hole with a whole peanut and saying, "It was nothing, duty, nothing more," and all the other ants standing around calling names in secret and knowing they been one-upped and saying, "Oh Marvin, you must be exhausted," and ole Marvin thinks he's the hottest shit in the ant hole because he's stupid enough to bust his ass over six feet of thick grass. A peanut for the queen. And I just going to give ole Marvin his right in the middle of his dreaming how he'll be the hero of the hole, and smash him peanut and all and grind him in so it'd take an ant to recognize the remains. And here's ole half ass, half female if you don't look close, half bright if she don't open her mouth. Wants to be king. Going to climb up on the wall there and say, "I am de king!" and be surprised when nobody bows. Here's old Grade C read in a book somewhere that mediocrity is a dirty word. Rise up out of the undershirt drawer, say, "I'm de king!" Going out to conquer the world in her old yellow jockey shorts and no use for the hole. Say, "I'm de king!" And Heydorf who isn't brilliant like I thought but dumb. Almost as dumb as me. And we're all screwed. So screwed I wouldn't even know what it'd look like not to be screwed. Going back and get a job in the Dairy Queen hawking soft ice cream and chocolate dips. Get old and fat eating soft ice cream and counting out change. Go home watch the TV. Get outraged when the phone service is bad. Die and never be heard from again and never ever have anybody wonder what became of me. Never once an old buddy to turn and remember my name and say, "Whatever became of her?" Every day dead and long and just waiting to go to sleep at night to get away from it. Say, "I want to be free," like it was magic or meant something. Eating all the candy you like and not having to brush your teeth. I feel bad. I'm sick and don't know what the matter is or what to do or even where it hurts.

All over. Every place. I'm ready to die now. It's too much. It couldn't be good enough to make it worth the effort. Steal a candy bar. Big fucking stick. And the dead comes over dark across the eyes and I'm not anymore. That's even scarier. When I think about that at night I can't sleep and get up quick and read a book and go the toilet and think very quickly about a lot of other things. Something would happen if I thought about it. I don't know what. Something would break like I went too far and can't get back.

But he's moving again, gets up and I follow him and we go back to the bus station and he's going in to piss so I do too. We come down the stairs again and he says, "See that spick?" and it's my little old spick in the orange pants still around. "He's the one who wanted to sell me the forty-carat diamond ring for sixty dollars." He's so smug 'cause he was too smart to buy it. Maybe it was stolen and really worth thousands. Cramp Heydorf's ass. And it's hot again and my eyes are really watering now. But then Heydorf's just strolling around town getting free food and candy and a neat new jacket and doing no real work. I don't even talk much that he has to listen to. He ain't so dumb. We go in a service station and Heydorf gets a map. Go back to the park. Sit down. Spread out the map. California. "What have you got with you?" He's all business now. Now it's coming. "Just camping stuff. A change of clothes, knife, hatchet, rope, stuff like that." "Where'd you think of going?" "Down the Baja, along the coast, walking. Fish and hunt for food. Like that." "Un-hunh. That's dumb." It hits and I swallow it and wait. "Look at this coast. All north of L.A. almost to San Francisco it's very bare. Just little towns once in a while. See, you go up the coast and locate near a little town but on the beach. Make your camp in an isolated spot and make raids into town once in a while for food and junk." His eyes slide and I nod enough to show. "Yeah, that sounds O.K." The two men are still giving speeches to each other down the walk. His long fingers are white on the yellow. The veins the same color as the Pacific. The map rustles and he slides the finger and stops. "Gaviota, just north of Santa Barbara." I look and it's a dot and small print on a yellow knob out into the blue. "Yeah, that looks good, nothing for miles around." "Let's go over to the bus station and see about a bus." And the map folds up the right way the first time and the sun's edging in on the buildings across the street, red shine in a bricky sky. He asks and there's a bus at ten and one at five A.M. A six-hour trip. He turns and starts explaining why it's better to take the ten o'clock bus, get there early in the morning, have the whole day to scout around, not have to pay for a night's bed. Yeah, yeah, I don't care, I don't know why you want it but I don't not want it so why not? I shuffle in my pockets past the rinky harmonica and a few half-mashed M & M's. The money's tight and square and flat with chocolate smears on it. Four dollars. "Are you coming?" I'm too tired to find out the question. "Yep." And I fork out the eight dollars and get the tickets and give him one and stick the other in with the money. So it's settled. That easy. He's coming. Make things easier. On my nerves anyway. And maybe he means more. Maybe he means it the way I want him to mean it. I don't know what he means. "You want to get anything at the Y?" "Naw, I'll call and tell the guy who shares the room. That's all." So I won't get to sleep in the Y. I thought I'd creep in a window or go past the queer at the desk and he wouldn't know I wasn't a boy and might even make a pass at me and I'd sleep on the floor in my sleeping bag next to Heydorf's bed. But I don't have a sleeping bag. Tarp. And I'd piss in the can and go out again in the morning still unknown, disguised, invisible. But another night on the bus and in the morning, I don't know what. A fried chicken place. Sawdust on the floor. I get fried chicken and Heydorf gets fried clams. Sit down on benches at a rough board table. Atmosphere. He's hungry and I'm hungry and it's fried goldy with a thick crust. Yellow squeeze bottle on the table. Sticky red oozing out of it. "Ah, ketchup!" and he starts squirting it on. It's too thin and pale and grainy. "Watch it, that's Tabasco." "Naw, ketchup," and he pounds it on, squeezing and covering it all thick over the french fries and the meat. I salt the chicken and wait. He bites and stops and his face turns red. "Tabasco?" He chews and gets redder. All his food is covered with it. I can't help it. I laugh. Laugh and laugh. First time I ever laughed at him. Got one over on him. Eat my chicken grinning and smacking. He chews away. Won't talk. He eats it all and keeps getting up for water. Takes the glass in the long flat hands and fills it at the cooler and drinks it there and fills it again and brings it back. I would have bought him more if he'd asked. Wish he'd asked. But he ate it all and I laughed.

Dark now. The speakers have all gone. The fountain is lighted. It's still warm and the sleepers haven't moved back to the bus station yet. He sits on a bench and I lay on my back on the wall in front of him. The moon is coming.

"Been studying hypnotism. Guy out in Pasadena. Professor. You have to be completely hypnotized a few times before you can do it to anybody else. There are seven levels of trance. At first it's just like concentrating on something. About the third level he can order you to raise your arm and it goes up no matter what. By the fifth level he can stick pins in you and you don't flinch. Feel no pain." "That'd be nice." "Yeah, they use that to drill people's teeth, cut off their legs. Not as much hemorrhaging, no danger of shock. I've gotten to that point in being hypnotized. By the seventh level he can make you think you're a dog or do about anything." Yeah, yeah, go on, the moon's coming. "Once you've been completely hypnotized you can hypnotize yourself. Put a red dot in a book. Hypnotize yourself. Read the book. Give yourself a

suggestion to wake up when you come to the red dot.
You'll have the whole part you read memorized. Make
studying easy. Anesthetize yourself whenever you need
to. Go weeks without food. Nobody could torture you.
Give yourself a suggestion that you can't be hypnotized by
anyone else and you're safe against brainwashing. Become a spy..." The moon is orange, hot mashed pump-
kin. Good to eat. His voice is low and slow with long
pauses and the bullshit is nice. Interesting and I wish I
could believe it. But it doesn't matter. It's still nice. People
outside the park. Tinkly laughs and footsteps and cars
going by and everything quiet and dark here. I could
sleep if I wanted to. It's good. He's stopped. The voice is
gone. I look and he's behind the bench leaning on a palm
tree. People going by. I go stand beside him and watch.
Fur coats. Tuxedos. Long dresses. I never saw a tuxedo
before outside a movie or TV. Dozens of them. High
heels clicking. Arm in arm. He helps her down the curb.
Long dresses and petticoats and their hair up. A big hotel
across the street. Doorman. Bright. They all go in there.
"Must be a graduation dance." Then I see they're all
young, our age about. I feel like laughing. It's very funny.
Heh heh. I don't laugh right anymore. Always because
something is dumb. Nothing is ever just funny. That's for
Heydorf I guess. Heydorf watches a long time. The
people all look the same. I can't really see them over the
suits and dresses. Go back and sit on the wall. The tarp
feels cold with the sun off it. A little brittle. Time to go
soon. He climbs back out of the bushes and sits down on
the bench. "Wanta go back to the station? We can piss and
get something to eat or a Coke or something before the
bus leaves?" "Yeah, O.K." He doesn't care. He's tired now.
Slow and tired and maybe old. Like I feel sometimes.

We piss and then go sit in the café. He orders coffee
and fills it up with milk and sugar. "It's an old bum's
trick. Enough milk and sugar and a ten-cent cup of coffee

can keep you going all day." I nod and drink my Coke. Go look at books for a while. I read comics and he looks at philosophy.

After a while I get the stuff out of the locker and go retrieve my bow. It's a different guy behind the desk but he thinks it's cute too. I don't grin this time. No reason to. I was going to throw the girly clothes into the garbage but he says to put it in a locker with two quarters just in case. He puts his raincoat in with it and takes the key. Sit on the bench waiting for the bus to be called. I want to break a window. One of those big plate-glass things. Heave a brick and stand and watch it all fall down. Not the time for it now though. Heydorf looking folded and flat.

The bus is there and we go out and get on. I sit next to the window with the bow between my knees. Careful not to let my leg touch him. Not touching him anywhere. It's all right. He's going with me. We'll be on the beach together and sleep together and eat and talk. It will be all right in the dark and something may happen. He may mean it some other way than it seems. He talks good and at night it won't matter who's there. Just somebody. She's worrying. She's probably not sleeping but she's over crying by now. She'll just sit up all night smoking and drinking coffee with that still look on her face. If somebody speaks to her she'll be pleasant but she'll be somewhere else. She was that way when Nick would be lost or hiding. Scared out of herself into someplace else. That hurts. Can't think about that. Still in the city. Lights but flat and dull. "This is Hollywood, ladies and gentlemen," the mike cracks. Driver showboating. Hollywood. Not much. Not much at all. Heydorf is sleeping. Time to sleep. Close my eyes and look at what comes onto the inside of the eyelids. An owl's face.

It's Santa Barbara but we're already moving out and there's just a flash of stucco arches and red tile. The road is on the cliff and the sea is bright and flat all the way to

the foot of the sky. Not far now. Thirty or forty miles.
Going north again. Hadn't thought of that. Bad sign.
He's still asleep. There's a shadow on the water. Long and
dark and it doesn't move. Makes my belly hurt. The moon
bright and everything dark but the water and the darkness on the water. I can see my eyes in the window.
Somebody's reading light on. Yellow flat glass and my
eyes huge and white all around the iris. Outside through
the iris. There's no face. Just the outside and then the
whites and in the middle of the whites little holes into the
outside and the outside goes past very fast and dark. I
put my face against the glass and the whites go away and
it's all outside again but the shadow is still long on the sea
and I can see far ahead, a long straight shadow along the
coast. Maybe a hundred yards out. It breaks and picks up
again and I can see it behind. I lay back and close my eyes
and wait for my belly to stop shaking. It's nothing. Just a
shadow. It'll be getting light and he'll be awake and I
won't be alone. The road follows the sea and the shadow
follows the road. There's black sky and bright water and
then shadow. Bright water again and then the dark nothing land and then me inside the window. My belly's a
hard knot and I feel all over as though I have to piss.
Tight and holding back. The bus starts to slow and it's the
same outside and then suddenly there's a light, white and
cold and the bus pulls into it. "Gaviota Store," the mike
mutters and I'm pounding Heydorf and we're grabbing
junk out of the rack and shoving down the aisle and we're
out and this is it. It's a gas station with a little store and
restaurant. Gaviota Store. We're out of the light down by
the road. He puts stuff down and stands up and looks
around. I stand waiting, looking, we ought to go in that
store and get some food. A cup of cocoa. Steady our
nerves. But he takes his hands out of his pockets and
picks up the tarp. "I'll take the packs," and I grab them
and swing them up dangling on my shoulders and the

bow and follow him across the road. Big highway. The
bus moves out and the lights go yellow and red in a little
square far off in the black. It's a little dirt road. Dust
road. Leads straight away from the highway toward the
water. The land slopes slightly toward the ocean but it's
flat. Sheds ahead. Three sheds. Picket fence and a dog
barking inside. Railroad tracks. Track tender's house.
The track runs straight along the cliff north and south.
Heydorf turns right, north onto the tracks. I follow,
twenty feet behind. Slow with the packs. They don't bite
through the rumble jacket. Just drag. It feels good to
walk on track again. My soles so thick it doesn't hurt to
miss a tie. The gravel crispy and somewhere light beginning, the moon low and new gray light seeping in. It's just
thirty yards to the edge and then water. I can hear it now.
Soft. Calm tonight. No wind. Maybe I can smell it. It's
supposed to smell but I can never tell unless it stinks.
And out there, a little further out, a half mile maybe,
long and flat and black in the bright is the shadow. I walk
faster. Tripping on my boots, on ties, nearly running.
Three feet behind him now. His hair gray and just the
noise of shambling along on railroad tracks. Far away
now behind, the little white light and the store. The
moon's down and it's gray behind the mountains. There's
a little wet in the air and I can smell sage, turkey stuffing,
and dust. I watch my heavy feet swing and fall, the toes
pointing in, almost hitting when they pass each other.
Hear my seams brushing, and my breath and my blood
and Heydorf's heels soft and spongy just beyond my toes.
In the movies the guy carries the pack. And she's always
falling down and her blouse comes unbuttoned and she
gets a dirt smear in the hollow of her cheek. Her hair
comes out of the pins in sweet curls and he helps her up
and pushes her behind rocks when the Indians come.
Right. I can carry the pack. I can walk as far as he can. I
don't fall down and I couldn't say, "I can't go on." Couldn't.

Want to but I couldn't. He wants me to carry the pack just because he doesn't want to carry it. Very simple. Reasonable. The gray light is mist and the light comes from the mist. It comes up out of the ground. Smoke from a buried fire. Slow and the wind gone. The dark shows through the mist and Heydorf's legs cut it and my boots go through and the rails gleam beneath it. Suddenly the ground stops and the rails go on. There is mist beneath the ties instead of gravel. The ties are closer together but the mist is solid underneath instead of shreds. A trestle. There's a fence on either side and the sea is still on my left and the black land behind but no ground underneath. Heydorf is still walking and I start again but watching and placing the boot firm in the middle of a tie each time. I can see the rails ahead but I can't see where the land begins again. He walks and I walk fast to keep up and the packs are getting heavy. The trestle is long, and there are platforms on the side to stand on when a train comes. Special for if you're caught walking on the trestle when the train comes. The ties are old and the wood wears off in long slivers under my boots. There are little lights in the mist. Four or five. Small and white. Flashlight bulbs. He is stopped, leaning against the rail looking down into the white. "It's a park campground." And I can see the shapes of cars and campers and a road coming down under the trestle. "Bet there's water down there." I can see the other end of the trestle. The slope is steep and brushy. "Yeah." I don't feel like climbing down and then up again. Don't feel like going into a campground. We walk to the end of the trestle and my stomach feels easy. Drop the packs and kneel down on the road bed to get the canteen. "I'll be right back." He's got it and he's gone. Down over the side. I can hear him for a while and then nothing. It's lighter but still dark. There are smells and bug sounds and dark all around with the mist sunk back and wetting everything. It's a little cold.

The water's striped. Long slow stripes, moving thin to-ward the beach and disappearing. It's a quiet sound, and the water is clear and bright in front of the trestle. At my end a jetty goes out, or a dock, a long dock. There's wet inside the jacket and inside the sweatshirt. It's cold sitting still and I stuff my hands into my sleeves and crouch rocking back and forth on the rails to keep warm. Crashes and gravel sliding and sticks breaking and Heydorf's back. The canteen's wet and I open it and drink a little. "There's barbed wire at the bottom of the hill but I got through. There's a water fountain next to a hot dog stand. State Rangers' cabin and all the rest campers." He sits down and takes the canteen and drinks a little. He puts it down and starts putting it back into the pack. "Listen!" He's stopped, head down. I can't hear it but I feel it. The buzzing in the rails, and it gets slower and deeper. I feel a grin, wide, and it leaves my gums bare and hurts after a while but it keeps smiling. I look at him smiling. He's looking at me I think but it's too dark to be sure. "Train coming." "Un-hunh." And we grab the stuff and pull it off the tracks and down into the side hill. Lay flat in long wet green shivering and listening to it come. From the trestle, very slow, and the light is small and yellow. The beam is high and narrow and doesn't touch us and the engine comes by at a fast walk and cars and cars, freight. The doors all sealed, going north. The rails groan and the wheels screech and our whole bank below the track shakes. We shake and hug into the ground. Something might fall off. Somebody might see us. And then it's gone. I can see the last red light going up a little hill and then it's gone. We climb out onto the tracks again. I feel strong again and the packs are light. He's got the tarp and there's a pink in the air. Day coming.

There's a long slope. I get tired again and warm again. At the top a dirt road comes from inland and turns and goes parallel with the track. A wide low gate and a tin trailer house beside the gate. Pick-up behind the trailer. Signs but they face the other way and I can't read them. We walk on by, being quiet. A guard, for something. The sun hits Heydorf's hair, turns it white. It moves down over his body and then I feel it hit me, warm, and we're at the top of the hill and the slope levels out and it's almost flat. There are mountains on the right, jagged, bare, a little sagebrush. The sage growing right up to the track bed. The dirt road angles off and goes away and the cliff on the other side gets rough and cuts in and the rocks look warm in the light and the sage soft. A little ways further. Another cut. Almost a ravine. A V in the cliff. Gray trees and a steep bank down and the bottom hidden. He stands looking down into it and then slides his eyes as I come up. "Looks O.K. We'll try it." And then he goes down scrambling with sand and little rocks sliding with him, grabbing things and falling and then he disappears into the brush. I'm coming down slow and quiet, planting my heels and stepping. The packs heavy, feeling good, I can do it without all that thrashing. I run the last few feet and the trees are small, just a little over me. It's narrow with the rock going up on either side and his smashed path ahead. Come out sudden in a little bare spot. Dirt. Daisies on the rock, brown and yellow daisies but the floor clear light dirt. A little wall comes up in front. Three feet, four feet and then climbs into the cliff. He's not here. I look over the wall. The stone drops flat and steep into the sand, six feet, more. Sand, a little cove. Rocks all around and the cliffs go out into the sea on both sides. Wild rocks and surf and in here a crescent of sand, white and hot. He sits at the foot of the rock in the sand with his knees bent and his hands dangling. The sun comes straight in hot and new. "It's great! We can sleep up here behind this wall, keep the wind out. Nobody could see us from up top!" I drop the packs behind the wall and climb up and over. Slide down the face on my

ass. The sand is soft and my boots sink in it. Fall down
beside him and the sand is cool on my hands and ass. It's
white and looks hot but it's cool. "Yeah, this is a good
spot." He lays back against the rock and the sun hits his
face and his eyes are really closed. I can't sit still. Mush
down to the water and it's clean and blue and the sand
goes out beneath it. Rocks and puddles in the rocks and
black shells hard on the rock, growing out of it. The
white water hits and sprays a few feet and then sucks back
out and the sound is soft and constant. Driftwood up
against the cliff. Beams and box ends and slats and sticks.
It's warm and I take off the jacket and throw it beside him
and the air comes in and dries me and I feel good. The
cove's only about a hundred feet across from cliff to
cliff. I can't hold it. "If the sun hits here this early it'll be
on the sand all day. Sink right in front of us. Think this
faces due west?" I'm looking at him and he shifts and
looks around and falls back. "Probably does." "Then
straight out there is China." And I look almost expecting
to see it. I see the shadow. Just barely. I'm too low to see
all of it, but the dark line is steady and gray on the blue
and it reaches as far as I can see both ways. It's farther
out than I thought. It was gone by the park but it's here.
There aren't any clouds. The sun is warm and the sand is
soft and Heydorf's awake and alive. But it hurts my
stomach. A coldness.

He's not looking at the shadow. He takes off his jacket.
A gray sweater underneath, his white fingers pulling at it
delicately. He never makes a fist. It comes off and the
white shirt underneath is gray and creased and there are
wet places under the arms. He rolls up the cuffs to the
elbow. Unbuttons the top button. Bends and slips off the
green suede shoes, the long dark socks. His feet are white
and the mung in the toenails is pale, inside of shoe mung.
He rolls his pants up below the knee and stands up. His
ass is funny looking, flat and high. He's thin but his

hipbones must be wide. "Um goin' in the water!" He goes down to the edge and stands waiting for a wave to touch his toes. He coughs and spits and puts his hands in his pockets, waiting. "Me too." And I take off my sweatshirt and undershirt and boots and socks and dungarees and go flying down to the water in my jockey shorts. Jump in and it splashes up to my armpits, stings and hurts so good I jump again. It splashes him and he moves back. Puts his arms up in front of his face. "Aarg!" But it's warm and he doesn't mind and I gallop and the water is only up to my knees but the splashes wet me and the jockey shorts get heavy and gray and droop down in a soggy bag between my legs where I haven't got what they were meant to hold. In and out and up and down and the waves are little and soft with a white edge as straight and fine as a wire. I jump and yell and show off for him. Run and beat my chest and slap my belly to make a rhythm. Then I step on something, hard but it gives and jolts me and I yike and jump straight out of the water. Run all the way to the cliff and back to the edge to see what it was. Can't see anything, blue sand. Look at my foot, nothing. Enough water. He's laying on the sand watching through his white eyelashes. I wring the water out of the underpants and go flop in the sand beside him. It grits and sticks and it's hot and I can wash it off later. The top of my head's hot, a little burned from my hair being too short. Rub it. My hands are clean. My feet are clean, even the toenails. "How come your belly's so big?" That stops me. Stops everything. Put my finger in my belly button, scotch it around. Soggy gray stuff under my fingernails. Rub it into the sand. He coughs and spits. "It ain't as big as my ribs." "Yeah, them too. Were you malnourished or something?" "Nope, just drink too much beer." Lay back with my arms over my eyes. Not interested. "You're built like a pygmy." Blowguns. Eat elephants. Live in holes in the ground. "Everything works, that's all I care." All very cool. Can't be offended by such things. He coughs again. "You got a cold?" "Maybe." "I got something that's good for that." Jump up, run over to the cliff. Plenty places to grab and stand. Easy climbing. Tear through the pack. Vicks VapoRub. Back down with the blue jar. "Take off your shirt." Got him now. Going to do something for him. "Whaddya mean?" "Take off your shirt. Rub this on your chest and back. It feels hot on, good, the smell cleans out your sinuses. Loosens up your lungs. My mother always does it to me." He's sitting up, the long fingers unbuttoning the shirt, slowly. He doesn't want to take it off. I go down to the water and whoosh the jar around getting the sand off it and my hands. Come back and his shirt is open but not off. "Come on, take it off and lay on it so you don't get sand stuck on you." He takes it off and he's white. No color at all. White and soft. Not fat. The ribs show and there's no pouch but it's all soft. No muscles, his arms flabby, shapeless. I take the shirt and shake it out and put it down behind him. He lays down limp and I get down and open up the jar and scoop out a glob of the jelly. The smell makes my eyes water and my nose run. Smear it onto him. On his chest, the nipples flat and pink and soft and no hair and no muscles, all soft. It gives completely and I rub it all on hard. "Turn over." He turns and lays on his belly without saying anything. Just turns and lays there with his arms limp at his sides. No elbows. He's got zits on his back. The skin white, no sun in years, and then red with little sharp yellow points. Zits all on his back and onto his neck. I slop on more Vicks and smear it around and the zits prickle sharp against my fingers. I don't rub hard. They might break and run on my hands. He doesn't have zits on his face right now. He never takes his shirt off. He's always covered up. Maybe he always has zits on his back. Sit back and put the cap on the jar. "You'd better put your shirt back on now and sit in the sun." Put your shirt back on. You look old or something without your shirt. He sits up and takes the shirt in the ends of his long fingers and shakes it out. The grease shines and smells. Makes him look melted. He puts the shirt on and buttons it up and turns his back while he unzips to tuck it in. I don't care. I don't want to see him naked. My back's hot and my shoulders like liver. Turning red and I can feel the old freckles popping out. Mush my hands in sand to get the grease off. Wash in the water. Not deep. Want to see where I'm stepping. Go put the jar back and take the shorts off and put my dungarees on. He's sitting in the sun. Slide back down and get our socks. Go stand on the big rock with the puddle. Tidal pool. Lots of things in it. See bugs. Rinse 'em out. Poke a stick up in the sand. Droop the socks over. Us mountain men always wash out our socks. Go lay down beside him in the sun. He smells. "You sure stink." "Yeah." "Come to think of it I don't remember that junk ever doing any good." I think that's pretty funny but he just lays there stinking. His shirt sticks to the grease.

"When the socks are dry we'll go for provisions." We could use the other socks but I don't feel like going now. Don't mention it. "We can build a fire at the foot of the cliff here and the smoke ought to be scattered by the time it's above the cliff. Won't start it till nightfall anyway." He's talking with his eyes low, sliding them to see how I take it all. I take it all. "Ought to be able to catch some kind of fish off those rocks." "Yeah, I brought some string. Had hooks but they were lost in the raincoat." He picks at the shirt, pulls it slowly away from the places where it sticks. It falls back and sticks again. The sun's high. His face is red, the nose and forehead red and the rest sick white. "You're getting burned. You better sit in the shade a while. It's plenty hot enough." He moves slow and old and clumsy. I want him to walk hard and talk mean but he shuffles and doesn't talk much at all.

The socks dry and are soft and smell good. The tops of

his feet are burned and the long toes go into the socks
very slowly. He stands up while I'm still lacing my boots.
"Get your shirt and the money." He picks up the canteen
and walks off toward the rocks. I run to catch up. "Figure
if we climb these rocks we can get past that gate on the
road before we climb up on the tracks." It's a long steep
rough wall. Not hard to climb but too long in the heat.
He starts up and I follow. He jumps toward the first rock.
Jerky, a broken toy move. His soft shoes hit wrong and he
falls back on his ass in the sand. I stop and lean on the
rocks and hide. He doesn't say anything, gets up and
jumps again and goes climbing using his hands a lot.
Scrabbling at it, doing more work than he has to. Must
have been a long time since he climbed anything. I follow
easy, walking and being careful not to use my hands
except when I have to. He fell bad, flat, hard. My fallen
hero. It's funny. It's long and I'm winded at the top.
Stand puffing and looking out over the water. Clear blue
and no line at the sky but the shadow is dark, greenish,
with straight sides. Runs all up and down the coast. I turn
around to go but it's solid sage. As high as me and solid.
Heydorf's in it. I can hear him crashing. Crawl up on the
brush. Sticky and rough. I can see the tracks. The bed
built up above the brush. A long way. I don't know how
far. I don't remember the sage being like this. The wood
is thick and the branches strong. I climb from one crotch
to another. It pulls and scratches and sticks. It's very slow
and I can't see the ground. A rock sometimes. Hot.
Rattlesnakes. Maybe rattlesnakes. Fat and fast and glittery
eyes. Not even the bite so much but it'd be so close and
it'd open its mouth and touch me. Touch deep. And the
hurt. And maybe it wouldn't go away after but would stay
where I could see it fat and do it again. Touch me again.
And I couldn't do anything. I'd just lay there and maybe
not even yell. Just lay there and let it touch me. If it
crawled on me I couldn't stand it. Something would

happen if it crawled on me. I'd break. Go off there where
I couldn't come back. I can see him sometimes, pale, he's
angling, not going straight toward the tracks. He comes
up and moves jerky and white against the dark gray and
then goes down again. I look each time I put my hand
down. I look where I put my feet. But it's too thick and I
can't see. Listen and the brush rattles in the wind. The
wood rattles when I push on it. It scratches my face and
it's hot and every time I feel a scratch or something
against my leg I jump and sweat. Can hear my blood in
my ears. I stop and lean against the brush and it pins and
prickles and pushes back. The sweat rolls into my eyes.
Skin over my eyes, their skin comes off over their eyes
and they're blind for awhile and get lost and wander into
towns and too close to the sea and they are mad and bite
and they lie in the brush, coiled around the rocks and
they are fat and fast and my guts come up in a wave and
it comes thin and hot out of my mouth, pale juice, and it
burns and tastes and makes me puke again, and there's
no cool place to put my head, put my hands on my head.
The palms are cold and wet and I can smell myself,
strong and feel better and go on fast not looking anymore
but jumping and running, charging and shoving and
knocking through the brush. Bite me for all I fucking
care but I'm getting out of here.

The track bed is gravel and I scramble up using my
hands, not caring and fall down on the clean oily old hot
ties and the clean rails and lay there with my tongue
hanging out staring at the rails. There's puke in my nose.
I'll smell of it for a long time. But with all his grease he
won't notice. He's still out there. Not far from the track
now. A ways ahead. Small and white. I spit until most of
the bad taste is gone and sit up. He's almost there. Stand
up and walk along slow, my knees soft, going in other
directions. Go slow and breathe. He climbs up and stands
puffing with his hands in his pockets. His face is red. He's

still not sweating. I can smell the menthol grease. He
slides his eyes at me. "Guess we'll have to find an easier
way." I nod. "Un-hunh." We're past the gate guard and I
can see the trestle long in the light. We stop at the
beginning and look over. A long way down. A hundred
feet. More maybe. They look like toys. Neat little roads,
neat little plots. In each plot a pick-up camper or a little
trailer or a tent. Picnic tables, portable radio music,
people in bright colors. I smell meat cooking. Lunch. I sit
down and lean on the middle board of the fence. Swing
my legs. Heydorf sits down and we look out. A little
cabin. Logs and rough-cut shingles. A patch of green and
a border of red and white flowers. Like a picture. Flag-
pole in front. Rangers' cabin. Girls in bikinis, motor
scooters. "They're roughing it." I smile and he nods.
"Yeah, with their air mattresses and stoves and portable
refrigerators." The dock on the other side goes out a long
way. People fishing. Beach next to it. Umbrellas, blankets,
people. All little and bright so far down.

Back along the tracks. The doors of the three sheds still
closed. A ratty hound sniffing behind the picket fence.
Up the dirt road and across the highway. Three miles,
maybe, from our camp. There are two small cabins behind the parking lot. People who work here probably stay
in 'em. A white shed with two doors. Ladies and gentlemen.
"I'm going to wash my face." Cement floor. Everything
wet and cool. A long piss and then wash. Cold water only
but soap, not for clean but to get rid of the puke. The
soap burns. My face is red too. The nose. Lots of freckles
sharp and splattered. Rinse my mouth out and let the
water run up my nose a little. A wad of toilet paper and
blow it, hard. White and clear and a few dry old green
snots. Sizzle some more water through my teeth. He's
sitting on the curb. Cars with trailers and surfboards.
Pick-ups with campers and bicycles. Inner tubes getting
blown up at the air hose. Lot of people. The screen door's

ripped and the Coca-Cola sign's bent. Not very big. A
counter with stools. Two picnic tables against the window.
Grocery section and miscellaneous. Postcards, sunglasses,
car deodorizers, fishing tackle, imitation sailor hats with
felt flowers sewn on. We go around in the groceries. I
look at Oreos. Got to have 'em with milk though. Dunk
'em and the black cookie part gets soft and the cream
filling's even sweeter. Fall off into the glass if you hold it
there too long. Spoon it out. Heydorf's looking at cheese.
I go look over his shoulder. "Good cheese." He waves it at
me. Slices in clear plastic. I don't like cheese. "Too expensive." "But it's good." "Then nick it, I don't want to pay
for it." He never nicks anything himself. Getting bitchy in
my old age. He puts the cheese back and goes on. Still we
ought to get stuff that's good for us. I put the cheese into
my pants and go look at canned stuff. He's looking in the
meat stuff. "How about hot dogs? Put 'em on a stick over
the fire." "Yeah, great!" So we get a package. "Ketchup or
mustard?" "Ketchup." He gets a jar of mustard. A loaf of
balloon white bread. He's looking at canned spaghetti.
I'm looking at pork and beans. "Spaghetti's good." "Yeah,
but we'll get rickets or something eating spaghetti. Beans
have a lot of protein." "Yeah, but spaghetti tastes good." I
stand looking at him and the spaghetti and he's looking at
me holding the beans. "Tell you what. Get some beans for
you and spaghetti for me." "O.K." Two cans of each. A
two-quart jar of peanut butter only a dollar nineteen.
"*Aarg!*" he says and I put it back 'cause I've been giving
him a lot of shit. "Wanta get some cake or something?"
"All right." He doesn't care. Big chocolate cake. Devil's
food but really chocolate. Lot of frosting. The box square
and the cake round and a clear plastic window in the top.
Lot of money but it'll go further than candy. "I want
orange juice." He's got a bottle and carries all his stuff up
to the counter. I take my load up and it looks like a lot
together. "Be heavy to carry. Better not get anymore

now." He nods and the man behind the counter rings it up. More than five dollars. The counterman goes in back to get a bag and I put candy bars into my pants. Heydorf goes outside. I can see him through the screen filling the canteen at the water hose. I pay and the man puts it all in a big brown bag. Lug it out. Not too bad. Heydorf gives me the canteen and takes the bag away. Goes off carrying it in one arm. "I can carry it!" "You'll break my orange juice." And he goes across the road very fast. Catch up and take the candy out of my pants and drop it into the top of the bag. Five bars. Three chocolate and two peanut and caramel. Not bad. I keep the cheese to surprise him with. We march single file down the track. The sage is close and the smell makes me want to puke again. The sun's slanted and the light red and cooler. We go down the easy way into the ravine. Take the bag down onto the sand and sit to rest. "Dig out some of that candy." He's looking at the bag. So I get it out and we eat one chocolate and one peanut and caramel apiece. Leave the other chocolate for emergencies. Drink a little from the canteen. He's saving the orange juice for dinner. It's all easy and warm and good. The shadow's just a line. "There weren't any stewardesses on the bus I took. Were there on yours?" "Naw, I was misinformed." "Lot of strange people on buses." "Yeah." And I go on and tell him about the people on the bus and how I got to the bus and all about the party I didn't go to and where I'd got all the stuff and how I'd spread the Montana tale around. I get excited remembering and talk well. It feels good coming out and he's listening, nodding and saying yeah and go on and that's a good one. "And I didn't have any trouble at all, with any of it." "Hmmm... That was a good idea. The Montana mountains business. They've probably got the Montana police watching all the roads for you. Never think to look for you down here. Cops probably think you were dumb to tell people where you were going." And he thinks the fake letter idea is good and I feel so good I get up and go around picking up dry driftwood for the fire. The sun's red and low, touching the water. And the tide's coming in. "Hey, the tide." He looks and walks down to the edge and looks back at the wall. "It's slow. Won't bother the fire. We'll sleep up in the crack anyway. No problem." He comes to help and we drag a big old gray beam up to our chosen spot. It's an eight by eight and twelve feet long. "A shipwreck, you think?" "Yeah, or a fire. Superstructure or a crossbeam from a fishing boat maybe." There are big bolts in it, bent and weird but not rusted. "We'll put it in back against the wall. Build the fire up against it. As it burns down we just shove it in." We lug and drag and push and get it into place. The sun goes into the water and doesn't make a sound. The sky is still blue but low and solid, and a pink cloud floats small far away. So perfect and pink I feel silly. He's careful with the wood. Small very dry thin pieces and the candy bar wrappers. I bring the matches and the knife from the pack. His long fingers strike the match and reach in under the twigs and slivers and the paper catches and the little red comes and the brown shiny paper turns silver and the yellow paper turns black. It's all lavender, the sand and the rock and then the little red and his white hair and hands. Pretty. Pretty. He takes the knife and goes to cut sticks for roasting wienies. I haul out the bread and mustard and lay the cheese with it. A little soft from being next to me. That's all right. It's a good fire. Small and hot and no smoke. Not a white man's fire. "Ah! Cheese!" and he picks it up and cuts open the pack not looking at me. We roast the wienies black and wrap bread around 'em and smear mustard all over and sit gorging while the stars come out. He wraps cheese around and lets it melt a little and puts on more mustard. Share the orange juice. Five hot dogs apiece and then cake. Gouging out chunks and eating with our

hands. "Good cake." "Yep." And more cake and the moon
up but it's white tonight. The water's just a few feet away.
I can touch it with my wienie-roasting stick. "Think it'll
cover the fire?" "Maybe. We can sit up high and dry on
the wall and see." Burn up the wrapping stuff. Put the
rest of the bread back in the bag with the canned stuff.
Close the half a cake back into its box. I climb up and he
hands me the stuff and I stow it behind the wall. Almost a
cave except no roof. He sits back down by the fire and I
stand above, leaning over the wall watching. He looks
pretty good. His face is yellow in the light and the
shadows are deep. Very clean from the side. Straight
nose, straight forehead, big mouth and medium chin.
The shadows cut in and make him look lean instead of
thin. He built a good fire. Make the bed. Pull the poncho
out of the pack. Spread it out. It fills the little clear spot.
Shove all the junk in back, behind where our heads will
be. Keep out drafts, rats, lizards, snakes. Flap out the
tarp, on top, fold the edges under. Glorious.

"You think there might be any rattlesnakes crawling
into bed with us?" I'm leaning over the wall talking down
to him. He looks up from the fire. His face looks enam-
eled. School bus yellow, but the shadows move. "Naw.
They don't come this close to the ocean. Salt burns their
skin just like a slug. There's always some salt in the air
and it settles on the ground and on plants and stuff. They
wouldn't come near here." "That's good." Makes me feel
better. But I know up on the cliff where the spray would
never reach, they'd come there. Probably millions of
them in the hills on the other side of the track. They
sleep in holes all together wrapped into each other.
Dozens tied in knots and squirming and if you stumble
on them in the dark you'd hit it and think it was a huge
animal and it'd roll a little way while they were getting
loose from one another. Hard to get loose. You couldn't
tell what was you and what was some other snake. And

the ball would fall apart into all separate snakes and they would all come after me, crawl on me, I'd feel them heavy and fat, long across me and their muscles moving and squirming as they bit me. I jump up on the wall and slide down fast into the light. Sit beside him looking at the fire. Breathe carefully so he won't know I was scared. He's got his jacket on. It's colder. Not cold but colder. I put mine on. Leave it unzipped so the fire can get to my belly. The water is right behind us. I could put my feet in it. It's quiet, shushing and hissing and shushing. The rock I washed the socks on is gone, covered. The firelight crawls halfway up to our hole, spreads wide and flat on the cliff face. The moon's high and small and the sky's blacker because of the fire. "Maybe it is tougher being a girl." I look up surprised but he's holding a stick in the fire. Not looking at me. "I don't know. Sometimes I think it is but you can get away with a lot of things a boy couldn't." "Yeah, but there are a lot of ready-made escape routes for boys. Army and forest ranging and the merchant marine. Nobody even thinks it's that weird if a guy wants to be a hermit. All part of the manly image. There's really no place in society for a woman like that. She has to either operate underground or else totally outside the society." He's encouraging me. Making me think I'm one of those women outside and he sympathizes. "Working underground is a waste. Unless you want to start a movement or save the world, or brighten your corner or some other such liberal bullshit. It fucks your private life. You're always going around maintaining a façade, spending a lot of energy keeping up your disguise. Gets in the way of doing what you want to." He's looking at me now, seeing if I understand. "Yeah, I get it. They're wifey and mothery and get their hair done and shave their legs and then they think they're accomplishing something in their secret lives by working part time or taking literature courses at night. Throwing clay pots in a hokey art school. Read

the *Wall Street Journal*." "Right, but they're fucking themselves the same as the guy who works his ass off fifty
weeks a year so he can go fishing for two weeks. Drink
beer, wear a red hat, big man, read *Argosy*." We're laughing.
A little. A little laugh. He doesn't smile. His mouth opens
a little and a "heh heh" comes out. "The secret is, that's
what they really want. It's comfy, see? They got the warm
house and the TV and washing machine. They just got to
play like they're alive sometimes to make it all worthwhile.
Come back from fishing with bug bites and poison oak
and be very happy to go back to the office on Monday."
Now I want the answer. Enough bullshit. Just tell me now
once. "So how do you get out of it?" The stick is burning.
He takes it out of the fire and waves it a little, the sparks
make circles. He shoves it into the sand and it's out. His
left hand lays dead on his knee and his right hand draws
in the sand with the stick. "Well, if they reject you, you go
mooning around missing what you haven't got. So at
some point it has to be deliberate. At some point you have
to decide it's not what you want. Even if you couldn't have
it if you tried, you've got to decide you don't want it, see?"
"Yeah, yeah, but what then?" The hand flops and the
stick digs and the waves come in small and quiet. "I think
there are some people outside of society. Not any particu-
lar system. Could be the best of all possibles and they'd
still be outside. I don't know if it's genetic or some weird
accidental combination of circumstances when they were
growing up. Doesn't matter which really. But somehow
they aren't social. They don't have an urge to live around
other people or be friendly or be like other people. They
may live near people but it's just for convenience, not
because they're afraid of being alone. They don't have the
morals or conscience of whatever society it is they're
surrounded by. They're totally egotistical. What's good
for them is good and what's bad for them is bad." He
stops and looks at his hands and digs more. I see he's

talking about himself now. Hopes he's talking about himself maybe. "A lot of people like that become criminals. That doesn't mean all criminals are like that, but some. Most criminals are pretty social I think. Maybe some of these outsiders work underground. They're probably good criminals and they'd likely be good at working underground. Be businessmen. Walk over everybody. Some of them are probably artists. But most of them I think are bums." I can see them sleeping. "Are they smarter than other people or something?" He digs and the fire is low and I zip my jacket up. It's taking him a long time. "No, not necessarily. They just think differently." He throws the stick down and turns his head at me. "See, these people don't really have to try to be outsiders. They just are. They couldn't be social people if they died trying." I'm scared now. It scares me. "Is there something wrong with 'em?" "No, no!" He puts his head down on his knees. His hands are limp on the sand and his voice comes from between his knees. "Maybe there is. Maybe they're throwbacks to really primitive times. Oughta be wandering around with a club looking for raw meat. Guess if there were too many of them it'd be dangerous to society and they'd all get killed off, persecuted. Have their iris prints taken and be put into concentration camps. Not allowed to reproduce. They're more dangerous than revolutionaries, see, they're all anarchists at heart. Thrive on chaos. Love it. There must be a constant percentage in the general population. Zen hermits, John the Baptist, gypsies, bums, pickpockets, Michelangelo. All them." He's not lecturing anymore. He's just talking. Doesn't know I'm here. "Do they all know? That they're that way?" He lifts his head and looks at me. His eyes are open and they look black in the fire. The shadows jump and the light changes. He's melting down. His mouth twitches at the corner. Heydorfian smile. "Probably not at first. But I'm sure they all come to know it if they live long enough." He gets up. Stiff, I can tell, and walks off into the shadow. He can't go far. The tide has us closed in. I can still see him at the edge of the dark. His back. He's pissing. I can hear it drilling into the water. He comes back and he's through talking. He stands and kicks at the fire with the soft sloppy shoe. But I need more. I know it's too much but I need it now. "But what if you're not one of the outsiders and you still need out?" He kicks and the sand sprays light on the wood but doesn't put out the flame. "Ah, I don't know, I guess you have to do something irrevocable." It's cold now. The wind's up and the waves break, small but the spray comes onto me and my hair's wet. Damp. He's climbing the cliff face slowly. I wait until he crawls over the wall and down into the shelter. Then I swarm up fast. Don't want to be alone down there. The tarp's thrown back and he's sitting on the poncho taking off his shoes. I walk past into the brush a ways. Dark. No telling what's there. Crouch and piss fast, listening and scared. Come back into the gray-lighted clearing still buttoning up. He's standing on the tarp in his socks, leaning over the wall, looking down. Sit down and take off my boots. It's a lot of work. The hooks and the laces and the buckles and the sand in the socks. Maybe too much work. Lay them upside down on a ledge in the rock. The wind comes in a little but soft. He's dark and there's a halo of white in his hair. Reflection from the fire. He'd like it if I said he looked like Satan, or Mephistophelean. Crew-cut Beelzebub. He'd snort a little and maybe do something daring. But I'd laugh. I couldn't help laughing. I could say he looked like a Roman emperor, one of the decadents, Caligula. Not that either. He looks like a statue. A wax head and wax hands on a rag body. "The water's gonna cover the fire." I jump up to look. Dark sea, dark and white lines and the fire tiny and red and the water inches from it, pushing. "Good thing we brought everything up here." "Yep." I'm too tired to stay and watch.

Time to lay down. Time to sleep. If he wants to fuck I could stay awake for that but nothing else. I sit down. Take off the rumble jacket. Cover my belly with it and wrap it around. The arms around my neck. My lover. My old khaki lover. He comes and flops down, slides under the tarp. His jacket still on. Lays flat on his back. It's hard. The ground is hard. I kicked the little rocks away but the dirt is hard. I lay on my back beside him, stretching, barely touching. Our sides grazing. He don't want to screw I guess. That's all right. I'm too beat to shit anyhow. The sky is black. Stars very small and far between. There's a hum somewhere, far way. It stays and doesn't go away. Not a bug, an engine. "Do you hear that?" "Yeah." My ears hurt, feel like they want to pop from listening. Then thunder, a hum and suddenly it's not a hum but thunder. A train on the cliff ramming past our ravine. It roars and rattles and then stops. A hum again and after a while the hum goes away. Can't sleep on my back. Turn on my side away from him. This stupid fucking tarp is going to freeze my ass. Freeze his too. Serve the mother right. Never gets cold in these parts. My poor tired ass.

I'm standing as straight as I can. The bricks are rough but the sun's nice. He'll just measure me once more. Green uniform, jack boots, the long chalk. He steps in front of me and sights with the chalk. I stretch my neck and lift my heels a little, just a fraction. He makes the mark and then marches off to the side. I can smell the dirt still wet from the dew. Chocolaty. Smells like dry chocolate. They are sitting, two men to a gun, five guns. All on tripods. I forget their name, with the belts of cartridges. He raises his hand and the chalk drops and I can see it breaking. White chalk and the dust flies up slow around the chalk. The lights come on in the barrels, bright blue, and I can see the bullets ripping into me. The holes pop out instead of pushing in and the holes look like belly buttons, little round ridges popping out all over me and I'm naked and it scares me the way the holes pop out like that and the guns keep making the noise and the blue light. "Stay down, it's a helicopter!" Heydorf's voice hurts and the whock of the blades echoes in the ravine. I can see the wheels and a glass ball and the blades so fast they look slow and it goes straight over out to sea and the cliff hides it. "I thought it was a machine gun." My voice is high and cracks and I stop and swallow and lay still. "I hope they aren't looking for you." He gets up and puts on his shoes and crashes back into the brush. My guts flip up and I have to piss. Jump up and plow into the daisies. Can't squat, they're too high. Lean and piss. No time to dry. Whip up the pants and back to the tarp. Grab the boots, shake 'em out, scorpions, centipedes, evil spirits. Sit shaking and sweating they'll drag me back and think I fucked Heydorf and give me all kinds of shit and I didn't even get to do it. The laces knot on me and I'm sweating and hurrying and he comes back slow, ducking branches. "There's an oil derrick out there. Up the coast a little and a half mile out maybe. That's where it was going. Probably carries supplies and men out there all the time." He sits down and I still can't undo the knots. The shake goes away gradually and the sweat dries and it's a blue sky and warm already. "They couldn't have seen us anyway. That green tarp makes good camouflage." He gets up and looks over. "Tide's almost out. It didn't touch the fire after all." Fuck it. Kick the boots off without untying them. Peel off the slept-in socks. Go get the toothbrush out of the pack. "I feel like brushing my teeth. You wanna brush your teeth?" He follows me down the cliff face. The sand is dry already, a gray line where the water stopped. The ashes clean and white and a black mark on the stone behind. The rock is uncovered. A little white breaker washing halfway over and then falling back. Roll up my pants legs. Heydorf following with his soft feet white and the cuffs too tight to roll. We stand on the rock. It's not in the sun yet. Still a little cold and the wind stronger. The wave breaks and I run forward and dip the brush in and scrub away with salt water and it stings and tickles and the dark brown taste washes away when I spit. Jump when the wave breaks and run in as it's sucking out. Scrub and spit and he's waiting for the toothbrush and the rock is rough and wet under my feet. The sea bugs going crazy in the pool. Tiny fish and crabs crazy back and forth in the water and the porcupine things open and waving and hungry. I hand him the brush and crouch by the pool poking at the anemones to make them close. He dips the brush once and stands very stodgy brushing his teeth and then spits and hands it back to me. I rinse it off in the pool and jump into the water to wade back to the sand. Get all wet. He slides in and comes back slow. "I don't usually brush my teeth. That's the first time I ever really liked it. Got to do it now though, and eat right. No old lady to pay the dentist, hand out vitamins..." It's going too far. Too much talk, and I stop. Silly stuff. I just meant to apologize for the hassle over the beans last night. He don't care. Crawls up the cliff and comes back down with the cakebox. "Time to eat cake." "Yeah!" And we sit in the sand hacking up the last half of the cake. A quarter for him and a quarter for me. I go back up for the canteen and we sit in the sun and the chocolate is a little harder this morning, fudgy. He eats it fast and sits sucking his teeth. I eat slow. Small bites and long voluptuous chews. It lasts a long time and feels good inside. "You ought to read Hobbes, and Rousseau. Have to wade through a lot of crap but the basic ideas are good." He plays with his toes. "I'd rather have you tell me about 'em. All the stupid big words. I'm sick of reading anyway. Never read again it'd be fine with me. You tell it better anyway, clear and simple. No phoo-phoo-rahs." "I

could tell you anything and you'd believe it. You don't
know I'm telling you the truth."

He's disgusted. No way to explain. It's dumb and I
know it but I can't help it. "I don't care if you're telling
the truth or not as long as you tell it nice. I don't see how
it matters whether it's true." "Haw haw." The old cold
"haw haw." "You're dumb." Piss me fucking off. Piss me
fuckety fuck the fucker off! "Jesus! You think it matters a
goddamn to me whether some four-hundred-year-old
politico with lice in his wig happens to agree with me
concerning the minuscule meaning of mankind? It's all
very pretty but it doesn't affect me more than this fuckin'
son of a bitchin' mosquito! What affects me is too many
damned mosquitoes. I like Santa Claus better than Rousseau
and I believe in him whenever I feel like. What's so
bloody fucking interesting about the truth all of a sudden
anyway? What'd the truth ever do for you?" I'm tired and
feel like crying. Make a fool of myself all the time. Lose
my temper. Talk big bullshit, and he's laying there flat
with his eyes closed not encouraging my hysteria. Lay
down and scratch my bug bites. Got a lot of bug bites.
Worse than zits. I don't want to think like that. Want to
think about eating and sleeping and building sand castles.
Everything simple. Scratch the bites, build the fire, look
at the moon, eat the cake. It's different somehow with
him, I thought he'd still be the boss and tell me what to
do and every once in a while I'd think of a surprise to
please him and the rest of the time just listen and ask
polite questions and think my own ditsy thoughts. But I
don't feel like being polite anymore and he's not really the
boss. He falls out of it sometimes. Lets me scream at him
like that. Probably over there thinking I'm a dumb shit
and he's gonna go off and leave me be a dumb shit on my
own.

"You missed the point." Naturally, I always miss the
point. I am a dumb shit. "The point is, you believe

anything certain people tell you. It doesn't matter whether it's war stories or interpretations of history or telling
you something that might affect you, even something
long-range, your whole life. I got to admit you're choosy
about who you believe but it can still screw you. If I lie
about some things that you know about what makes you
think I don't lie about things that could wreck you? You
just believe whatever you want to." "Yeah, but I only
believe it as long as it's handy. See, I need you to tell me
things now and I listen and I think I understand, but that
doesn't mean I just eat it up. It's just there. Like a
grammar rule. If I run across something that disagrees
with it, that's an exception to the rule. If I run across a
shitload of exceptions it's a dumb rule. Throw it out. Like
if you tell me to do something I don't just go do it. I look
at it and if I can figure I can do it without getting
screwed I do it. Or if there's a fair chance I won't get
screwed and it seems worth the risk, I do it even if it's a
little hairy. But see, I judge for myself. Like when you
wanted those fancy chocolates in the Woolworth's. That
really pissed me off. You knew that was impossible. What
were you trying to do? See how far I'd go to please you? I
used to think I just did things without thinking. Grabbed
and ran. But now I don't think I do and I don't think I
have for as long as I've known you. I don't know." It
makes me tired when I talk. He's just sitting there in the
sunshine fiddling with the sand and I'm blowing my brain
around through a pea shooter. I give up. Shut up. "I
wanted you to *buy* those chocolates in Woolworth's." He's
grinning, kink in the mouth. Heydorfian grin. He thinks
it's funny. It is kind of funny. Buy 'em. "I never thought
of that." I'm grinning too and it's all right. It's pretty
funny. Buy 'em. Didn't think of that.

Sand fleas hopping around. Short disgusting little hops.
Hot sun and we lay in it for a long time talking about all
kinds of things. "Knock off the Vatican if you had a

helicopter and a submarine. Two people could do it.
Land on the roof. Kidnap the Pope. One holds a gun on
him while the other goes down into the vaults and makes
the monks carry up bullion and candlesticks, pieces of the
cross, St. Augustine's left ear in a silver box. They'd all do
what you wanted so the Pope wouldn't get it. Pope wouldn't
be too gutsy even if he really believed all the heaven crap
because he wouldn't want the church to suffer such a blow
as having the Pope knocked off in his boodwar by a
couple of atheists. Put all the booty in the helicopter, fly
off. Lock the Pope up and by the time they've got him out
safe you've landed on your submarine in the Atlantic,
transferred the goodies and submerged leaving the helicopter to sink. Evidence eliminated. Head for Red China.
They don't care about the Pope." "Yeah. Get millions. I go
live in a cave cut into a mountaintop. Never come out.
Have cannons built into the walls, all on one string so I
can sit in my command post and blow hell out of anybody
who comes near. Pull the handle and they get drenched
in boiling oil. Leave 'em out there for the bugs and birds.
Layers of skeletons piled around the mountain. Scare
people off. Come out once a year in my flying machine.
Land in Portland or Omaha or Galveston. Go down the
street on my mad elephant. Paint him red. Gold harness.
I point and say 'Kill!' and the elephant mashes cars,
wrecks stores, crushes people, picks 'em up and throws
'em into the river. I so rich the cops running along
behind saying yessir nosir making sure nobody gives me
any trouble. Chief of police coming along behind with a
spoon and a sack picking up the elephant shit, put in the
museum, sell little packages to tourists, souvenir of the
visit of the king. De king was here! President sends me an
invitation to a White House banquet in my honor and I
wire back, 'What's for dinner?'"

"Naw, naw. You set up in New York, see, or Paris or
London maybe. Develop a network of spies and skillful

criminals. Finance fantastic jobs all over the world. Influence world politics, start wars. Sit in a study with a big rug and a lot of seegars. Throw darts at the map. Nobody knows you exist until finally you control the world." "Aah, that's work. You got all that money, why work? I ain't going to work at all. Sit on my butt. Go blooping around in my flying machine. Have my own movie theater with a built-in popcorn machine next to my armchair. Go to New York City and get in one of them horse carriages in the park and say, 'Take me to San Francisco.' Pay no attention to anybody. You'll blow all your money on your power game, land in jail and come out twenty years later with thirty dollars and a Good Will suit. Come begging to me on the street and I'll say, 'Do I know you?' I'll fly into Portland, hire a wrecking crew. Flatten the city. People coming up saying, 'Remember me, I was in your class,' and I'll say, 'Do I know you?'" I'm grinning and digging Mayor's running around trying to find the key to the city in the rubble. Come up with the key all bent and the ribbon torn, gilt scraped off. 'Please accept this token...' and I'll say, 'Do I know you?'" I'm grinning and digging in the sand and he's laying there with his hands crossed and his eyes closed and I feel good and cozy and silly and it's fun but it's slipping away. "I was thinking I ought to build a raft and sail to Tahiti. Or Samoa. Be the first lone woman to pull the Kon-Tiki thing off. Go around and get companies to give me money to do testimonials afterward. You know: 'I sailed the Pacific in my Virgin Form panty girdle!' or 'Sunny Jim Peanut Butter crosses the Pacific!' It don't matter that I never sailed before. In a raft you just float along with the current and keep your head up. Besides, if it's going to kill me it won't matter if I've studied navigation. It'll kill me anyway, go down spouting numbers and flexing my sextant. And if it isn't going to kill me it just won't."

"Yeah, that's right. You can't worry about things like

that or you'd never do anything." "Besides, I've had experience. Floated all the way down the Tualatin River to Lake Oswego my sophomore year. Borrowed Vic Coles' two-man rubber raft. Box of twenty-four Hershey's with almonds. Walden Pond. Read *Walden* all the way in the sunshine. Leaning back with a wet ass and my feet over the side. Had to get up once in a while to shove off a snag or get away from the bank. It was nice. But I didn't know there's a fall into the lake. Lost the book. Broke the raft. Cost me four dollars to get it patched." "You like *Walden*?" "Yeah, in those days, when I was young, you know? Didn't get to finish it. Lost it." "That's good. Dumb man. Well, he knew some things but it's all so obvious. Report to Congress. Six-million-dollar study. Five hundred professors for forty years. Decide healthy people are happier than sick people. Rich people have more money than poor people. Everybody's very surprised. 'Ah! A revelation!'" "Yeah, they don't believe they got an asshole unless you can show 'em statistics. Everybody got an asshole. I'm a body, so I must have an asshole." "Aristotelian logic." "Great stuff." "Yeah, floating down a river would be nice. Easier than rattling around in the ocean." "Yeah, I oughta do that again sometime." "When I was in Missoula I went up to Helena to visit somebody. The Missouri starts near there. Very rough and small for a ways until it gets big in the plains." He wants to go I think. His idea. Good idea. "That'd be great. We could build a raft at the head and float all the way to the Mississippi. All the way down to New Orleans." He's nodding. It's right. "Yeah, then get a job on a boat going to the south seas. Jump ship and be a beachcomber." It's getting serious. My belly knows and my hands are cold. Red in the sun and cold. "We could do it with just the stuff we've got. The hatchet's good. More rope to tie the thing together. Fish off the raft for food. Stop in towns on the way and steal goodies." He's nodding, digging in the sand now. His hands make a

ditch and it crosses the ditch I've made, breaks the walls
and I scoop the sand back and make walls for his ditch.
He's talking fast trying to convince me though I'm con-
vinced. He ought to know. "Keep a journal, see, sell it to a
magazine when we're through. America's heartland, human interest. Take a bus to L.A., then a bus to Helena.
Not a lot of money. Forty bucks apiece maybe. You got
that much left?" "Sure, and more for a grubstake."

The day goes and night comes and he builds another
good fire. His cough is worse and the stink's gone from
his chest but he doesn't want anymore. My bug bites itch
in the heat from the fire and we bring down the knife to
hack open the cans. Spaghetti and beans and the knife
blade for his spoon and a smooth stick for mine. Gray
from water and smooth and the bean juice turns it red.
Dig out the grommet tool to use as a pot holder. Stick the
open cans in the fire and take them off holding them with
the grommet tool. I'm hungry but there's something
wrong with the beans. Maybe Maw puts brown sugar in
'em. His spaghetti looks like worms pale on the knife.
The beans taste flat. The can's too big. Too many beans.
Thick. Hot at the bottom and cold on top. The stick is
nice but the beans are no good. "If you'll give me a bite of
your spaghetti I'll give you the rest of my beans." "If
you'll eat all your beans I'll give you a bite of my spaghetti." Got me. The beans are heavy and hurt and I finish
and throw the can into the water. He holds the can out. I
scrape out the spaghetti and it's smooth and sweet and
light and I feel better but he got me. I'm a little glad. The
water's white far out. Too rough to see the shadow in
the dark. Wind. We sit by the fire with the rumble jackets
zipped and our backs to the wind. All the talk is gone for
now. He's sitting on a beach in front of a fire and I'm
sitting on a beach in front of a fire. Accidentally the same
beach and the same fire. The water comes too close and
we climb up to the tarp and lay on top still separate

looking at the stars. It's too cold and I take off the boots and crawl under. Can never find anything in the sky. The big dipper, sometimes, but it all looks like the big dipper to me. When I fell asleep he was still on top of the tarp.

I want it. His jacket's off and just his shirt and sweater and my sweatshirt and it's cold, gray. It's gray and he's warm. I can feel him and his arm's under my head. He must have put his arm under my head and come close and made me feel him. I on my side away from him and he on his side toward me and his arm under my head and his belly against my back but not his prick. His belly but not that low. It misses my ass. My legs are curled and I straighten them and feel his legs but not his prick but I want it. The hand is asleep. If he is awake he put it there. It hungers between my legs and runs and he's got to give it to me. He came out here with me and he sleeps here with me and if he weren't here I could do it myself but I can't do it with him here so he has to do it. It almost hurts and the empty runs wet into my pants seam and he's got to. Turn easy. Turn careful and look. The arm stays beneath my head and my head turns and my body lifts and turns and I want to spread my legs and be touched. Touch. His eyes are open and the arm stays beneath my head and I look and the eyes stare into the gray. They are gray and look up into the gray and they slide. Nothing moves but the eyes sliding and he sees me. He felt me and now he sees me and he sees it. That I want it. It's there and he must see it. And the arm doesn't move and the head moves. It turns away but the arm stays and the white skin turns away and the eyes are gone but he has to look and give it to me, but he's afraid. He's afraid. But he has to and I reach with my hand and it's square and dirty and black in the creases but it reaches and touches and turns his head back and I say, "It's all right. Don't be afraid." But he's still afraid but he reaches. His head reaches a little ways, an inch, and my head reaches the rest of the way and his mouth is open and I put my mouth on it but it's too soft and falls away and my lips touch teeth but I open my mouth and take his mouth and I won't let it go because I need it and he has to give it to me. His mouth gets hard and pushes back and I fall back and his mouth is still hard and pushing and he puts his hand on my arm but it is heavy, not tight but heavy but it doesn't move and the arm behind my head doesn't move and I move all over trying to rub against him but he is heavy and holds me down and pushes my mouth with his mouth and I can only feel his arms and his mouth and I want to rub but he won't let me and his hands don't move. It's not right. He won't give it to me and his mouth pushes on my mouth and I can't breathe and it is only heavy and not good. I practiced kissing on the inside of my elbow but it's not good and I stop trying to rub because I can see his head against the gray, dark, and I don't even close my eyes. I don't know whether his eyes are closed. Maybe they are open and he sees me looking at his head but not his eyes and I lay still and stop pushing back with my mouth and he pushes and his mouth touches my teeth and his mouth slides away onto my face and doesn't push anymore but just stays there against my face and I'm looking at the sky. It's gray, not blue. It's cold and I feel sick. The hungry's gone and I want to puke. The slime between my legs is cold and sticky and the crack in my ass is stuck together with the slime and he lays on his side and his arm is under my head and his other hand is on my arm and his mouth is against my face.

The helicopter goes over. I can't hear it till it gets to the ravine and then it's loud and sounds like a machine gun and when it passes the ravine I can't hear it anymore. When it's gone he rolls onto his back but his arm is still under my head. He says, "We'd better get up." I roll up from the arm. Walk barefoot in the brush back to where I can't see him anymore. Pull the pants down and piss.

There is wet inside the pants. It makes the cloth dark, nearly black. I look for leaves to wipe it away and between my legs but I don't know what they are, bugs, poison oak. So I pull the front of my sweatshirt till it reaches and wipe my crotch and wipe in the crotch seams and pull the pants back up and let the sweatshirt hang outside. The wet is against the pants and I don't feel it. He's down on the washing rock brushing his teeth. I go down and wade out slow and climb up to wait till he's done. Crouch by the bug pool and the crabs and things are still crazy. The water is white on the rock. He hands me the brush and I stay crouched and dip it into the bug pool. They flash away and I scrub and spit into the pool and then get back down into the water. He follows me onto the sand and I sit down and he runs up for the bread and the mustard. A faint green metal taste but we put the mustard on thin and eat all the rest of the loaf. It's not really cold now but the gray and the water is dark and the sand is gray and his hair is pale gray. He's telling me how since the northbound freights go right by we might as well ride them and save the bus fare. I nod and say the right things. Probably the right things and grin and whirl a stick in the air. "Whoopee, sail a raft down the Missouri." And then he takes the canteen and goes to fill it at the campground.

I go crap behind a rock and bury it in the sand. Wash my ass in the bug pool. A train goes by on the cliff and I wonder vaguely if it hit him.

It's a start. So he was scared. Maybe he never did it before. Maybe he was afraid of getting me pregnant. A laugh. Maybe though. And we'll ride the freights to Helena and truck out to the river. A creek there, and a canyon he said. Build a big raft. A good tight tough one and I'll get a bunch of food. Collect it in town and keep it for provisions and we'll stop at night and build a fire, or maybe on the raft. What was it? A layer of dirt or mud or

something so you could build a fire right on the raft. And
we'll lay together every night and he'll kiss me again and
maybe it'll be better. He'll get used to it and then he can't
just do that all the time he'll have to do more and touch
me and give me that. He comes down the cliff with the
canteen and he drinks and I drink.

"I've got some money coming to the Y. It's from an
insurance policy I cashed in. It ought to be there by now.
I figure I'll go back into L.A. and pick it up and maybe a
few things to take with us. I'll go tonight, catch the bus at
the store." The cold comes over me and I'm scared. He'll
go, not we'll go. "I'll get that stuff out of the locker in the
bus station and sell it or ditch it or something so nobody
runs across it and begins to wonder. Maybe send that
letter to St. Ignatius for you." I'm sitting in the sand
beside him and the sky is gray and the water is dark, no
color, and the tide's beginning to creep. I snuggle up
next to him. I can't help it. Put my shoulder into his
armpit and nudge and he lifts his arm and lays it across
my shoulders. The hand hangs down to my elbow loose
and not touching but it's warmer and makes me feel
better. I can feel him all along my side and he's warm and
soft. I feel like crying. I'll be scared. I know I will. I don't
really like being scared.

The wind comes up and it's cold. We climb up and sit
inside the wall on the tarp and I sit apart, facing him,
better now. He explains how all those really deep-sea fish
are very tiny, the ones with lights and electric tentacles to
zap their prey. I'd seen the pictures. I thought they'd be
as big as salmon but he says they're very small, an inch,
two inches. With bony foreheads, their eyes round and
deep in the sockets, strung out from being electric.

It starts going, fading out. A shiny spot in the gray and
it starts to go away and it gets colder. He's zipping the
jacket. "How much money have you got left?" I dig it out
and count. It's wadded and ragged and takes a while.

"One hundred and thirteen dollars and seventy-five cents."
He takes it and folds the bills around the change and
sticks it into his pocket. "Probably best to get traveler's
checks. I'll get about three hundred from the insurance
policy and we can go quite a ways on that." "Yep." He
looks around and feels in his pockets, the long hands not
going in all the way, just the fingers bending in and
reaching to the bottom and the whole backs and palms of
the hands outside. "Here are some matches." The box
comes down and lands on the tarp next to me. "I'll be
gone at the most three days." I stand up, he's going. I
want to grab him and say, say something. I put my hands
in my pockets and look at my feet. "I'll be scared while
you're gone." I didn't mean to say that. I really didn't. He
looks and the hand waves once in the air. "Naw, you
won't. Take it easy." And he goes on up the path. I slide
down and start the fire quick. I've been watching him but
the bread wrapper's some weird kind of plastic and melts.
I get the brown paper bag and it's a little better. Not
much. My pyramid of slivers caves in and I have to start
over. Careful to use dry twigs. The gray makes everything
wet. I'm clammy and the rock sweats and the spray tastes
salty. There's a little crust around my nostrils, salt and
snot and it scrapes off like old skin. He does it with one
match. Boy Scout training. Start at the back and light the
paper all over, bend and spread the jacket out around it
to keep the wind out. There's salt dried in the wood and
it pops and sizzles and I put the bigger sticks on it and it
all falls in and the little sticks blank out in the sand, tiny
black spots on them where they had scorched but not
burned. Fuck it. More work than it's worth. I'll go back
up out of the wind. Wrap up in the tarp and eat cold
spaghetti.

The knife is heavy, black blade, not shiny, for night, and
the tops of cans are thin. Stab in the point and pull and
dig and the metal tears and the juice oozes out onto my

fingers. Tomato, or red anyway. Lick the fingers and the sides of the can and cut at the metal and bend it back. I get to use the knife tonight. Eat his spaghetti. It's not as good cold. Grease on the roof of my mouth, thin and the tongue can't get it off. Eat it all anyway. Lick the knife off and rub out the last of the sauce with my fingers and sit full looking into the can. Yellow inside. It's too dark to see but I remember it was yellow inside. The light went away and it's dark. I can hear the water but I'd have to sit up in the wind to see it. They sound the same. The wind and the water. Shushing and cold. No stars. No moon. Clouds. The sea dark. Do they sleep? Do they go to sleep in there? Fishes? Maybe the light doesn't make any difference. Down deep it's always dark. No eyes. A place for eyes but they've healed over. In the land of the blind, but not if it's dark. If it's dark everybody's blind. It's all dark and it moves. The rock is still but the trees in the wind dark and the sage up top is moving. The daisies are dark and move. They're pretty in the light, dark in the middle and yellow all around. But they stink. And in the night they're not pretty and the wind blows the stink away. The sky is dark and the clouds a different dark moving on it. All the different darks all moving against each other and the dark is not light and a dark thing is not the same as a light thing. A thing in the dark is not the same as that thing in the light. I don't know what it is. It's too dark to tell so I can never know because if I bring a light it changes back in the light. It is different again in the light and you can never see what it is in the dark. Could be anything. Possibilities. All the possibilities are different or at least worse than possibilities of light. There may be ghosts in the daytime but there could be bogeymen only at night. If there were things like that. If there are. And snakes. Anything could be a snake at night when you can't see. Like in the sage up there, too thick to see. But if it had bit me I probably would have seen it. Now it would

move and touch me fat and fast and I couldn't see and it
could crawl on me. There could be more. A dozen. All
sitting around disguised as sticks and at night they soften
and move and get fat and are waiting until I step or they
will come and find me. Crawl on me. If I went to sleep
crawl up on my chest or under the tarp on top of me and
if I woke up and felt him heavy it would break, in there.
I'd go in there and not be able to get back. I'd be gone
away then and he'd still be heavy and soft on me, getting
warm from me. Waiting for me to move so he could bite.
And I'd be gone, so I'd move and scream and my mouth
would open and my arms would go up and my body all
sick and tearing away, trying to tear away from the heavy
on top of me and he'd bite, reach and touch my face,
deep. It would hurt. His face against my face. Maybe my
tongue because my mouth would be open screaming and
his head would reach in with the long jaws open and the
fangs and the fangs would go into my tongue and my
mouth would snap shut, close on his head, my teeth
touching his eyes and the bone cracking between my teeth
and his teeth would still be sunk deep in my tongue and the
yellow shooting through his teeth into my tongue and his
body would roll and jerk on me heavy and long and soft
and he'd throw himself against me and the long body
jerking and coiling and come up and wrap around
my head and his head still in my mouth with the eyes
broken and running down over my teeth and the fangs in
my tongue and his pale scales grating, sliding like metal on
my teeth. I die then. At least I'd die. The body would die
and not feel the heavy anymore and the body would
send a message and I'd lay down in there wherever it is
and not get up anymore and not know it had happened.
That would be good. That would be the only way because
I couldn't live. Even with the bridge broken, even with the
eye-mind gone back into that other place, I'd know. I'd be
so scared and sick all the time shaking and puking and

screaming because that had happened. Not being able to touch myself anywhere because he had touched me. Screaming until the sound stopped and still screaming and never close my mouth again because that had happened and die slow of screaming and knowing all the time slow. It would be better to die fast when the poison hit and not have to know anymore. Can't sit here anymore. They could come down from on top, from the sage. Come down here out of the wind with me. Jump out of the tarp and onto the wall and down, sliding fast and jumping to the sand. Wet and clean. The strip is narrow, a foot, two feet some places, and the water comes to the edge shushing. Four steps and turn. Four steps and turn. They don't like loud noise. AAAAAAAAAAAAAAAAAAAH! Holler and yell and bellow into the night but the wind catches it and tosses it up and thins it out and it's gone, weak and blown away. Four steps and turn. Toward the water. Always toward the water. It's darker than the sand, and there are white lines on it. They're white but dark. Dark dark because that's the way they are in the dark. Four steps and turn. He's on the bus now. Warm and soft seats and he'll get there early before day and eat something before he goes out to the Y and when he gets there he'll take off all his clothes and get into a bed with sheets and warm. There are things moving in the sand. Little things. When a wave draws back they are left on the sand and are running toward the wave. They're dark on the dark sand and disappear in the black water but they are on the sand running toward the water. If I light a match I'll see them. But if I don't I might step on them. Crouch and fumble with the matches. They go out in the wind. Shelter with my hands, a cup and crouch lower. Bugs! Sea bugs! Armadillos, potato bugs, legs, my thumbnail, millions, all on this little sand running toward the water. It goes out and it's darker and my eyes burn from looking. Can't stand on the sand. The bugs running and the sand full of

bugs. The wall is clean. The wind is hard and cold and
the salt lays thin on the flat face of the wall and thick in
little ridges, white. I've seen it, layers on the little knobs in
the wall. Back up the wall, halfway, crouch sideways on
the wall and rest on the clean bare rock where nothing
grows and nothing comes because of salt. Were there
bugs on the rock where the guy had his liver eaten every
day? Bugs crawling and snakes crawling would be worse
than having your liver eaten. That'd just hurt. Maybe it
was high up and no bugs, cold, but when the eagle came
lice would jump out of his feathers into the inside where
the liver was. They'd stay in there when the eagle flew
away and there'd be lice in the guy's insides biting and
squirming and itching around on lots of feet and the liver
growing so it could be eaten the next day. I said pigeons
were dumb and good only for eating and there's this
dumb pigeon limping around, couldn't fly and I said,
"Probably good eating. Squab. Cook 'em up." And they all
said, "You wouldn't do it." So I hadda go get the dumb
pigeon all quaking and shaking and its eyeballs rolling
around and shitting white and green behind me as I
carried it and some shit got on my sneakers and they all
laughed and made me mad. Shit on my sneakers. Pigeon
shit. Dumb gray pigeon shaking and shitting and I hit it
against the curb but it bent its neck and squawked but
didn't die so I went and got a rock and they all ran away
and didn't want to see and the pigeon was lying there
shaking and its legs up in the air and the wings not
moving, the eye just going in different directions but I
was mad so I got down on my knees and swung the rock
up and whammed it down and things cracked and the old
gray pigeon body jerked around but I held the rock down
so it couldn't get away and the crazy old wrinkled pink
feet got all tight in balls like little pink fists and the old
pigeon body womped around but couldn't get away because its head was under the rock and I held the rock

down hard. And after a while the old body stopped moving but the feet stayed tight and I stayed holding down the rock and after a while bugs started coming out of the pigeon. Black bugs, little and skinny, running like crazy away from the pigeon and I was afraid they'd get on me so I jumped away and that old pigeon body gives another jump, straight up in the air and the rock rolled off and there was the pigeon's head all flat and spread out and the beak cracked in two so I ran away.

The wall is clean and the wind is cold. Hard and it hurts and the wall is hard and hurts but it's clean and doesn't scare me. I can hang on this wall all night until the water goes back and the sand is clean and all the bugs will go back down with the water. I thought the water was clean. If you put your hand in with a cut and the cut stings and gets clean and when I play in it all the dirt comes off me, even the toenails and fingernails and the scudge on my elbows and after when I'm dry there's just salt like dust all over me and if I rub it it goes away, falls off. But there are bugs, right on the edge like that. Right where you put your feet in and run. All those bugs, running toward the water. Probably more bugs in the ocean than on the land. More water than land and millions and trillions and godzillions of bugs. I thought they'd all be crabs and little fish and such, not real bugs. Maybe the water kind of bugs are clean to the dirt bugs and the dirt bugs are clean to the water bugs. If I go in the water I get clean and maybe if they come up on land they get clean. But they die. And I die, and they run toward the water, I go in just a little way and then run back to the dry sand, maybe they just come up a little way and then run back to the water, to get clean. Some bugs are all right. Ladybugs and daddy longlegs and moths and some others. Clean bugs. Don't bother anybody. See 'em one at a time. Not by the army. One-at-a-time bugs don't bother me. The millions bother me. Ants and roaches and all the ones I see too many of. Bees. Bad as too many people. Two people in a room and it's O.K. Me and somebody else. Three gets confusing. Two always siding against the other one. After that it's all out of control. Can't see what's happening. Classrooms and assemblies. All ready to break open and they'll run at me and rip and tear and pull and break me and step on me and I'll be in pieces spread all over and my eyes rolling around crazy looking for the rest. Too many. It ain't the dying. That's not right. That's not what bothers me. It's they killing me. Taking pieces and throwing them around. Break off a finger and chew it a little and then play with it. Toss it up and down. Forget all about it. Leave it laying on the floor someplace. Nobody knows where it came from. "Hey, who left this old mungy finger lying around?" Wouldn't know it myself if I ran across it. They chew and change it and I can't put it back on. Even one other person. They say, "Give me your finger," and I like 'em right then so I take it off and hand it over and they treat it right when they're in front of me but who knows what they do with it when they go away? Give it to a shark, at least he eats it. Glom. Too small, doesn't even notice, but he eats it. Sharks and eagles. Wade out too far, splashing around and the shark comes at me upside down. Just see his belly and his crooked smile. Womp. I'm half gone. Whole bottom half gone away into shark. None of this nibbling and tasting. Big bite. It's all over. Least I know what happened. Know where the other half is. "Oh, I left it in that shark, Maw." He wouldn't take the rest. Too bony. And he grinds it up and shits it out. Shark shit, which is probably very watery. They wouldn't give up anything solid. Hang onto everything. Greedy. So he uses it all. Turns it into shark. So I'm now half shark. Lead a double life. You are who eats you. Rather be one godawful mother shark than forty million fucking bugs.

Have to piss. Can't climb down. Can't climb up. Stay

here. Prop my feet against the wall and lean back against it, pull down the pants and piss runs down the wall and makes the wall darker. The wind dries me but it's cold. Pull up the Levi's. Goose bumps on my ass and belly. Cold. Move over a little, away from the piss. My knees hurt from crouching and my hands are stiff, hanging onto the rock. Lean my face against it. The wind burns cold. It's cold and it burns more than the sun. Frying in the wind. The snakes come back but I push them away. They couldn't get down here onto the salt rock. The night's long and the water stops coming in and begins to go out. I lay against the rock and my head goes off to weird places. To when I'm rich. To when I'm old. To places I don't know anything about and can't tell about because my mouth is shaped wrong or the words are shaped wrong, something. It comes finally. Gray and colder at first and then pink and the water's yards away now. I could just stay here. Not move. Stay lying on the rock like this. If I don't move it won't hurt anymore. It's past hurting now. My hands don't feel and my legs are asleep. Not tingling anymore but really asleep. The place where my face is against the rock is warm now and a spot out from my mouth is wet where my breath condenses on the cold rock. It's light enough to see my breath now. Smoke or steam or clouds. I'm the puffed face with the bug eyes that blows the serpents back into the sea. Icicles on my eyebrows so they know I'm from the north. I could just stay here and the salt would coat me over till I looked like part of the rock. Picnickers snickering by. The twisted figure, bas-relief curled and clinging to the stone. Go back to their tin trailer houses with the double bed in back and the convertible dinette. "We saw the most marvelous folk sculpture off there on the cliff." But they'd come up and touch me. Get a uniformed guard and a red velvet rope to hang in front. I'd just hang here forever, white and salty on the clean old rock where the bugs can't get me. The pink goes away and it's gray again. Gray day. But warm and the wind eases off. Time to move. I knew I'd move again all the time. But it doesn't work. I'm saying move and they just stay the way they are. Have to concentrate. Have to really want to. That's the trouble, don't really want to. Grunt and pull and the hand comes off the rock but it's white and curled and doesn't uncurl. Claws with the thumb hooked and it doesn't move. The arm moves and aches and stings but the hand doesn't move. It scares me and I push against the rock with my other arm and fall out and feel the sick of falling and can't remember how far it is but it's three feet. Four maybe. And the sand is soft and cold and my legs bend falling and the pain comes, not from falling but from the legs moving when they were ready not to move again. Knives and pokers and needles and all the pain they talk about only it's mine and it hurts. It just hurts and I yell high, once, and lay in the sand and the pain doesn't go away. It gets worse and I groan and they won't move but the pain gets worse and the water starts out of my eyes and the hurt comes out of my lungs and I lay there crying, "Wah wah!!!" out loud like a baby because it hurts. It gets worse for a while and then starts to get better. My belly's cramped and the hand still doesn't move but that hard coming-back-alive pain starts to go away. I sit up and suck the snot off my lip. Wipe my nose on one sleeve and my eyes on the other. Stretch the legs out in front of me wincing and grunting and feeling sorry for myself. The hand is white and doesn't move but it doesn't hurt and it's interesting. Maybe it'll stay that way. My left hand anyhow. Wear a black leather glove. Almost as cool as a hook.

The sun on the water far out and it comes in fast. The gray water turns blue and then the gray sand turns yellow and the sun is reaching for the rock and it will turn from gray to yellow.

I can move and get up and walk around in the sun. It stings and tingles and aches but it's better and the sun is warm. I walk close to the water. The bugs are there still, washed up and left on the sand and running back to the water. They're only in one place though. Not along the whole beach like I thought. They are gray and armored and the size of the last joint in my thumb. Lots of little legs. But they just look running and digging in and getting washed back and running in again. Too many of them, that's all. I unzip the jacket and turn into the light to warm my belly. I'll brush my teeth in a little while. But for now I'll just get warm again.

Go up to get the toothbrush. Everything messy. Tarp flopped all over where I dropped it getting away from snakes. Pack open and spilling. Spaghetti can laying there with an ant in it. Tidy up. A neat camp is an efficient camp. Junior Woodchucks' rule number one. Find the bow laying in the daisies. Forgot all about the bow. Get a rabbit. Forget about beans. Show Heydorf the skin. Mighty warrior. Bye, baby bunting. Have to go up into the sage. Beans tonight. Rabbit tomorrow. Some for Heydorf too that way. Practice with the bow today. Dig out the arrows and the tooth-brush, slide down. The sand's hot and I come back from the rock and dry quick with sand behind my knees. Scratches when I bend. Take off the jacket and the sweatshirt. My face is burnt from the wind and I can't shoot into the sun anyway. White arrows. Hammered tin tips. Target tips. Hokey striped fletch. Stand perfect and shoot at the beam across the fire. Hit every time from twenty feet. They are all sticking out of the soft old wood. Weird angles crossing each other and meeting each other. Lay in the sand with the bow under my chin, looking at the arrows sticking out of the wood. Bet that shit in the movies is phony where the Indians ride around the circled wagons shooting arrows from under their horses' necks. My ass. They hadda make the things by hand. Don't go shooting 'em at the sides of wagons. Don't go leaving 'em at burnt-out homesteads so the hero can pull it out of the door and say, "Unh! Apache!" Dig 'em out of doors with their knives. Pull 'em out of bodies. Put your foot on her belly and pull and the head comes out with guts wrapped around it and you shake the crap off and take 'em home. Dry 'em and rub the rough stuff off and use 'em again. Mostly use spears anyway. More efficient. More satisfying. Feel it when it goes in and give a good twist and the little kid throws up his fat hands and rolls his baby blues. "Oh, Mother, I am murdered!" Damn right, you little punk. Serve ya right. Goldilocks in South Dakota.

The warm makes me sleepy, and I'm hungry. Can't eat until tonight. The stomach rolls around and gargles and grumbles. Kind of nice. Loud sounds and it doesn't hurt. Just lets me know it's there. The wind is up again and the sand blows. Hits my burnt face and stings. Find someplace out of the wind. In the sun. Take a little nap. The shelter in the cliff is shaded. Chilly. Go through the brush and on up to the top. Still got the bow, two arrows, just in case. Climb up onto the tracks and lay down. The sage cuts off most of the wind. No bugs or snakes up here. Creosote and gravel and trains coming through. It's hot and rough and I lay across the tracks with my head on my arm. Turn the burned side away from the sun. My eyelids are red when I close them and it's warm and the stomach mumbles and trickles and I drift off and sleep and wake up a little bit and sleep again.

Helicopter comes over late. Sun low and I'm almost finished with the castle and the machine gun sound comes rocking out of the canyon and the thing goes over and swoops over the cliff and is gone. I was digging in the sand and made a good ditch in a circle so I decided to put a castle inside. Moat and thick walls with a ditch in the top to stand in and shoot out of. Room to build fires to boil the oil. A tall keep. The orange juice bottle with sand piled around and a couple of other buildings inside and I lay down and look through the gate and can see them riding in and out on fat old horses and they've got leather shirts and swords that I couldn't lift and the swords would break if you hit 'em against a rock.

The sun begins to go and I rush around getting dry stuff for the fire. Lean it against the beam instead of trying to be cute with a pyramid. Slow and careful and drape my jacket around to give it a chance and then fan like crazy until it licks up and I can feel the heat and the flame moves deep and blackens the wood. Not great but it'll do. I go get the beans and hack 'em open. Careful not to spill any. I feel a little sick to the stomach and eat a knifeful of cold beans to hold me till they're hot. They're good. Better than cold spaghetti. Eat slow and chew everything and my stomach stretches and aches a little and quiets. Lick it all clean. The knife and the insides of the can and my fingers and sit tasting the bean juice in my teeth and thick on my tongue. Looking at the black paper burned away all around the can. Bury the can in the sand and sit nursing the fire. The castle is down closer to the water, out of the light. There are stars but no moon and it looks far away and like a ruin already, dark and low and all its edges soft. He may come in the early morning like when we got here. Or maybe around noon if he takes the five A.M. bus. He knows we haven't got any more food down here so he'll probably bring some. More cake maybe. He likes it as much as I do. The fire is hot and burns against my burned face and I look into it and not at the dark and I see what hell's about. They got it wrong. Nobody knows anymore how hot fire is. The preachers talk about hell fire and the people nod and think of central heating, radiators. Nobody sits by a fire anymore and feels the hot blasting his face and his back and ass freezing. I can feel it all and see how the fire makes the dark darker and the cold side colder because it is hot and bright. He's in there dancing with his feet in hooves so he doesn't burn and he's laughing and jabbing or maybe he's a spider like in the movie and he sits and waits and sends out little tremors and tremors come back to him and he sits and interprets and sends out orders and waits. The house burns and the roar is blowing more than the wind and the black frame of the house is clear against the yellow and their voices come from inside and I reach up and can see them screaming, "For god's sake, throw me a gun!" And I turn and walk away from the heat and the screaming until I can just stand in the cool black and watch and see the black twisting and falling into the bright and the red going up beyond the yellow and sparks flying off getting mixed up with stars. If they had gone away I wouldn't have had to. They wouldn't have had to die. Just go away and I would stay in the house and sit in the fireplace and sleep in my own bed and go down to eat alone and quiet and piss and shit in a nice clean toilet and even bathe once in a while. I'd never answer the door or the telephone and could read all day and all night and get up whenever I wanted or stay in bed or go around naked and never speak. Never open my mouth and never hear the stupid come out but let it stay inside where it's still clear and bright and there's nobody, and never see anybody so I wouldn't ever feel bad. Never make a fool of myself. Never hurt anybody's feelings and never be hurt. Get up at noon and eat cake for breakfast and read all day until night and eat cake and peanut butter and chocolate and hot dogs all spread out in front of the TV all night and go to sleep when the sun came up and be warm and comfortable and quiet with no bug bites and no snakes and nobody. I don't know why I always think I want a man, anyway. Just lay down and rub and imagine and it's good and the feeling is nice and I feel better after and think about other things. I wouldn't bother anybody. I wouldn't hurt anybody. If I had all I needed and was comfortable nobody would ever even know I was there. But I can't do that. They wouldn't go away and I'd have to pay bills. But I could do it all by mail. Phone the grocery and have the stuff left on the porch. But I'd need a lot of money. I'd have to go out and work. Go out early in the morning no matter how I felt or what I wanted to do and walk and take the bus and say good morning and do something all day. Carry plates full of food and be nice and polite and smile and listen and talk and all the people talking and listening and they'd be there and in the night I'd go home aching and tired and eat and watch TV and wake every morning hating it and have to do it. Every morning and on weekends knowing that I had to go back all the weeks and months and years and it would all be so I could be comfortable at night before I went to bed and alone and comfortable on the two days out of every seven. And for two weeks a year. And Christmas Day off. I couldn't do it. Maybe for a few weeks and then the new would be gone and I'd want to be alone again and if I couldn't stop I'd break. Break as much as the snake could break me. I could get married and stay home and he would be gone mostly and I would only have to be nice for a while before he went to sleep. That might be easier. I wouldn't have kids. I couldn't do that. They'd always be there. I'd kill them. They'd be too easy to kill. Too small and soft and I'd hit and they'd die. But who would marry me? Nobody. Not even a service station attendant. They like 'em with tits and ass and hair in knots. Nobody would know I was a girl and when they found out they wouldn't want to marry me. That's pretty funny. I never thought about that. Heydorf was wrong. I won't marry the service station man because he wouldn't marry me. Even if I wanted to. That's pretty funny. That's not what will happen after all. That couldn't happen. It will be something else. Something different. I don't have to worry about that at all. It hurts. Good. Like not being invited to the party. I know it's a dumb party and I don't want to go but not being invited hurts. And I couldn't do that other. Couldn't work like that. Have to figure out something else. But at least I don't have to worry about that anymore.

The water is cutting at the castle. It doesn't cover it. It washes around and fills the moat and slices under the walls. The sand crumbles and washes away and there are gaps and holes in the walls and the moat is gone. Filled in already. I thought it would be faster. A crash and it would all fall and not be there anymore. But it just wears away.

It's cold. The wind cuts under the jacket and through the Levi's. I hold my hands and my face to the fire and the palms burn and the backs sting with the cold. The dark is solid and the wind blows on it and I'm tired. Too tired to be afraid. Climb up and wrap in the tarp and the jacket. Pull the tarp over my head and it's all my private dark inside. It might be light out for all I know. This is just my own dark, warm, or warmer. The wind brushes on the tarp but doesn't come through. I can feel the ground hard and rough beneath me. My bones hurt against it but it's all far away and easy and I don't really care.

I guess he took the later bus. He'll come about noon. He'll bring a lot of goodies. Cake and candy and real food and we'll sit in the sand and he'll tell me all about L.A. and I'll tell him I wasn't scared after all. Go up and sleep for a while on the tracks He'll find me there when he comes. Think it's cool.

* * *

I'm stupid. He didn't mean to count that first night as
one of the three. He'll come in the morning. I sit by the
fire and put the canteen into it. When the water's warm I
drink it fast and belch and straighten so my stomach can
stretch. Have to fill the canteen when he gets here. He'll
probably bring something to drink anyway. And chocolate
cake and more spaghetti. Maybe canned stew. Bread and
hot dogs. Eat all day tomorrow. I didn't shit today or
yesterday. Must be using it all.

My stomach wakes me up all night and it's very cold.
Get up and put on the other sweatshirt and curl up tight
with the jacket and the tarp wrapped tight and tucked
under. Still cold. It hurts to breathe. My lungs ache and I
shiver and chatter and feel sorry for myself.

Gray. No sun. The sea gray and the shadow broad and
dark. Probably all the bugs sitting out there waiting for
the right time to charge the land. All those little ones are
just spies, couriers. He won't come till noon. Better go up
out of the wind and sleep.

He might hop a freight instead of taking the bus. Save
money. Or he'll come in the morning. Have to go down to
the campground and fill the canteen. Hot. Best go while
there's plenty of time before dark. I leave a note stuck on
the pack. "Heydorf, Gone to get water. Back before dark.
Dutch." The tide's out. Go around by the beach. Not as
conspicuous as sliding down the bank from the trestle.

Dig out the web belt. Hang it around the outside of the
jacket. Canteen in one loop. Knife in the other. Looks
cool.

The cliffs fall rough into the sea and the rock is new
and sharp. Edges and grain and the white spray high
against them. The surf rougher than in the cove. Climb
and jump and my belly hurts but my feet know. The boots
grip and the hands grab without sliding and the bird shit
baked onto the rocks white and smooth as enamel and
the birds in the air and the rocks all clean and rough with
salt. A long stretch with old round rocks. Smallish. My
head size. Rolling and sliding, heavy walking with my
ankles tired from stepping and slipping. The rocks go
straight into the water and the water slops up on them
and sucks back hard and they rattle and roll in it. Rattling. Sea bones. Not bones in the sea. Bones of the sea.
Old sea bones rattling. Makes me nervous and I run and
fall and get up and go along carefully. More rock, solid,
and pieces of cliff jutting out. The canteen banging on
my hip and the web belt slipping down. I can see the pier,
little figures and long poles jutting out. High above the
water. A sand beach. Little kids with shovels and buckets.
Shirts on over their bathing suits. A brown girl. Yellow
hair, flowery and high on her head. Hips and tits and a
neon bikini and curves all down her legs. She turns and
looks at me trudging in the sand. She has white stuff on
her nose. White grease. I look at my feet. Water fountain
next to the hot dog stand. The beach goes on past the
pier and the pier ends under the trestle. The trestle, high
and dark. Dark legs and black beams and the long little
track running across. I can see the sky through the strips
between the ties. It's gray and there are ladies on the
beach in pants to their knees. Pink and lavender and big
hats with flowers. Sunglasses. Picnic tables under the
trestle. Brick fireplaces with grills. A wooden trellis for
shade. Parking lot. Cars with surfboards and kids run-

ning and yelling. A little kid comes running down from
the pier with a string of fish. Flat silvery fat fish. He looks
at me, his eyes open and he stops and looks with the fish
hanging down. "Hi." He moves as though to go and then
stops. "Hi." "What kind of fish are those?" "Surf perch."
"They good to eat?" "Yep. We're gonna have 'em for
dinner!" He grins and shoves his bare feet into the sand.
He's nine, maybe ten. His belly's pooched just a little and
his shoulders skinny and his head big. "How'd you catch
'em?" He puts his hand in the pocket of his shorts, cut off
cords. Pulls out string and a hook. "Just sit on the beams
under the pier there at the end. Use mussels for bait. Just
cut 'em off the rock. The perch are there always, but the
grownups want big fish." He's grinning and I'm grinning
and I feel silly. Look at my feet. He comes up close and
hands me a little hook. He's as tall as I am in his bare feet.
Just a little kid. "That's a number ten. Same's I caught
these with. There's always a lot of line caught down under
the pier. They get tangled up with each other and cut it."
"Gee, thanks." "Naw, see ya." And he's off running with
the fish flopping and shining. Cars and trailers and tents
and campers. People everywhere. All mincing along on
the gravel in bare feet or thong sandals. Wincing and
taking short steps. The hot dog stand. A little white box
with a wood flap propped up. Shade in the daytime and a
locked door at night. The water fountain stands beside it
running. I unhook the canteen and unscrew the cap.
Rinse it out once and drink a long time from the fountain. Swallow and swallow and stop and stand up and
breathe and then swallow more. I can smell the food. Hot
dogs. Hamburgers. The grease is in the air and coats my
tongue and my jaws run wetter than water. Fill the
canteen to the top and cap it. Hook it into the belt again.
There's orange pop and grape and Coke and candy. Lots
of candy bars and Life Savers and a man comes up and
goes away with a paper cone full of french fries. It's all in

glass cases. No way in the world. Just make myself sick standing and looking. Heydorf'll probably be there when I get back. Have all kinds of good stuff. I look up at the trestle to see him walking across. Nothing. But it's long. The cliff looks low at the other end and there are cars and trailers almost all the way. Little trees planted in rows. A tree and a picnic table and a brick fireplace to every camp site. Johns and showers in the center. One water faucet to every ten camp sites. It's gray and not warm enough to swim and they're all out here. Guess this is when they get their vacations. Got no choice. The gravel turns into dirt under the trestle and the dirt is a ramp leading up to the pier. Boat winches at the end. Thirty feet out of the water. Drive the boat up there on the trailer and pay the man three dollars to lower it into the water for you. The pier is old gray wood. Cracks between the planks. The water dimpling below. Light and dark. Catching the light from the gray sky and throwing it white up through the cracks. My boots thump loud on the boards. I walk softly, putting them down carefully. They thump and clomp and scrape. They turn and look as I pass and then turn back. They are tall and fat, short and thin. They all wear hats. Red peaked caps, baseball caps with bills, old canvas hats. There are hooks and feathers and flies stuck into the hats. They stand leaning on the rail or sit in canvas chairs or on collapsible stools. Each one holds a long pole and the pole is thick in their hands and arcs far out over the water getting very thin. I can hardly see the tips. Each one has a basket or a tin box or a net sack full of stuff. Boxes and spools and paper cards with something on them. An old lady and an old man in red slickers with red slicker hats with hooks in them sit on canvas chairs with matching poles and drink from cans of beer. A neat triangle cut into the top of each can. An old hand with brown spots curled around each can. And from under each red plastic hat short gray hair

curls out as innocent and crisp as a pot scraper. It's gray
and wet and the wind hurts my face. The top of my head
is burned. I can feel it shrinking and wrinkling under the
hair. They all turn and look and the faces are blank and
then they turn back to the poles. I touch my head with
my fingers. It's sore under the hair and the hair hurts it.
There is a rail across the end and their poles are black
and thin against the gray sky and on the edge, far out on
the edge, there is nothing, and between the end of the
pier and the edge there is nothing. China maybe, beyond
the edge. Old gray wet steps leading down under the
pier. Black piles and long beams diagonally bolted between the piles and the deck of the pier. Dark and the
wood old and wet but oiled and inoculated against the
salt. Creosote or it feels like creosote. Railroad ties and
telephone poles and the piles of the pier. Oily and black
with struts and crossbeams and bolts as thick as my arm.
The steps end and a metal ladder on hinges goes further
to a floating platform. Get in and out of your boat after
the man has put it into the water for you. I sit on the last
step and rest. Yards of green hard line looped and
tangled in the piles. Knots and nests and webs of line
trailing in the water. Walk out onto one of the support
struts. If I fell it's not far to shore. But with the boots and
the jacket and the canteen. Too late. I reach a knot of line
and lean on a pile tugging at it. It's wet and tight.
Unhook the knife and hack at the hard parts and pull
and long loops come loose and trail away in my hand. Put
the knife back and walk slowly back with the half the line
in the water. Sit straddling the beam and coil it up. Yards
and yards. Plenty. And strong enough. Not old. Just lost.
The green hard twine in a smooth ball in my hand. The
hook is in the belt and I slip it out and tie it on. No
leader. Don't matter. Mussels on the piles. Climb down to
the floating dock and reach long over the water to the
piles with the knife. The shells are long and black and

rooted hard to the wood. Brown hairs growing from the shell into the wood. Cut and pry and pull and get a few. The shells are smooth and the edges sharp. Go back up to my beam and crack them. Hammer with the back of the knife and water shoots out and the shell breaks open and it's pink and mushy with white snot floating on it. My tongue before I spit. Too soft. Slips off the hook. Use the lip. Rubbery, tough. Scootch it on, layer on layer, accordioned mussel lip with loose ends. Drop the hook into the water and sit back. The waves slop against the line and it moves softly in my hand and the light shadows move on the bottom of the dock. The water all around is gray but under here it's green and clear and bubbles run in it. Sheets of bubbles from the surface. There's a tug and I tug back joking and it's still there and I panic and yank and the fish comes out silver and its tail flapping and its head shaking. It's below me between the water and the beam and the twine is the same color as the water and the fish floats up to me, swims up to me shaking and waving and it's little and flat and clean and its eyes are yellow and black in the middle and I hope it'll jump off the hook and go away but it stays and lays down on the beam and the tail flaps against the wood and the gills pump up and down and the eyes stare not moving. It's silver and the scales are small and the fins are soft and it won't hurt me. I hold the knife tight and bring the butt down on its head and blood runs out from under the eye. The eye is yellow and black in the middle and a thin watery red runs out from underneath. The tail is still flapping and the gills are still opening and closing and I hit it again and it stops. I lift the line and his mouth opens and the hook comes through his nose. Put the knife point in and pry and pull at the hook and the fish teeth ragged and white and tiny give and bend on the knife and the mouth breaks. I can hear the bone break and the hook comes out and the mussel lip is still on it

but pushed down. I pull it around into place and drop it
into the water and my back doesn't touch the pile before
there is another jerk and another fish floating up toward
me, trying to come to me and I lay it down and hit it over
the eyes with the knife and one eye breaks and the
movement stops and rip out the hook and put another
mussel lip on and drop it into the water and the water is
flat and white with the light shining on it and the light
moves back and forth on the beams and I can see the
long lines going down all around in the water. The long
lines from the long poles. There's another bite and I kill
it quick and sit looking at them. They are soft, silver
bellies and gray backs and the fins lay clear on the wood.
Longer than my hand and broader but flat and not as
long as my foot. I'll take 'em back and he'll be there with
goodies and I'll show him and then throw 'em away and
we'll eat the goodies. Untie the hook and put it into the
belt. Run the twine through the gills and out at the
mouth. Teeth in the gills, rows and rows of little teeth.
Hurt. Almost cut. Tie the string onto the belt. Look cool.
Back up on the dock and the heads turn again but they're
looking at the fish. Wet against my leg. Soaking through
the denim. Silver fish bodies against my leg. Clomp clomp
and the heads turn and look and then turn back. There's
a cleaning tray built into the rail. Water faucet and a hole
at one end to throw the guts in. Hole drops down into the
water. Throw the guts into the water through the official
hole. Sun's about halfway down in the sky. The gray solid
and the bright spot about halfway down. Tide coming in.
Across the beach and up into the rocks. The children stay
on the sand. Don't go near the rocks. Not allowed. Don't
run. Don't climb. Don't go into the water. Play nice in the
sand. They're all gone. I can hear the voices but not the
words. All rock and water now. The guerrilla and the
rock and the water and the pier is gone and the hot dog
stand and the kiddies and their mommies. All gone and

me and the wind out here along being tough on the
rocks. The tide's in quite a ways. Harder work. Rougher
climbing. The sea bones are still rattling. Louder now and
longer. The water higher and white all along. It breaks
on the rocks and roars breaking and then sucks out
rattling for a long time. Climb around on the cliff. Don't
try to walk on them. The next ledge juts far out into the
water and there's no dry way off. Sit down and breathe
and look. No dry way off. The cliff is flat and goes
straight up. Go back or stay here or go through the
water. Have to think about that. The rock is warm and
the spray doesn't reach me. Lay down. The wind blows
across smooth and wet and hot but it doesn't sting if I lay
down. The fish lay beside me on the rock and I sleep a
little.

It's not getting better, getting worse. Water deep and
faster. Don't want to stay here all night. Heydorf waiting
with goodies. Freeze my ass off. A little boat out there.
Two men. Red hats. A chugger engine. It comes closer.
Toward me. An arm waves and I lift my arm and wave a
little. Lay back down. It's still coming. The chug bounces
off the rock and rides on the water. Coming here. I can
see them clear. Fishing in their little boat. Been out
fishing. Got the man to put it into the water for them.
Got in with their red hats and their long poles. The man
stands up in the bow and cups his hands around his
mouth and the sound drifts lazy toward me. "Want a
lift?" I sit up and shake my head. He can't see that. Cup
my hands and shout, "No thanks!" My voice yells good,
low and loud and he can hear it. He waves and sits back
down and I wave and watch the other man turn the boat
and the engine gets louder and they go bouncing back
toward the pier. Assholes. How'd they think they were
gonna get close enough to give me a lift? The white
breaks on the half-hidden rocks beneath it and the water
is rough and dark and I can see the shadow dark and

long on the bright gray. Have to get wet. No other way.
Climb back in toward the cliff to the shallowest point.
King's X. And jump and it's up to my knees and fills the
boots and the gravel slips and it splashes to my waist and
it's cold and I run, heavy, pushing through the water.
The canteen is heavy and the fish are heavy and I climb
up on the next rock and the water runs out of the boots
and my pants and feels slimy in my socks and the wind is
cold on me and wet and I don't stop but climb and jump
and run and climb and scrape around the last point and
there's the cove. The sand not covered yet. A few yards
left for a fire. Get wet again to the waist wading to the
sand. Cold. Windy. Nobody. "Heydorf!!!" Yell and the wind
tosses it away. Run up the cliff, scraping and hurting
and my lungs aching. Fall over the wall and sit breathing
hard on the dirt. Making mud in my wet. All the same. The
note tucked into the pack strap. Nothing changed. Nothing added. Nothing taken away. The note flaps in the
wind. Rattles. Rip it out and crumple it. Throw it over the
side. I thought he'd be here. I thought he'd have food.
My belly hurts. Part hunger, part cold, part coming so far
so fast. I'm tired and cold. Stand up and the wind hits
my face and I'm wet and it stings. Dig out the other underpants, socks, thin old grayed-out Levi's. The other
sweatshirt. Another tee shirt. Strip and the wind dries
and hurts, stings everywhere, hurts. Drape the wet stuff
over the stone to dry. Put the boots upside down sopping.
Brush the mud off my feet and dress and it's warm for a
minute and then cold again. The jacket's too wet to wear.
Wrap up in the tarp. It hurts, it's cold and it hurts. The
fish are hanging against the rock. Build a fire and cook
'em. Feel better if I eat. They're stiff. They curve flat
together and they're stuck together and they're stiff.
Shoulda cleaned 'em at the dock. Thought they'd look
cooler to him with the heads and guts. Bigger. Now
they're stiff. The blood is frosted on the scales and they

look dull and gray. Kill me probably. The eye is broken
and the blood crust all around it. Fuck it. He'll come in
the morning and bring food. The water's close in. Five or
six feet of sand and then water. Cut the string off the belt
and swing it far behind me and throw far out and they
turn together, stuck together in the air and fall gray into
the water. Go piss in the bushes and pull the pants up
while I'm still dripping and come back and curl up in the
tarp. Cold. Cold. Cold. The gray beats around the sky
and the daisies thrash against each other and petals fall
off and blow yellow against the green tarp. My head hurts
and my belly hurts.

We'd all go to the beach in the car. Drive a long time
warm, singing hokey songs and talking nonsense and stop
halfway for hot dogs and mustard and orange pop and
then we'd get there. Deserted hunk of beach and Maw
and Dad would carry blankets down and Nick would
wade and I'd go off and climb rocks and sit high up in
the wind and think about eagles and wolves and sea
horses and feel cold and alone and powerful and she'd
bang on a pan and we'd come running and they'd have a
fire in the driftwood or behind some rocks out of the
wind and we'd all sit down on the blankets and it'd be
warm and friendly and she'd haul out peanut butter and
jelly sandwiches and tuna or ham for Dad and cold fried
chicken and potato salad thick and yellow with onions
and mayonnaise and a dozen boiled eggs and pop for us
and beer for them and celery and carrots for vitamins
and salt for the chicken and we'd eat and eat and when
we couldn't move there'd be cake. Always chocolate with
the frosting an inch thick on top and in between the
layers and we'd eat and eat and lay moaning and groaning and feeling good in the sunshine and then we'd all get
in the car and he'd drive and she'd talk to him and Nick
and me would be asleep in the back seat, kicking each
other now and then for room. And in the dark about

halfway he'd say, "Who's for ice cream?" and we'd be so full we couldn't see and say, "Yeah, me, me!" and he'd stop and we'd get twenty-five-cent cones with four scoops and he'd get a milkshake and she'd get a root beer float and Nick would bite and his would be gone fast and I'd lick and it'd last a long time and he'd look at me and hate me 'cause I still had ice cream and when I was through I'd fall asleep and he'd be asleep and we'd wake up when they were carrying us into the house and mumble and she'd wash our faces and hands with a warm soft cloth— "So you don't get ice cream goop in your beds." And then we'd stagger into our pajamas and in the morning be hungry all over again. He would be gone to work already and she would have already made pancake batter and eggs and junk for him and do it all over again for us and we'd kick each other under the table and tell jokes while the other one had a mouth full of milk to make him laugh and spray it all over the table. Fried eggs and pancakes with maple syrup. Put the eggs on top of the pancakes and pour syrup all over the top and more syrup when that soaked in and cold milk by the quart and a flaky white mustache from the milk.

It hurts. My belly hurts and my head hurts and I feel a little like puking. He'll come in the morning and bring food. Stand up in the wind to get rid of the puke feeling. It's cold and burns and there's a little moon in the clouds, riding between the clouds. Sliver of light in the dark. The water is black and there's a path on it, white path runs straight to China. The lady dances and her long skirt sweeps in the water and her white arms bend and are thin and her hands arch. She's very tall, almost to the moon, and she's white. The dress white and her shoulders and arms and neck but her hair is black and she doesn't turn her face toward me. Her hands rest on his shoulders but he's too dark to see and she whirls and her dress swings in the white path and I can almost hear the music, almost. But the path breaks where the shadow is and she isn't looking, doesn't see it and he whirls her around and she falls and her white arms go up and she sinks into the shadow with her long arms waving like snakes and he goes down with her and the shadow closes and I lean over the wall and my stomach heaves and I want to die and a little water comes up, thin and clear. A teaspoon and dribbles down onto the rock and I stay leaning and heaving and nothing comes up and I fall down, mean to but fall instead of doing it careful and pull the tarp over me and my throat and mouth burn and my belly cramps and loosens and cramps and it's cold and I'm shivering and my lungs shake with the cold air in them and it hurts and I go blank. I can see but it's all still and quiet and cold and all I know about is the pain in my belly and the cold.

Gotta get some food. Even if he comes at noon, can't hold out. Fish, meat, anything. Staggering on the rocks, lights moving in front of my eyes. Can't see. I fall and hit against rocks but it doesn't feel. Only the stomach hard and burning and the rat chewing and the stomach shivering. Keep the water to my right and keep going. Too slow, too slow. A piece of bread. Something to keep it down until I get the fish. Fall and the lights go bright and flare around and I'm dizzy and the stomach comes up. The whole stomach jerking up flat and the acid running out onto the rock white and it burns and I lay looking at it and it hurts and I choke and cough and it comes up again and blinds me and comes flooding thin out my nose and between my teeth and it steams on the cold rock and runs into the water on the rock and my head is in it and it burns my hand. My nose is full and my throat is full and I can't breathe. Roll onto the rock and the stitch in the stomach harder and tighter and it runs back down out of the nose and the nose burns when the air comes in and the acid running down the back of my throat burns and I gag and heave again. The whole body closing below the stomach and wrenching up and I can't move but lay on my side doubled up and holding the belly and holding doesn't help. It all goes away and I'm someplace warm with a pain in my stomach. I can't see or hear but it's warm and soft and there's a little pain in my stomach. I can't see or hear and I'll die. I'll die. Just float off into the warm and the pain will go away. But the pain gets bigger and I open my eyes and the rock is wet in front of my mouth and there are flies. Where did they come from? Wading in the acid and buzzing wetly. The pain is solid and clean now. No puke. I can feel it on my face and hands and in my mouth and nose but I can't taste it or smell it. If it's just the pain I can take it but not having to puke. Not that feeling. Roll into the puke and lift up slowly to my knees and double over the stomach. My legs are watery. Never quite knew what that meant before. Watery. Bend any way if I don't watch it. Stay bent to keep the pain in the stomach, don't straighten. It will spread and burn me up and I'll just lay down and not get up anymore. Rocks and they scratch and cut and bang against me and I can see blood bubbling through the scrapes on my hands. Little bubbles of blood coming through where the skin got too thin, but it doesn't hurt. Only the belly hurts. It's slow. I'm very tired but there's no use stopping. Starting again would be harder than going on. I can't walk over the loose round rocks. I get down on my hands and knees and hold my belly in tight to keep the pain from spreading, and crawl across the sliding stones and up onto the solid rock beyond and further and I climb around the last big rocks and the pier is black and long against the gray and the little figures pose against the rail with the long poles arcing out. Children in the sand. Have to straighten up. Can't look sick. Somebody'd come and ask questions and I couldn't say anything. Couldn't even lie and they'd be trouble and I'd rather hurt than have trouble. I straighten up and the pain flames up all across my chest and down into my legs. Don't look at anybody. If they spoke I'd yell, scream, fall down and heave again. Straight as I can. Only hunched a little. Look at my feet. Boots still wet from last night. Dark wet leather. Feet squish. Sand crusted on the wet. Walk walk walk. Don't look up. Just walk. Up the pier. Almost there. Boards and clomping. They slide today, not a clean sound. Long walk and then the steps and the cool dark and the water. Can't go out on the beam. Too dizzy. Fall. Sit under the steps. All the ache fallen back into my belly now. All the pain round and tight when I sit down and double over it. The string and the hook. I forgot the mussels. God, I forgot the bait. I have to go get some bait. Can't stand up anymore. No-body down here anyway. Crawl out from under the stairs and down to where I can reach the mussels on the piles. Too far. I hold my breath, press it hard down on the stomach to hold it and reach and grab. Can't bother with the fucking knife and pull and yank and tear and the mussel comes off and I crawl back up and smash it and bait the hook and drop it in. A long time, hours. They were quick yesterday. Maybe I took them all yesterday and I threw them away. There aren't anymore. The tears come and I sit blubbering and rocking over my belly and snorking the puky snot and keeping quiet so nobody up top will hear me and then the jerk comes and the little fish and I yank him up and slam him down on the wood and grab the knife. Smash and the blood runs and he's still and I turn the knife and whack and the head comes off behind the gills and falls down into the green water. Now it's not "him" anymore. It's meat. Rip down the gut line and run my finger in to push it all out into the water. It's open and empty and clean and my fingers reach in and tear and the white meat comes off tender and clean in little slabs and I shove it into my mouth and chew fast and tear off more and swallow and chew the bones and they are little and thin and crack easily and scrape going down and my mouth stings and burns from food and I eat all the white meat and the skin is left smooth on the inside and scales still silver on the outside and the little fins attached and the backbone with the white string running through it and the little shreds of meat and bone hanging white from it and stained pink where the thin fish blood comes. I throw it away and lean against the wood and close my eyes and wait for the pain to ease.

I catch three more. A little bigger. Clean 'em quick and carry them back to the cove in my hand, walking slow. Tide's out and it's easy. A little fire. Slow built and all right. Run a wienie stick through the three fish and toast 'em, fins and skins, no heads, no guts. They're black and fall apart and I pick the littlest pieces out of the sand and eat them swallowing the sand and then lie down and don't care who sees the fire in the daytime, or the smoke, and sleep.

I don't wash anymore. Rather be my own kind of dirt than wash it off and get sea filth on me. Sea bugs. In the morning I go up and sleep on the tracks. It was sunny again one day but it's mostly gray all the time. Later I go catch fish. After noon. If I need to fill the canteen I go down to the pier. Usually I fish off the rocks here. Takes longer. Sometimes I don't get anything. But it's closer. Easier. No

people around. Always get something eventually. Black
'em up a little. Don't taste like anything anyway. No use
fussing with 'em. Sit by the fire at night. Sometimes most
of the night. Too cold to sleep. Huddle on the little sand
that's left by the tide with a little fire. Sleep up on the
tracks during the day. Trains don't come too often. Just
the helicopter. Hide when the helicopter comes.

The shit comes out hard and slow. Two little chunks.
They'd bounce. Drop them on a floor and they'd bounce
and roll. Dark brown. Not even wet. Rubber. Not even a
smell. Tough shit. My ass is grungy and there's nothing to
wipe on. Have to wash it in the water again. Filthy bugs in
the water crawl up my asshole. Tall lady in a white wig.
Flour in the wig and earwigs in the flour. She strolls in a
long dress. Watch close and shining earwigs flit in and
out of the curls. She lifts the glasses on a stick and looks
through them out the window. No, into a mirror that
reflects a window. "Let them eat shit." And the ax falls
and the earwigs go looking for a new home. 'Cause if I
ate my shit I'd have even less to shit next time and less to
eat and less to shit and very soon nothing at all. Poor
feeble little shits. I cover them up with sand and go wash.
Cold crawly water. The salt dries and itches later. My
asshole itches.

I was singing a little song in the fire at night and it
sounded good and deep and beautiful and there was

nobody to hear but me and I could hear how beautiful. Remembered the harmonica. Go dig it out and come back to the light with it cold and bright and warm it a little and put it to my mouth to blow. Going to make beautiful music. I'm so full it has to come out. But it doesn't. The breath goes through the little holes and comes out buzzing and dull. Slide it along my lips and hum but it hurts. It tingles and my lips are burned and dry and the holes rub and the noise comes out buzzing flat up against the rock and makes me think of bugs buzzing and beating in the air. My voice was good off the rock. It came off low and slow and rusty and warm. My own voice was good and the little metal thing tins it out and there's no music, only noise. It makes me mad and I slide it hard across my mouth blowing hard it hurts and the noise screeches up high against the rock and echoes light and it scares me and I stop. Put the thing into my pocket and huddle close away from the cold, but it's my back that's cold and my back is always the same distance from me. Try to sing a little but the voice is gone and cracks and is ugly. Ugly.

The snake came shooting off the cliff top and fell slow. Its long fat twisting and bouncing off the rocks. I was laying in the sand watching the top of the cliff and the snake came shooting off gray and gold and I saw it fall and I rolled fast and sick almost into the water to get out of the way. It must have got lost. Been chasing something and jumped right off the edge and it will lay there in my white sand with the long spine broken and the head moving and the tail moving but the long body still and dead in between. Wrenching along with only the head and the tail and the mouth open and the long teeth pale and thin, dripping yellow. I ran down to the other end of the sand and shook and sweat pouring and I found a stick, old gray washed stick, and came back to kill it but it had gone away. Buried itself in my sand. Now I'm afraid to walk on the sand. It is buried lightly waiting for me to come near.

Found an abalone shell this morning. Big storm last night. Rain and wind. Scared shit out of me. Put the fire out. Wet clean through the tarp. Sunny today and this abalone shell washed up on the sand with a lot of other crap. Seaweed and wood and cans and this half shell. Big. Can't reach across it with one hand. Pink inside and smooth and green and silver outside. The holes in one end. Never figured out what the holes were for. Just a half shell, not a whole shell. I'm kicking around in the junk, see it and pick it up. Rinse it off and it's not broken or chipped and it's pink. Maybe I'll sell it to a tourist. I'm a beachcomber. Sell shells to the tourists. Go up to the store, look around. Maybe wash. Fill the canteen. So I go trucking off to the store. March over the trestle looking down at the pier and the beach. Sunny and they're all getting burnt and picnicking. See the smoke coming up from the grills. People in the water. Hope a shark gets 'em. Up to the store and the trucks go by roaring fast and I'm scared to cross the road for a while. Wait till there's a good open stretch and run across. Go take a piss in the real toilet, and wipe. First time in a long time. My face looks like meat. Nobody I know. Red. Freckles look pale and the skin around them red and dark. White patches, peel soon. Going to wash my face and hands but the

water stings and the soap burns. Makes my eyes water.
Rinse it off. Forget it. Rinse the shell off once more.
Looks better wet. Out to the front. Not .many cars stopping. People in 'em. Fill the canteen at the hose and sit on
the curb watching. Wondering how to sell the thing.
Knock on the window, "Hey, mister, wanta buy a abalone
shell? Fresh from the Pacific storms?" "Get away, kid."
And he'd drive off in his Hawaiian shirt and madras
bermudas. Can't do that.

He's long and gangly. Tan work clothes. Finishes cleaning
the windshield and the car drives off. Sticks the greasy
rag in his pocket and comes over and sits on the curb
near me. "Hot." He's grinning and nodding so I nod
"Yeah." His hair's rusty and scraggy and grows out of his
ears. Blue eyes. Pale in his brown face. His face wrinkles
all over when he smiles. "What's that ya got?" He's reaching
and I hand it to him. "It's an abalone shell. Found it on
the beach this morning." "My, that's pretty." He turns it
and touches the smooth inside. His long brown finger
with black under the fingernail. "Yeah. I thought maybe I
could sell it to a tourist." He nods, feeling the shell and
turning it in his hands. I look out over the road and past
the cliff. The shadow's dark on a sunny day. I can see for
miles up and down. The blue and the white sky and the
gray shadow on the water. "What are these good for?
Abalone." "Eat 'em. Very expensive. Abalone steaks. Suppose to be great stuff. I don't know. Never tried one.
People make ashtrays and lamps out of the shells." He
nods and turns and grins at me. "See, I ain't from around
here. I just come out from Kansas a month ago." "You

like it?" "Yeah, it's real nice. I'd never seen an ocean before." The shadow stops off there in front of the park. Have to go fishing later. Have to go down there on my way home. Walk back on the rocks. "Hey, do you know what that shadow is out there?" My guts turn a little. Shouldn't have asked. Think I'm a fool. "Oh, yeah. I asked about that first day. Kelp beds." "Kelp beds?" "You know, seaweed. They got a barge goes along and harvests it. Use it for iodine, medicine. All kinds of things." I'm laughing a little. Grinning and giggling and he's laughing softly, not opening his mouth much but really laughing. "That's a relief. I thought it was sea monsters." "Yeah." He laughs more. "So'd I. That's why I asked my first day here." I feel strong and good and it's funny. "If you put some water on that it looks even better." We go over to the hose and he puts water on the shell and holds it up and the sun gleams red and pink and deep in it. It's pretty. "That's really nice. I like that. How much will you take for it?" It surprises me. I didn't expect that. "I don't know. I'll tell you, if you'll buy me a candy bar you're welcome to it." He gets a little red. I can see the blood coming up in his ears with the sun behind him. "Naw, now, I wouldn't feel right about that." He looks at the shell and holds it in the light. "What if I give you a dollar for it? It's probably worth a lot more than that." I don't want his money. Want him to have the shell. "That's too much." "Naw, now, that seems about right to me." He pulls out a ragged old cardboard billfold and gets out a green paper dollar. Hands it to me. I look at it with the light on it and look up at him and grin and he grins and I feel really silly. "That's great," I say and feel even sillier. I'm red. I can feel it, and he's red. Don't know why. It's just silly. Another car comes in and he puts the shell on a cupboard with the oil cans and goes to wait on it. I stand around trying to decide what to do with the dollar. Food.

I wave and he looks up from the gas pump and grins and waves. I run off across the road and truck down to the park. Climb down from the trestle, under barbed wire. Get out behind the hot dog stand. A line. I get in at the end and don't see anybody or anything, looking at the prices. My turn. "I want a hamburger with everything and one order of french fries and an Almond Joy and one Hershey with almonds, nickel size." It comes in a sack, wet with grease seeping through. It's hot. I can feel it. I take the red squeeze bottle off the counter and open the bag. French fries on top. Squeeze half the bottle on them and carry it off to the pier with the top open so the ketchup doesn't make a mess. Climb down under the pier and tear open the sack. It's hot and greasy with pickles and a sliver of tomato and shreds of lettuce and mustard and ketchup and mayonnaise and the meat is thin and brown and done and the french fries have a lot of salt on them under the ketchup. Eat very slowly in the green light. The water whispering against the piles and the light moving on the dark boards. I can hear people walking on the pier but they don't come down here. Nobody will come down here. Bite and chew and the old dear taste and the sweet sadness of eating something I like again. A few french fries soggy with ketchup and chew for ten minutes to get all the flavor and then swallow and a little little bite of hamburger warm and juicy and greasy. I take a very long time and then lick all the ketchup off the french fry paper. Sit picking my teeth and thinking how great that candy bar is going to be and when the time comes and I open it and eat it, it's finer than I'd remembered. I sit comfy in the shade under the pier for a long time with a full belly. Take the other candy bar home. Save it for dessert tomorrow night. Then I get up and walk easy on the rocks back to the cove and sit up late by the fire thinking how good that hamburger was.

* * *

Hard night. Very cold. Snake's back. Couldn't sleep at all.
A little sun in spots so I climb up to the tracks and stretch
out. Head on one rail and legs propped on the other.
Warm. No wind. I just close my eyes and drift a little. Not
really asleep. "Excuse me." Eyes pop open. He's crouching
on the track next to me. Brown. Goldy brown. Khaki
clothes with insignia sewn on. Brown skin. A wide white
smile. Young. Older than me but young. "Hi." What else
do I say? He comes waking me up on the railroad tracks.
"Hi, I'm the Ranger down at Gaviota State Park. Could I
ask your name?" I sit up and look at him. Nice smile.
"Dutch Gillis." He's nodding. "Is that Jean Gillis?" "Uh-
hunh." "Hi, I'm Dick Foster." He sticks his hand out. Dale
Carnegie. Hooray, Dick Foster. So fucking what? I take
his hand anyway. Let it go quick. "There are a couple of
men up at the gate asking about you. I wonder if you'd
come with me and speak to them?" "Sure." I don't care.
We climb off the track. He's got good boots. Not as tough
as mine though. He's big. We wade through a little sage
and there's barbed wire. He lifts it and I slide under and
then he steps across. Show-off. Fucking beach boy. Should
have known. It's the dirt road, even, must grade it once in
a while. Round a curve and I can see the gate. Tin trailer
house and the pick-up behind. A car parked on the other
side and two men in suits. My stomach drops out and my
knees get funny but I keep walking. I can smell the sage
and the wind runs across me and up into the hills. I look
and they're rocky and bare except for the sage. Snakes up
there. The snakes weren't so bad. Look out to sea. The
kelp beds long and stiff and dark out there. They're big.
Broad with bellies and hats. I don't know 'em. Thought

it'd be Dad and my brother. I look at the Ranger and he's just marching along feeling fine. We get to the gate and a thin gray man opens it and we walk through. The men come forward and look at me. The Ranger says, "Jean Gillis, this is Detective Ranelli and Sergeant Mears of Santa Barbara." I nod and look and they are looking at me and I can see the little quirks starting around the mouths. Ain't he a cute little fella? Big fat sons of bitches. Come waking a person up and making trouble. The biggest one clears his throat and rubs his cheek. "What do your friends call you, Jean?" "Dutch." What's it to you, motherfucker? "How old are you?" "Almost sixteen." They smile. They just crack their fat old mouths open and flash their plastic teeth. "What are you doing out here?" "On vacation." "Runaway, hunh?" "Nope, just on vacation." "Your folks know where you are?" No answer. Why play games? Fuck 'em. "Well, we'd like to have you ride into Santa Barbara with us." Gotta get my stuff. Can't go off and leave everything. I'll need it. "Unnh. Ah." My throat doesn't want to work. When the words come out the voice is even lower than usual. Too low, breaks, "I've got a camp in the ravine down there. Can I get my things?" They look at each other. "Is it far?" He asks the Ranger, not me. "No, not far." The Ranger's easy. Big picture smile. Lives in a log cabin with red and white flowers. Talks to brown girls in neon bikinis. Get grease all over if he kissed her. Sun tan lotion. It's all like a party or something. Grownups tossing your hair. "You've grown, hasn't she grown?" The gate opens and the big one and the Ranger come with me. We walk down to the place in the wire where we crawled out. I slide under the wire and the big one edges under and the Ranger steps over. I climb over the track and the big one's stepping along carefully, hurrying to keep up with me. He's got patent leather shoes. Shiny anyway. I go charging down the hill into the ravine and he hollers, "Wait!" and I stop and he comes up red and puffing. "You wouldn't try to get away, would you?" I grin "Naw," and go on. He follows me into the little shelter. I pack all the junk together and go to lift it. He reaches out. "Here, let me help you," and I pull it away. "No, I can do it myself." Pile it all on and go out and clamber up to the top. The Ranger's waiting there. Posing in the sunshine. The big one comes puffing up, using his hands. Dust all over his shiny shoes and on his sleeves and pant legs. He's red and sweating. "I'm not dressed for this kind of work." He giggles a little and the Ranger smiles. I turn and go out to the road. They follow and I go through the gate alone. The back door of the car is open. Not marked. I throw the stuff in. Climb in after it. Sit there on the soft lush seat and lean back and feel a little like puking. The two men are talking to the gate man. Shaking his hand. Shaking the Ranger's hand. The sign on the gate says "Therman Ranch, No Admission Without Pass." Must be a rich man. Millions of acres of desert. Big house somewhere in the middle. I coulda gone and stole from him if I'd known. Just follow the road. Must lead to the house. Lives out there and nobody can get to him. Guard at the gate. The detectives get into the front seat. Roll the windows up. Air conditioning. They are clean. Their necks clipped and the flesh rolls spilling over stiff white collars. I can smell after shave lotion and a little sweat. The big one sits on the passenger side. The car turns and goes slow down the dirt road. Dust. Rough. Trees at the bottom and another sign. Rustic carved wood. "Gaviota Beach State Park." Two sea gulls. Very cute. A big road and we go past the store. I look to see the man who bought the shell but there's nobody outside. The kelp beds black on the water. I'm going to puke. "Can I roll the window down?" He turns and looks and he's suspicious. Thinks I'm going to fling myself out onto the road at sixty miles and hour. Signal to truck drivers. "Please, I get carsick." "Oh, Jesus, go ahead." He turns around disgusted and I crack the window open and suck at the hot wind. Let it beat on my eyes. Lean my face against the glass. A bell hanging on a pole. A little sign. "El Camino Real." I am de king. Right.

The big one turns and looks at me. "You know a guy named Heydorf?" I pull away from the glass. "Yeah." "Where is he now, do you know?" Very casual. Very cool. What the fuck? "L.A., I think, why?" He's still looking and he sees me looking and he's very cool. "When did you last see this Heydorf?" "I don't know. What day is this?" "Saturday." "Then it must have been last Tuesday. It was Tuesday when he left the beach to go back to L.A." "You sure it was Tuesday?" "Yeah, I know it was Tuesday." He looks at the other guy. Looks back at me. "It couldn't have been last Tuesday because the L.A. police picked him up last Sunday. How long have you been out there anyway?" Picked him up. Picked him up. That's why he didn't come. "I guess it must have been Tuesday before last. Guess I kind of lost track of time." He turns all the way in the seat. Leans against the door to look at me. "Dutch, what've you been doing out there all this time?" "Nothing. Fishing." "Fishing. Yeah, I go fishing out there at the park whenever I get a chance." I smile. He looks at me funny but I smile anyway. I can see him in a silly hat with feathers and flies and a big long pole propped under his belly. "When did you get out there to the beach?" I don't know. Some time ago. "Sunday morning early. Took the night bus from L.A." "Sunday morning." He makes notes on a pad in his lap. I can see his hairy ankle. His dusty gray pants leg is rucked up and there are blue clocks on his socks. Pants rucked up. Socks rucked down. Fat old hairy ankle sticking out. "How long had you been with Heydorf before you left L.A.?" "I don't know. Coupla days. Since Thursday I guess." The seat's soft, warm. Just the little breeze from the window. First time I've been out of the wind in a long time. "The stories check out completely." He's talking to the driver. The driver nods. The big one turns back around and starts talking to me. "Heydorf was picked up originally on suspicion of burglary and/or transvestism. He was walking around downtown L.A. with a standard burglar's kit, a .22-caliber pistol and a paper bag full of women's clothing." "Those were probably my clothes." "Wait. Then he played cagey about where he had been and what he'd been up to. After two days in the cooler he said he'd been up here on the beach. The guy's some kind of weirdo, right?" No answer. Fuck him. "Anyway, they connected him with the murder, see?" I can feel my eyes pushing out. "What murder?" "You mean you haven't heard about it?" I shake my head and look and he's glad and he settles in to tell me all about it. My tongue gets dry and the sick's back in my stomach. I hold my stomach and look at my grubby paws so I don't have to look at him. "It seems two kids, a boy and a girl, ran away from their high school graduation party. They went to the beach just below the park there. Their bodies were found two days later. They had each been shot twelve times with the same .22-caliber pistol. That means the killer had to empty his revolver and reload and fire again. They were both nude. The girl had been raped. You know how the tide comes in down there. All the traces had been washed away. No footprints, no shell casings, nothing." He loves it. He thinks he's scaring me and he is. Because he loves it. He isn't glad they're dead. He's glad they died the way they did. He can't get the smile off his face. He really eats it up. "They were both seventeen." That's his final touch. He's looking to see it hit me. What if I told him I'm glad? Good riddance. Kill 'em all. The younger, the better. Then they won't have a chance to turn into horses' asses like you. Befouling the air. Probably going to get a promotion when he solves this case. Lieutenant, get a new refrigerator and an electric fishing reel. "Could we stop?

I think I'm going to throw it up." "Stop, stop! For Christ's sake!" and the car pulls over and the gravel pops against the fenders and I open the door and sprawl out and heave. Nothing in there. White liquid. Burns and stinks and nothing. He gets out and stands by the car watching, so I don't run away. He'd have to follow me in his patent leather shoes. Stop or I'll fire. Once over my head with his .38 Police Special. Then into my left buttock. Hit me in the ass and blow my head off. Antipersonnel weapon. It doesn't feel bad. Just a little puke to clear the air. The gravel's hard on my hands. I lift them and look at the red and white pocks in my palms. "You O.K.?" "Uh-hunh." Wipe my mouth and spit. And stand up. Crawl into the car. "Jesus, kid, I didn't mean to scare you that bad." He gets in and the car sags on that side and the driver's looking back at me worried I'm going to puke on his plastic upholstery. "You didn't scare me. I told you I get carsick." We go again and they're not talking. I lay back against the seat and close my eyes. But wait. School let out Thursday. I left Thursday night. Got into L.A. Saturday. Not Thursday. Saturday. Only in L.A. one day with Heydorf. Lean forward but not too far. Don't want to hit him with my puke breath. "When did that murder happen?" "June third. That'd be Thursday of that week. The night they graduated." I can feel my face going white so I say, "Wow... the day I got into L.A." "Yeah. Let that be a lesson to you. That killer's got to be a maniac! Might be wandering around on that beach still." "Yeah. But what about Heydorf? Did he tell you where to find me or what?" "Yeah. He gave you as a witness that he'd just been up here coincidentally so close to the crime and that he'd been somewhere else when it happened. Your story checks with his. They'll let him go now." Lean back and close my eyes. "That's good." "You pretty worried about him. He your boyfriend?" He's leering and nudging the driver and rolling his fat greasy eyes at me. I'm too tired to be

mad. Too sick. "No, just a friend." Lay against the seat
and rest. Tired. Didn't sleep good last night. "Might as
well take her straight up to the juvenile center. You can
witness her statement." They talk to each other and some
of it's about me but it doesn't matter. It's all off there in
the front seat. There are cute houses. Imitation something or other with red tile roofs and a lot of shrubs. A
turn and we go up a little hill and there's a long low
building. Red brick and a lot of good grass and palm
trees. Looks like an old folks' home. The car stops in the
parking lot and the big one takes my arm and the driver
carries my stuff. They lead me into the lobby. A desk and
chairs and potted plants. A medium ritzy hotel. They talk
and give my stuff to the guy behind the desk. Have a
good laugh over the bow and the five arrows. Yeah, it's
pretty funny. I sign something about the pack and they
ask me my address and I'm going to forget for them but
it'll just mean trouble so I give it to them. They say they'll
contact my parents. I don't care. A tall pale lady in quiet
clothes leads me down a hall and invites me to wait in a
small room. Wire mesh on the window but a good red
leather chair. I go to sleep in it. She wakes me up nicely
and takes me to another room where I get a skirt and
blouse and pair of underpants, white cotton. New. And a
pair of bobby socks and white tennis shoes. Not good
high black big-nosed sneakers, wimpy white tennis shoes.
She leads me to a big bathroom and I take off all my
clothes and she leaves me alone and I get into a shower
and the water's too hot but then I get it right and stand in
it for a long time and even put soap on. In my hair and
on my face and all over where I can reach. It stings when
I rub and a lot of the skin comes off. Rolls off in scrudge
and peels off in thin icky sheets. But it's kind of nice and
the water's clean. No bugs in it probably. I stay for a long
time and all the black comes off my hands and feet and
the crust rubs off my elbows. I come out and rub and pat

myself with a towel. Easy so it doesn't hurt my sunburn anymore. It's all pink tile and there are panties and brassieres hanging around. I put on the clothes and stand in front of the mirror. I look like a mistake. I feel naked and cold. Short sleeves and a skirt. My hands look red and the arms and legs white and the face like cheap uncooked hamburger. Need a haircut. Starting to curl. All I need is kinks. Bundle my friendly old clothes and go looking for the tall lady. She leads me to a door in a long hall of doors. "This is your room while you're here. I have to lock the door but if you want anything just call and I'll come. I'm Mrs. Graham." I thought it would be cells. It's small and not fancy but it's not a cell. "Dinner is at five-thirty. It's about two now so you can rest until dinner." She takes my old clothes and I nod and go in and she locks the door and I don't care. There's a bed with a mattress and sheets and a pillow and blankets. A chair and a table and a chest of drawers. Brown wood. Plain brown wood. The walls are plaster over brick probably and green. Light green. It's all green. Like a hospital. A little window with wire mesh and the light bulb with wire mesh. The switch is by the door. I thought it'd be cells with twenty people in each one. Take off the clothes except for the panties and crawl into the bed. Cool and soft and warm. I cry a little. I admit it. I cry. It's nice. I'd forgotten.

At dinner everybody files into the dining room. It's just like the school cafeteria. Except the boys are all on one side and the girls are on the other. It was mostly that way in school anyway. They're always bitching about the food. It seems all right to me. One nice thing is they got a pot of peanut butter and a pot of jelly on the table at lunch and a whole lot of bread. You get a hot meal too but you can have all the peanut butter you want. The jelly's just jelly. But the peanut butter is the cheap soft oily kind that spreads easy and has just the right amount of salt. The cheap kind of peanut butter is always the best.

The doctor who gave me the physical didn't talk. He moved slow and didn't hurt me and he put some good stuff on the bug bites and sunburn. Not greasy and they stopped itching and hurting. The skin still comes off but it doesn't hurt.

There aren't any lectures or anything. Nobody bothers you. Get up and get dressed and they open the door and we wash and go to breakfast. Got to make my bed and sweep the floor but that's nothing. School for three hours in the morning. The boys go in the afternoon while we play volleyball. They aren't dumb. I thought they'd be dumb. They talk about South America and news. They know a lot of stuff I don't.

Don't have to talk at all. Nobody asks you questions in school time unless you put your hand up. I sit and listen and watch. Don't have to because I don't care if I pass or anything. Don't have to make friends. Just do what everybody else is doing. Do what they tell me to. Don't have to talk at all. Just be there. They bring books and paper and stuff back to their rooms. I just lay on the bed and look at the ceiling. Sleep a lot. Seem like I could never get enough sleep.

He's the art teacher. They call him Mr. Voorhees. Leather carving. Hammered tin. Stuff like that. I gave him the card because I was new. He took it and took a pencil out of his apron and smiled at me and wrote on the card. He looked up and smiled again and said, "Are you here for parole violation?" I didn't know what parole violation was. He smiled nice and I wanted him to think I was young and innocent. So I put on this bewildered look and he said, "I see by your face you don't even know what that means." I felt bad. I'm not invisible anymore. I put on faces. I didn't know what he meant but even if I had I would have put on that face so he'd think I didn't know. It's too bad. It was nice being invisible. They can touch me now. I have to defend myself.

My chest came off today. Two big sheets the size of my hand. Almost square and a round hole in each one because the nipple doesn't peel. The belly is still flaking. Always looks dusty. Maybe it won't come off like that. It doesn't hurt when the skin comes off. It just looks funny.

The place underneath red and cooked and the sheet of skin thin and the light shining through. Weird. I hold it up and try to think, "That's my skin." But it isn't anymore. I put the pieces in the waste basket or flush them down the toilet.

He was late. No matter what. He was late. He left Tuesday night and he said three days. Three days means Wednesday, Thursday, Friday. They picked him up on Sunday. He knew I only had food for two nights. Maybe he wasn't going to come back at all. He had the money and he was going to ditch the clothes or sell them or something. He was just going to disappear into the sunset with my money. I was a sucker to give it to him. I know better. I know him better than to do that. He figured I'd wait three days for him and that'd give him a head start and I wouldn't bitch to the cops. He knows I couldn't do that. He'd be safe out of it. Probably decided him with that horny pass. That was it. He turned his face away. He wasn't afraid. He was disgusted. He just went along with it that far so I wouldn't make trouble and so he could get the money. I said, "Don't be afraid." He probably died laughing inside. Or almost puked. Big-bellied, knobby, bald-headed frog pooches its slimy lips out. Bugs its eyes. "Kiss me, big boy." And I so horny trying to rub against him. Begging for it. No pride. Where was I? Why couldn't I see? He wouldn't let me rub or do anything himself. He didn't want me. He wasn't afraid of getting me pregnant.

He wasn't afraid of anything except puking in my face and blowing the money. Other girls tried to flirt with him. With tits and asses and hair and nice faces. I've seen it. And he looked and didn't do anything. What made me think I could make him do anything? "You're built like a pygmy." He knew how ugly I am. And I came and sat beside him and made him put his arm around me. I feel sick and ashamed and I'll never speak to anybody again. Never look anybody in the eye. It's disgusting. I'm disgusting. No pride. I'm a lover. Everybody loves me. Aaaaarg. Probably had a ticket to Mexico in his pocket when they picked him up. Figured I'd wait three days and then go running home to Mama. Or he figured I'd nick stuff and get by and not be bothered about food. I could've taken stuff from the store. Stolen picnics. Fat guy in his Hawaiian shirt comes running up to the pretty Ranger. "Somebody stole my picnic!" That's what I should have done. Been a picnic nicker. Too bad I didn't think of that. Swipe picnics. So he figured I'd get by or go home or anyway not give him any trouble.

Or maybe he had to wait for his money in the mail. Maybe it didn't come until Saturday and he was going to come out Sunday. Figured I could get by so he'd wait till the money came and not have to make another trip. But if he was gonna take the bus he'd have taken it Saturday night. Or early Sunday. No, he was trucking out with my money. One hundred and thirteen dollars and seventy-five cents. Big haul. Knock over the hot dog stand you'd get that much. But you might get caught and he won't get caught robbing me. Pretty smart. They probably let him go by now and he's in Mexico living high. Cheap in Mexico. Never meant to go on the raft at all. But it was his idea. Maybe he just thought of the money and taking off when I made the pass at him. Maybe everything would have been all right. I could have pretended to be going to piss and gone off and rubbed myself to get by. My own fault. Blew it. Another Gillis Miracle. But he talked or they wouldn't have found me. They weren't looking for me here. I could have stayed there all summer. He must have been pretty visible himself to get picked up just walking around. How could that happen? What was he doing? I was just laying there sleeping and old pussy boy comes sweet-footing up and he's got me. I could have tried to get away. But why bother? But he found me so easy. Must have known I was out there all the time. Saw me walking on the trestle or down on the pier there. Maybe saw me going off up the rocks with my fish and not coming back. Heydorf probably didn't tell them about me at first because he thought I might tell them about the money. Or maybe he was trying not to squeal and got hit with that murder shit. Enough to make anybody squeal on anybody. But his neck's out of the trap. And I'm in. One way or another I have been screwed by Heydorf. Not what I had in mind.

It's just like school except they leave me alone. People just the same. Little girl here stole twelve cars and was driving the thirteenth over the Mexican border when they got her. She's twelve. Just joy-riding. She's about the worst. Rest "incorrigibles." Skipped school. Runaways, like that. There's this one. Angel. Real pretty. She doesn't talk either. Long yellow hair, and a sweet face. Angel face. Everybody gets two cigarettes a day if they want 'em. Except Angel. When she gets a cigarette she holds it there and smiles her sweet angel smile while it burns away. She's got a lot of scars. They don't like her doing it. They won't give her cigarettes. She wears long sleeves and it don't show but she goes to the doctor every other day to see if she's been doing that. It stinks a little while she's doing it but she always goes into the can or does it in her room where she don't bother anybody. It makes holes. Real holes and they're all black for a while and the doctor puts some kind of gawp on 'em and after a while they're red and white stuff comes out of 'em. Maybe I know why she does that. The tall quiet lady says she's either trying to get attention or she's guilty about something. Feels guilty and wants to punish herself. I don't think that's true, I think maybe she does it because she can feel it. Maybe she can't feel anything else. Anyway I always get two cigarettes and give 'em to her. Figure it's not any-body's business if she wants to do that or why. Long as she don't bother anybody else.

The tall lady opens my door. "Jean, your mother's here." Oh, lord. I get up and follow her out. It's rest period and the hall is empty and the big room with the chairs and the TV is empty. She leads me down another hall and there's an open door and an office. The blinds half drawn and rug and big chairs and a big desk and a big white-haired lady sitting behind the desk. My mother gets out of one of the chairs and runs up to me. "Jean, Jean, baby, are you all right?" She throws her arms around me and pulls me close and I can feel the wet coming from her face onto my hair and she smells of lotion and cinnamon and she's soft and warm. A soft little woman. She's got her good dress on. She spent a lot of money on the cloth and got a good pattern and spent about a week making it. She only wears it on Christmas and like that. "Yeah, I'm fine, Maw, really." And she pulls back and grabs my hands in her soft red freckled hands and touches me and feels my bones and runs her hand over my face and hair and down onto my neck and holds my neck and tips my chin up and looks into my eyes and her soft gray eyes with red all around and water on them and sliding out of them and she looks into my eyes. "Are you sure? You're all right?" I'm sorry. I'm really sorry. I didn't mean it to touch you. Not really. I didn't mean to bother anybody. I can feel water coming out of my own eyes and I grin so she can see I've still got my teeth. "No, I'm fine. They were fine, Maw. Everybody's been fine. I'm glad to see you." I don't know whether I'm glad. I put it on. I tacked it on to see her smile and she smiles her silly soft old smile and the gray eyes fold into the wrinkles and the water keeps coming out of the wrinkles. She takes both my hands in her hands and pulls me down beside her on the big old chair. Plenty of room for two and she looks at me and feels me and clucks over my sunburn and I ask how Dad and Nick are and she says they're fine, they're outside and she's laughing she's so glad to see me. The big lady behind the desk pulls her chair forward and clears her throat and we both look at her and Maw is still holding both of my hands in her hands. "I see that you have no speech impediment." Her voice is hard and clear and the words click off her tongue officially. "No, of course she doesn't. What do you mean?" My mother is bristling over her chick and her soft eyes get cold and glittery. The old lady probably been giving her a hard time. "Jean has not spoken a word since she arrived here. This is the first time anyone on our staff has heard her voice." "She's accusing me of something. Showing off something." I didn't know they wanted me to talk. Nobody said they wanted me to talk. She looks down at the desk and taps a yellow pencil on a green blotter. Green leather corners and the walls are a light green. I look at Maw and smile and she smiles and squeezes my hands and the tears are sitting on her cheeks and she doesn't wipe them away. The big lady looks up at us from under her eyebrows. "I'm Mrs. Rast. I am the counselor assigned to your case. It is my duty to decide whether you should be released in your mother's custody or be remanded for hearing. I would like to know why you ran away. Were you unhappy at home?" The breath comes up long from inside me and I don't know what to say. "No, not at home." "You wanted to be with this young man Heydorf, is that right?" I can feel my eyebrows going up in the middle like my mother's. A little tent, and the cooked skin wrinkles in a tent. "Not exactly. I just wanted the adventure." Maw squeezes at my hands. She believes me. The big lady doesn't believe. She smiles and it's dirty. I want to hit her for smiling that way in front of my mother. "Really. And what were you going to do, 'for adventure'?" It's foul. It greases out of her mouth and shines into the room and I'll kill her. I'll take a hatchet and swing it hard and cut her and cut off the slime. I open my eyes pretending not to see the filth. I look at her and say, "We were going to go to the headwaters of the Missouri and build a raft and float down to the Mississippi and then to New Orleans." She isn't listening—not really. She's looking at me to see the filth answering her filth. "And this Heydorf, you are in love with him?" I laugh. It just pops out. It rolls around in my belly and juggles out. She doesn't think it's funny. I've offended her. "Oh, that's humorous, is it? But you liked him very much?" "Like him...I don't know. I never thought about it." "You never thought about it and yet you ran off to be with him worrying your mother to distraction and causing untold heartache at home?" She's really angry. She's trying to get my mother on her side. But she's *my* mother. "And you are trying to lead us to believe that you were out on that beach with this young man, spending nights with him, and had no relations with him?" "That's enough!" My mother stands up and goes to the desk and she's the wolf bitch. She's not gentle. There's nothing soft about her. She leans and her voice is as cold and the words as precise as the big lady's. "Your doctors have examined her. You have on your medical report that she is not yet pubescent and that she is physically a virgin.

Now I have had enough of this disgusting innuendo. I know my daughter and what she says is true. She would do this for adventure. And I'm sure she intended to float down the river to New Orleans." I didn't know she knew that word. Innuendo. I never heard her use it before. The big white lady puts down her pencil. She still wants my mother on her side. "Madam, all I can say is that if my daughter had done this and then told me that cock-and-bull story I wouldn't have believed her for a moment. I would know that there was a sexual motivation behind it." She's still hard, my little mother. I didn't know she could be that way. "Then, Mrs. Rast, I pity you, and I pity your daughter. I'd like to take my child home now. Her father and brother are waiting outside and very anxious to see her." Maw to the rescue. Get them pesky Injuns! I feel silly and light and want to dance around and cheer. Good goin', Maw! Way to fly, Maw! Mrs. Rast knows when she's licked. She picks up the pencil and starts filling out forms. "It will take some time to process the release. It's eleven-thirty now. If you'll return to the lobby at two P.M. Jean will be released to your custody. Is that satisfactory in your eyes, Jean?" She looks at me as though I'm getting away with a mortal sin. I'm grinning all over. "Yep." Maw comes back and gives me a big hug and whispers in my ear not to eat much lunch. We'll celebrate afterward.

I liked this room. Nothing in it is mine. Nothing I'm wearing is mine. All borrowed, but from nobody. So bare and clean. The pale lady brings my old clothes. New washed. Everything washed and folded. I put them all on and leave the skirt and tennis shoes and stuff on the bed. Feels good. My good old clothes that cover me. Feels like

I ought to be goin' someplace. The Missouri, New Orleans, China. I walk out and the pale tall lady leads me down to the lobby. The man at the desk has all my stuff piled in front of him and Nick and Dad are standing there looking at it. Nick's got the bow in one hand and the harmonica in the other. Maw sees me and comes running over and grabs me and kisses me. She's not crying any- more. She's laughing and looking at my rumble jacket. "My God, what a roughneck! I've got to get a picture of that! Look at this child, George!" and Dad comes over all shy and bumbling and pats me on the head and Nick comes saying, "Wow! Can I play with the mouth harp! Where'd you get all this stuff?" It's my stuff. My things. I worked and scraped and stole and cadged to get it. All of it. I want to jerk it out of their hands and scream. It was all with me out there. The canteen still has water in it. I grin and shuffle and take the bow from Nick. Sound eager and remorseful and cheerful and glad to see them but I want my things. I don't want them to look into my packs and touch the stuff and talk about it and ask me questions. "We ready to go?" I'm eager. They under- stand. "Sure, honey." Dad tries to help me with the stuff and I pull it away and grin stiff and put it on. Can't bite him. Spoil it. "Naw, I'll take it. I carried it this far." And we go out and they're talking and laughing and the sun is shining. The car is different. A yellow station wagon instead of the old green DeSoto. "Where'd you get this?" "Oh, we traded the old car in. Didn't think it would make it all the way down here and back. 'Bout time anyway." We pile in and Dad goes driving out the steady way he always drives. Just sitting there. Not moving. The car does what he wants and he doesn't do anything. Nick's blowing into the harmonica. Noise. Soft noise.

"...All the time we thought you were in Montana. Every- body seemed to think you'd gone to Montana." "Hmmm... Hey, Dad, who's in the service station while you're away?"

Casual, change the subject. I made a mistake. He
shifts in the seat and looks at me in the rear-view mirror
and smiles. "Well, dear." He's so slow. Always slow. Never
wants to hurt anybody. Something's wrong. "Well, dear,
I decided to give up the station. I'm going out to the
shipyard when we get back. The hours are shorter."
Maw looks at him and smiles and I feel like shit. Nick
grunts and pretends to retch. "Whyn't you tell her the
truth?" He loves the truth. He always liked the truth.
"They went bankrupt! Had helicopters flying over the
Mission Mountains looking for you." He thinks it's funny.
He expects me to laugh. "Hundred dollars an hour!
Helicopters!" Mom turns around laughing. She won't let
him hurt me. "You know how I always wanted a helicopter. Well, I just thought 'Here's my chance!' and we had a
marvelous time. You should have seen Dad tinkering away
alongside the pilot. One of the things wouldn't go and Dad
gets down in his good clothes and crawls into that engine…" She goes on and on. One of her better stories.
They're all laughing and I'm laughing and the road goes
past with the black bells, I am de king. Sure you are honey.
The kelp beds are black. The sky is blue and the sea is blue
and the long shadow runs up the coast and we go north.

"We've got a surprise!" she glows. Her cheeks pink and
her eyes still wet. She keeps reaching back to touch me
and hold my hands. "We're going to have a picnic. You
know where? At *your* beach. At *Gaviota* Beach!" She's
looking to see if it's all right and I pull my face into a
good smile and a good voice. No half-assed acting now. A
good voice. "That's a great idea. I'd like you to see it."
And she's happy and he's happy because she is and Nick
is blowing on the harmonica beside me.

I can see the tracks as we pull into the store. I lean back
in the seat and put my head down. He fills the tank and
doesn't see me. His long bones wiping over the windshield and I look the other way so he won't see me. I

wonder if he still has the shell. Dad comes out of the store with a six-pack of beer and another of pop. Sticks his huge old head in the window and smiles at me, "You still like orange pop?" and I crack across the face grinning for him.

It's great. Fifty cents' admission to the park and a dollar fifty overnight. The beach boy Ranger in his starched khakis takes the money. "Well, hi there, welcome back," and the big flashy grin and Maw waving at him as we drive through. Didn't cost me anything. Find a parking spot and pile out. "I didn't stay here, Maw, I was up on the coast a ways." And she takes my arm and we stroll out onto the dock. Dad talking to the people with the poles and a long white fish dying of suffocation next to an old lady in a sun hat. Nick running up and down looking at people's poles. My boots are heavy on the wood and Maw's heels clicking and Dad's shoes hard, his good shoes. None of the heads turn this time but the boots sound heavy and slow and hollow. It's different. I don't remember it. Very crowded. We get to the steps and Dad and Nick are talking to a fisherman. I take her down the rough wood steps into the dark beneath the pier. The light is yellow moving on her face and she looks around at the wet dark wood and looks at me and her face is soft and afraid. I take out the string and hook and show her how I fished. "But how did you know they were good to eat, dear?" "Somebody told me, Maw. They were O.K." "Well, you're awfully thin. I'm going to get you home and feed you up good." That's what I wanted. I remember wanting that. Food and Maw. Maw's food.

* * *

He lights the fire for hot dogs. A bucket of fried chicken
from a place in town and hot dogs with mustard and
ketchup and mayonnaise. We sit at the table under the
trestle. The trestle is black and I can see the sky in little
slits through the ties far up. They are laughing and
telling me all about their tribulations. It's a joke already.
As soon as it's over. A joke. "Maw didn't sleep for three
nights running. Sat up smoking and looking mournful
with a squeaky voice and the third day she put sugar in
the Scotch broth instead of salt so we tied her in bed." All
funny. She blushes and laughs and Dad is laughing and
squeezing her arm and Nick makes fun of us all. He's
outside it now though she does the same for him when
he's late or runs away to stay with a friend. Then I laugh
and we are all laughing and the hot dogs are brown and
bubbling, not black, and she spreads the rolls and fits the
wienies in and hands them around and it's good. I can
taste it hot and sweet and sour and fine fine. Three hot
dogs apiece and orange pop and then chicken and she's
got bananas and oranges. Dad goes to the hot dog stand
for coffee and she's got a big cake. Dark chocolate six feet
high and "Welcome Jean" in pink frosting in the middle
and Dad brings back ice cream. I didn't know they had
ice cream. It says "Welcome Jean." "We were in Santa
Barbara three days waiting to see you and I knew they'd
let you come home with us so I ordered it. I'm sorry I
couldn't bake it for you myself." I can see her and the
cake coming toward me with ice cream piled on top of it
and this is what I remember wanting but I don't want it
anymore. They shouldn't have come here. I would have
told them about it. Now I can never tell about it. It was

mine and now it's not mine. It isn't theirs. They don't want it. It only isn't mine anymore. They want me but I'm not theirs anymore. I don't belong with them. I forget when it happened. Maybe I'll remember later if I think about it. They are foreign and the beach and the pier and the good food. All foreign. Her face is soft and I can remember touching it and aching over how soft it was. I can remember caring and wanting and needing but I don't anymore. They touch me and talk and I hear and feel and see but I'm not here now. This place is different now. I can feel my face grinning and hear myself laughing and they are all laughing and talking to me. They belong here and they're good. Even Nick. I can see it. They laugh and their eyes laugh and the sound is good and they aren't pretending not to hate me. They love me. But I'm not here. I went away and I didn't come back. I'm up on the trestle, invisible, and the people are pretty on the beach. I can see them laughing at the picnic tables. They're far away and small and I can see them and hear them but they can't see me and they can't touch me. I'm invisible. I'm glad I'm invisible. I'm glad. It feels clean and hard and powerful and I look at them and feel sorry for them. Silly little people. So visible. But it hurts. I'm glad but it hurts. I don't want them to see me but then they can never see me. I can see all the times coming. They'll come. I can feel them in me. I'll be aching and crying to eat and be warm and clean and have somebody love and take care of me but no matter how much I want it they can't give it to me. No matter how much they want to give it to me they won't be able to. I'll be far away and alone and for hours and days and maybe weeks I'll ache that way and hurt and nobody will be able to help me because I'm invisible. Because some little while back, I don't know quite when, I decided to be invisible. There's no getting out of it. I don't want out but it wouldn't make any difference if I did. The cake is thick and the chocolate sweet and heavy and so good, so good, and I know all those times coming when I won't have cake or even bread and I feel so sorry for myself. I feel so sweet sad sorry for myself. Poor me. Oh poor me. It hurts good and the cake is good and my old eyeballs go running water and my nose starts running down into my mouth and I'm crying and choking on my good good cake and they all stop laughing and Maw comes running and holds me and wipes my nose with a paper napkin and sits holding me and saying, "There, there, little one, what is it?" and Dad is leaning over the table and holding my hand and patting my square grubby old hand with his big dark rough hand and even Nick is patting my head and they're all so worried and the little tents are up in their foreheads and it's funny. All of a sudden it's funny and I start to laugh and the cake sprays out onto the table and I can't help laughing and they smile a little but the tents are still in their foreheads and I catch my breath and stop "I..." but I can still see them and they look so funny and I'm so funny and I laugh again and the tears are rolling but from laughing now and Maw is patting me and I stop and say, "I'm just so glad to be here with you," so they can laugh too and the tents go away and they laugh and it's all right. Everything's all right for now, right now. The rest doesn't matter, what comes later.

"I want to call L.A., Maw. Find out what happened to Heydorf. He was in jail, you know. I want to find out if they let him go." "Of course, Little, I understand." And she's rooting in her purse for change. It's outside Sacramento. A diner. She goes to the can with me every time. She doesn't know why. She doesn't even notice that she does it. I know. She's afraid I'll run away again now and be gone just when she's getting to breathe again. I don't mind if she always comes to the toilet when I do. She still thinks it was all a momentary impulse or something. She doesn't know about all the months of planning and all the money and how I planted the Montana story on purpose. She gives me the change and I get into the phone booth and close the door. She stands outside. I don't like to see her standing and waiting but she will. Information and operators. A buzzing and another queer voice. Not the same queer. Another queer. I wonder if my mother knows about queers. "I'm sorry, Mr. Heydorf checked out more than a week ago." Ah ah. I don't know why I expected him to be there. "His roommate is still here if you'd care to speak with him, sir." "Yes, please," and there's a long wait. He might know. I can ask. Maybe he'll be queer too and I'll know why Heydorf turned his face away. "Yeah, this is James P. Barton Esquire speakin'. Who's this?" Not a queer, a cracker. A flat-A'd cracker. "This is Dutch Gillis. I'm a friend of Heydorf's and..." "Yeah, he told me about you. You O.K. an' everything?" "Yeah, but..." "Heydorf joined the army. Enlisted the same day they let him out. I saw him when he came around here to pick up his stuff. Scared the shit out of him. Yep, think they did." No address. Don't know where he is. In the army. He always said, "Screwed in the army. Get your ass shot off." He was scared. He got scared and joined the army. My maw says, "Well, maybe it's for the best," and Dad and Nick are finished eating and we go out of the tin shining diner with the neon sign and we go north again. He joined the army. Maybe he did it. Maybe that's why he was scared. Maybe I scared him. He was scared I'd make trouble. Maybe he killed 'em. We are going north in the dark. Maw is asleep beside Dad. Nick is blowing softly into the harmonica. He was always good with music. He's got the first few bars of "Pop Goes the

Weasel" and he plays them softly and then reaches around blowing softly and listening for the next note. It's black. I can't see myself. Can't tell where my hands are or how I'm sitting. He said, "Maybe you have to do something irrevocable." Maybe he had already done it. He could do it. I could do it in the right mood, at the right time. But the girl was raped. I don't know him. Could he do that? He is walking on the beach. Chilly. Wind. Dark water breaking in a long white line like machine gun fire. The moon makes his hair white. They are laying in the sand with their clothes off. White. He can see them white and they don't hear him. He walks up soft and slow, to see. Just to see. And they are touching, maybe more. Maybe the boy put it into her and Heydorf was watching in the dark and they moaned and whispered and we were watching and the wind sound and the water and they didn't hear us, and we walked soft, not giggling, not breathing, and I pulled the trigger and he jerked. His body jerked on top of her the way it had been jerking before and she yelled and I pulled the trigger again and the pop and cream blowing off thin in the wind and I pulled the trigger slowly again and again and then I hand Heydorf the gun and he reloads and starts firing with one hand in his pocket. They are only lumps now, not moving. I get bored watching him pull the trigger and go around picking up the shells. We walk farther up the beach and it's dark and the white lumps are still and the tide comes up around them. They are too heavy and the tide cannot move them but the sea bugs wash between their legs and run back to the water and the marks in the sand go into the sea and the sea forgets and the lumps forget and we are walking on the sand, invisible.